Praise for Exposures....

"With vivid detail, *Exposures* wraps the reader into the lives of two incredible characters who open our eyes to the world around us, as well as to the inner landscapes defined by heart, soul and life experience. I wept, I cheered, and I could not put it down. *Exposures* throws the reader into the detailed world of a world-class photographer Jess Cappello, mesmerizing the reader with true exposures of the heart and soul. Inspiration, heartbreak and true courage will keep you turning page after page and leave you wanting more! Remarkable!"

Yvonne Smith-Blair, Founder, Bella Design Group

"I read *Exposures* in one sitting. I was caught by the combination of the characters, their interactions and the insights into them, and the lovely fragments of description teased with art history. The story is so clean, and clear. Understated, I think is a good word. The relationships are allowed to evolve and aren't predictable. They seem real, true to whom the characters are."

Patricia Rogers, M.D.

"Jess Cappello is brought to life through the eyes of one who must have known and experienced the inner workings of a photographer. The exquisite detail developed to expose his challenging life is a wonderfully delightful read. By the end of book I was convinced I would want to exhibit the work of this amazing, more real than life, creative soul. Bravo! Bravo!"

Dennis High, Executive Director/Curator, Center for Photographic Art, Carmel, California

Exposures, a novel

Glenda Burgess

author**HOUSE**™

1663 LIBERTY DRIVE, SUITE 200
BLOOMINGTON, INDIANA 47403
(800) 839-8640
WWW.AUTHORHOUSE.COM

First published by AuthorHouse 05/16/05

ISBN: 1-4208-4064-9 (sc)

Library of Congress Control Number: 2005902441

Printed in the United States of America
Bloomington, Indiana

This book is printed on acid-free paper.

In memory of Kenneth Grunzweig
who taught me the truth of Willem de Kooning's words
"Content is a glimpse"

For Katherine
and Mikhail Gelfandbein
in your hands mere wood and strings sing

If I could tell the story in words, I wouldn't need to lug a camera.

Lewis Hine

The Photographs Described by Chapter

Seoul Moon, Jess Cappello, 1953

Snowbank, Jess Cappello, 1981

Triangles, Ruth Bernhard, 1946

Jean Chalot and His Wife, Edward Weston, 1933

Moonrise over Hernandez, Ansel Adams, 1943

Woman Behind Cobwebbed Windows, Wynn Bullock, 1955

Redding Stream, Connecticut, Paul Caponigro, 1968

Remnants of Resonance 8, Brad Cole, 1988

Tide Pool, Wynn Bullock, 1957

Drizzle of 40th Street, New York, Edward Steichen, 1925

Sir John Herschel, Julia Margaret Cameron, 1867

Georgia O'Keefe: A Profile, Alfred Stieglitz, 1920

Wendy, Northern California, Jock Sturges, 1987

Baskets, A/P#2, Linda Butler, 1974

Untitled, Kathleen Barrows, 1989

Le Violon de Ingres, Man Ray, 1924

Composition

Seoul Moon, Jess Cappello, 1953

The cold intensity of light.

The photographic image *Seoul Moon* is a sharp cut of heat on the tongue. A simple selenium black and white image enlarged to 10 x 14, and framed in black. The lens perspective is distant, deliberately so. The eye immediately absorbs the landscape and its dominion over the scene, and simultaneously, the human devastation. A village on the valley floor lies in smoking shambles under the light of a raw moon glittering off the fresh snow, and beyond, a mountain range locked in ice. Here, in these black rocks, the world might end.

Note from the Daybook:

Captain sent word last night that Louis is dead–somewhere at Inchon near MacArthur's landing. Makes it through Heartbreak Hill and steps out of a tank to take a piss on a detonator? Told Cap to send my brother home to Aunt Shelby in Kentucky. She's the last of Mom's people left, she'll know what to do. Korea is taking us down...one at a time.

Jess Cappello stood on a slight rise and surveyed the valley below. The Communist North Korean and Chinese troops had hit scattered villages in the night, in the midst of a blizzard blowing in from the east–a time when the sounds of artillery wagons and tanks moved within the faint whisper of the wind itself across the crusted snow. On the valley floor what might have been huts and stables, low lying structures of wood and brick, littered the snow. Plumes of ash filled the night sky, thin gray smudges against the brilliant moon.

Artillery fire garbled sharply across the snowfields, followed by the bright flash and distant boom of a shell exploding. Jess clutched his padded jacket to his neck and shivered in the eerie light. He pulled his camera bag around, slipped the 35mm Leica out, clipped off the lens cap and removed his wool gloves. The base was behind them, to the southwest. Quickly he made a mental grid, and bringing the Leica up, ticked off several shots covering the valley--north, northeast, east, southeast, south. Should he finish the roll? He decided not. He had thirty-four shots of casualties and artillery placements already in the can. How much information did the Command need beyond the basic body count? His job was done. He pulled his gloves back on hurriedly.

"What the hell you doing here, grunt?"

Jess turned on his heel and smartly saluted. A huge man, bundled in heavy winter issue overcoat, the fur earflaps of his cap pinned up with a Lieutenant's insignia, leaned out of the cab of his jeep. The scarred metal door was emblazoned *The Buffaloes, Seventh Infantry Division*: Quinn's regiment, Jess thought, taken aback.

Windshield wipers flicked clumps of snow right and left as the officer screamed at him again. "You're Air Force recon aren't you? What the hell you doing on this ridge on foot? Enemy troops in the valley!"

"Airman First Class Jess Cappello, sir!" Jess responded, his teeth clacking in the cold. "On orders to photograph the damages to the valley, sir!"

"From up here? In the middle of the bum-fuck night? You nuts?" The officer stared at him in disbelief, his mouth see-sawing at the ice crystals crusted in his mustache. "I'm radioing base to haul your sorry ass out of here, soldier. Idiots! In the way of real fighting men. Recon! In the fucking snow!"

Jess dropped his eyes, waiting.

"Bastard sons o' bitches lurking around...cow-eyed tourists." The lieutenant poked his driver roughly in the shoulder and the jeep lurched over the ridge toward the nearest demolished village, feathers of white rising in it's wake like long commas of breath.

Jess shrugged. Fine with him if he got a quick ride back to a warm cot and a cup of lousy coffee. He stamped his feet, growing numb in his boots. They were never warm enough, not any of them. Another winter, playing hockey over the 38th Parallel. For two years Jess had been assigned to the Joint Forces Recon Operations Center outside of Seoul–even though Command kept saying the war was ending, and that once the POWs were exchanged the Armistice would be signed. Bloody Ridge and Heartbreak Hill led to more soldiers dead, heaped up like jacketed briquettes as the negotiations foundered.

He hated Seoul. Dark and freezing, bleak as the slag piles of the worst Breathitt County coalmines back home.

A flick of snow hit Jess' cheek, and he remembered the camera suddenly, held tight in the grip of his wool gloves. He pressed the box inside his coat, warming the mechanism, praying the aperture would not stick in the cold, or frost leak behind the lens. Last thing he needed was to explain to the Cap how he'd screwed up another camera.

Cracking gunfire echoed across the long traunches from mountain ridge to valley floor. Maybe that asshole in the fur-flaps was right. He'd better clear out.

Jess looked once more at the damaged hovels. They were all so ugly, he thought, blowing his breath into his hands as he hugged the camera against his wool undershirt. The war was ugly. He ought to snap off a few more wide-angle shots, the reflection of the moon on the snow was light enough for a decent exposure, but he was hellishly sick of the vast and repeatable ugliness. Bone-tired of grisly scrapbooks of troop damages and failed maneuvers for Command reviews, prissy public relations photos for the newspapers back home. All shot from low flying planes so the geeks in covert operations could pore over them with magnification lenses, looking for hidden military stockpiles, new signs of the Chinese mole.

Jess spit angrily on the snow. His spit froze, cracking with a ping. It had to be fucking forty below zero. Had to be. It made no sense. And Louis dead.

For an eerie second the valley fell silent, the sounds of gunfire swallowed in the wind from the bitter mountain. The beginnings of a new snowfall edged the far horizon, moving in fast. Jess surveyed the steep rise of the ridge, his eye drawn back to the villages, snow-mounded and oddly humped together, empty of even a cry. The round moon washed the entire valley with a scalding luminosity. Jess withdrew the Leica and raised the camera slowly, adjusting the focus and exposure for the waves of moonlight bounding back from the snowfields to his lens. He clicked, shifted his angle, and shot again. Capturing the uppermost ridges of the silver mountains above the dark sorrow of broken town, the benign indifference of drifting snow.

Jess lowered the camera and zipped it back into his jacket, gazing across the still valley, silent witness to this odd wonder in the battlefield, the effect of the moment's light. Jess stood,

4

transfixed, snow filling in over the tops of his boots, confused at the enormity of what he had not apprehended before. There below was human death and futility, fresh on the snow, or the most astounding natural wonder of light and landscape he had ever witnessed.

The burning awareness inside him felt huge, and Jess understood that he must choose one of two realities. Stand witness to the very foulest of things, or in a deft shift of perception, choose distance: level himself at the periphery of truth. The language of object was above all not human, but the purest shape of life, abandoned of meaning.

What Jess saw before him compelled him toward beauty.

Standing above the battlefield, ice blistering the skin of his face, Jess Cappello, aged nineteen years and alone in the world, experienced exquisite damnation. The thumbprint of destiny marked his soul, and in his possession, two images of beauty.

Genesis

Snowbank, Jess Cappello, 1981

W hat befell in a glance.
Winter and night. A woman, back to the camera, reclines on one hip within the wooden frame of an opened window. Beyond the log cabin, clinging to the eave is the odd fact of a twist of icicle, a spike of watery light. A wash of moonlight amplified by deep fields of snow, falls across the woman's bare shoulders. Her face is half-turned into the darkness of the room's shadow. One hand reaches to the hidden moon. There is no separation in this image between the lens and human heart, and the things neither can say.

Note from the Daybook:
I made an unforgettable image today. Used the old M3 Leica—no time for exposure compensation—no light meter! Opened the 50mm lens all the way, and set the exposure at 1/8 of a second. Even with Kodak's new TRI-X film, knew I would have to coax the image because of extreme contrast. (note: HC 110, heavily diluted 1:20, to compensate.) Negative contrasty, but printable—damned hard to do. Selected

Oriental paper, Grade 2, and developed the print slowly, in baths of Dektol and Selectol. Repeated test prints to get detail on the cheek right, and the shadow detail in the hair. But I knew! Knew the moment the shutter opened....

Jess stood slightly behind the stage curtain, squinting into the lights. He fingered the collar of his black dress shirt, tugged at his jacket. On stage, the curator of the Photography Department of the San Francisco Museum of Modern Art was speaking, waving her hands enthusiastically; referencing her remarks to the image prominently displayed to one side of her on a large easel.

"This is an image so recognizable today one might almost say it has become the author's signature piece. Our museum is thrilled to have acquired an early print, directly from the photographer himself. *Snowbank, 1981,* forms the cornerstone of our retrospective of Jess Cappello's work. The tradition of the fine black and white landscape and portraiture of the West Coast School, our own Ansel Adams, Edward Weston, Imogen Cunningham and many others well known to collectors throughout the world, continues today as the museum is *deeply* pleased to open this exhibit of work by Jess Cappello." She paused for effect. "Introduced tonight by none other than the artist himself!"

Applause in the grand exhibit hall and the wide, wide smile of Cynthia Withers, the curator, beckoned Jess on stage. Cynthia nodded encouragingly as her assistant nudged Jess forward.

"Directly to the podium, Mr. Cappello. The microphone's set, no need to pick it up."

Jess stepped into the focus of lights, hesitating uncomfortably as Cynthia rushed forward and clasped him by the hand. She tugged him to the podium, gushing big smiles all around.

"Ladies and gentlemen, please welcome Jess Cappello!"

Jess gazed out at the assembled guests.

"Just make a few remarks, Mr. Cappello, and entertain some questions if you will," Cynthia whispered. She removed herself to the far side of the stage, standing by the displayed image; his name emblazoned from above in neon tubing.

Jess cleared his throat, bending to the microphone. "Well, I'm not sure how many living artists are asked to guest their own retrospective, but I'm hoping the move isn't a bad one."

The audience tittered and Jess looked down. Portions of the left side of the room had shifted oddly, assuming a murky shadowiness unless he narrowed his vision to the right. He straightened to his full height, a skeletal six foot three.

"Well, thank you for being here. I'd guess an artist loves approval about as much as a dog likes a good belly scratch." He half-grinned, rubbing his chin. "I've been asked to make a few remarks, but frankly, in terms of collecting art, and the value of any artist's work, I believe you folks have more to say about that than I do."

A spatter of clapping rippled around the room.

Jess took a deep breath. "In my life as a photographer, I have known two motivating influences—the astounding aspects of the natural world around me, and my own need to record and document beauty. I haven't had much formal training, but I have had life, lots of life. And I've come to know the same elements of art exist in the field of war as the field of wheat... and the human face is in every way as complex and unique as the shadows and elevations of Half Dome in Yosemite." He glanced around the room. Faces of every kind looked his way, waited on his words.

"A photographer, myself at any rate, is first an observer, and then a craftsperson. The art of the image, what art there is, I believe, lies in its meaning. Not in the application of a selenium tint, not in the object photographed–although these may be highly technical or quite beautiful–but in the brain's interpretation of the whole. And meaning, like the brain, is ultimately personal. My work is a synthesis of object and craft, but you give it meaning." Jess slipped his hands into his pants pockets and looked out earnestly. "I am honored that the museum has chosen to mount this exhibit, and hope San Francisco continues to support photography."

He ceased speaking and fell silent. That was the extent of his prepared remarks. He could only hope to God the audience was ready to let him off the hook and hit the wine bar. Trickles of sweat crept down the neck of his shirt: all black, the jacket too. To hell with what Cynthia assured him was the expected look for artists of film and camera. He was absolutely roasting, cooking under the hot halogen spots. Thank God he'd gotten a haircut, otherwise there he'd be–the spitting image of Willie Nelson at a funeral.

A hand went up in the audience and a youngish fellow, a standout in a silk chartreuse shirt, a nick of beard dead center on his chin, stepped forward. "A question if I may? Your image *Snowbank* is remarkable, even after twenty years it still has legs." He nodded around, inviting the others in attendance to second his opinion. "However, there has been some speculation in the past about the model. Is it true photographers particularly photograph nude subjects known, shall we say, intimately?"

From the corner of his eye Jess saw the curator grimace slightly. This must be the critic from the San Francisco Chronicle she'd warned him about. He cleared his throat.

"Well, thanks for liking the image. As to your question, I'm not sure what you're asking, but I can say that after roughly a thousand printed images, I can't vouch for any stamina, intimate or otherwise, beyond a good pair of hiking boots."

Laughter rolled down the aisles.

"Yes, but who is she?" The reporter persisted, jutting his chin peevishly. "Why the big secret about her identity?"

Jess shook his head. "There's no secret. But there is privacy. The model is also a painter, with a career of her own. In my work, I make it a rule to focus on the success of the image itself. There is no celebrity value in an individual subject, to my way of thinking, which outweighs light, composition, and chemistry. *Snowbank* is a photograph—that is the point of my work."

Another question on *Snowbank* followed a few touching on the southwestern landscapes and Jess early work in the Point Lobos area, and finally, a question regarding his workshop training with Minor White. Jess answered each in turn, gravely giving his most honest opinion; unsure how to explain that the art behind his images was for him, entirely different, and necessarily so, from what these strangers perceived. Yes, *Snowbank* was about the snow, and beauty of Catalina's back in the half-light; but it was also a haiku of everything between them present in the room that night. Yet ultimately, the monolithic picture displayed to his left was, as a photographic image should be, a public field for imagination.

"Mr. Cappello, would you comment on the possible role of teaching in your career? Does the old adage that those who can do, and those who can't, teach, dissuade you?"

Jess looked at the questioner: a sturdy, middle-aged woman in a crisp azure suit, wearing blunt cut hair. Her accent was English, and standing beside her was a girl with hair the color of a penny: a new penny, shining under the lights.

"Well, I hope not." He coughed wryly and shifted his weight, peering down from the podium. "Art is one of those mediums where mentoring is a significant gift. Creative frustration drives one to art—or crime—to begin with."

He waited a beat for the laughter to pass.

"An old hand, anyone who has learned a way to create from inner chaos, can help a student find their own way. I sometimes find myself doing no more than pointing out to a gifted beginner the presence of his or her own unique point of view. Reflecting back to them what they have made." He hesitated, thinking. "Teaching in the arts is both the learning of craft and helping students master a personal language...so to speak."

The new-penny girl spoke up, stepping apart from the woman in the suit. Her voice had the timber of a temple chime, high and light. "Who was your teacher, Mr. Cappello?"

Jess nodded gravely. "Life, young lady. Life, and the friend that gave me my first camera. And every great photographer before me who has let me study and absorb the greatness of their work. Some of us learn from exposure, and I am one of these."

"To your left, Jess," Cynthia called out, and Jess turned slightly, realizing a field of hands was waving from the left side of the room. He grimaced apologetically. He hadn't seen them.

"Sir, what does a retrospective mean to you?"

"A well-earned pause," he grinned. "A little bit more money."

Another voice, carrying across the room.

"Does this mark the closing arc of your work, the definition of your image-making?"

"I hope not! One's vision is always changing—it's in the nature of the work. For example, many of the places I've photographed over the last decades no longer exist as they were. Continued construction, more roads and people erode their isolation. New geometries lie between our cities, and in them, as a matter of fact—a web of horizontal and vertical angles. I hope to be making images as long as the world offers something to see."

11

"The great Miss Bernhard of San Francisco stopped making images in her nineties...will you stop at some point as well? Are there limits to craft?"

Jess shrugged simply. "Well, certainly age changes things. I don't venture into the foothills as far as I used to with a sixty-pound pack. But no, I can't ever see myself not making photographs. That's how I live in the world."

He turned to Cynthia with a look of appeal. He was exhausted with questions, each one aimed at the heart of him, all asking for explanations of what to him was visceral intuition.

Cynthia stepped forward.

"Let's thank Mr. Cappello for his remarks! I'm sure he'll welcome any more comments you might have as we enjoy wine, so generously donated by Blue Creek Cellars, and delicious hors d'oeuvres, provided by Delectable Bite."

She steered Jess offstage in the wake of an enthusiastic applause. "A few preliminaries Jess, with the press, and then I'm afraid you can duck out...much as I'd like you to stay. You're half the draw, you know," she said looking at him speculatively. "The whole world wonders who you are, this photographer with such an exquisite and painful view of our world. Do you realize you have no interviews or essays on record? We had a helluva time preparing a bio on you!"

"I'm a photographer, Cynthia," Jess apologized. "Couldn't begin to tell the story in words."

Alone on the Starlight Express, riding the passenger train from San Francisco to connections southwest out of Los Angeles, Jess nursed a beer, watching as the darkening cliffs of the Pacific shoreline fell away. His thoughts bumped with the shifting weight of the train car against the rails, nudging against hard, tight feelings many of the evening's questions had roused in him. He was not a man prone to introspection, but tonight he was finding some of his thoughts difficult to quell. A damned retrospective. There it was, a visual essay to the past. The simple weight in an undeniable narrative of so much of his work assembled in one place; in the chronology of the work, the migration of images, like film, from scene to scene. A story associated with memories he treasured, and those he had wished away.

Jess dimmed the reading light above his seat and let the darkness beyond enfold him. The train rattled south at a high speed, bending shadows flashing past the window. Jess considered again the significance of Cynthia choosing *Snowbank* as his signature image. Had he not wondered, these past twenty years, if Catalina herself was not the painful essence of that photograph? Wasn't it there, in black and white? Who was he to claim differently? He knew his work. It was always two parts chemistry and geometry and one, very large, unknown.

Camera Obscura

Triangles, Ruth Bernhard, 1946

A still, silent mystery.

Before Jess ever picked up a camera, Ruth Bernhard defined the photographed nude. Her silver gelatin image *Triangles,* suggests eloquence and secrets. What is this unknown woman thinking, her head bowed into the privacy of her arms, sunlight caressing a smooth canvas of arm, breast, and bent knee? The image captures human vulnerability, yet calmness radiates from the cloistered seclusion of her face.

Jess proffered a soft "good morning" as he passed the averted countenance, as he had for nearly thirty years, and let himself out the front door of his adobe with his first cup of coffee. He sat down on the log under the spindly juniper, his shoulders brushing branches heavy with the odor of pinesap and sage that by mid-morning, would be a garland of bees. Jess balanced his coffee on his knee, and as he did most days, watched the first swell of color fill the eastern sky.

Note from the Daybook:

Tossing more negatives! Dozens ripped from the drying racks. Am I misjudging the light, missing the focus? How could that be? I have taken apart the cameras, calibrated light meters and cleaned the lenses, timed out and recalibrated the shutters, checked, and rechecked chemistry and process...but nothing.

Jess shifted against the bumper of his old pickup, removing and shaking his field boots one at a time as creek slime and loose burrs emptied onto the ground. He tilted his face toward the east, gauging the rising sun with a practiced eye, scanning the wilderness. The dry winter grasses bent low under the press of the wind. Narrowing his eyes, he randomly framed the distant silhouettes with the edges of his palms. Nothing.

His fingers had grown numb with cold and were clumsy as he tried to remove his wet socks. He tugged hard, wringing out the wetness, and laid the socks neatly along the dimpled chrome of the bumper. He scrounged around the back of the old pickup, a Ford 1950 F-1, for the spare running shoes he kept and slipped them on. The goose-nosed truck, caked in reddish dust, sat parked at the edge of a shallow streambed swirling with torrents of winter run-off. It was early spring in the arroyo, and feet dry, Jess leaned back against the tailgate and waited, observing the pale browns and reds of the desert deepen with the rising sun. Stalks of hollow reed and spiny agave glistened fiercely in the early light as the hard earth steamed.

He sighed, throwing the wet socks and boots into the back of the truck. The flat, early light was gone and he hadn't gotten what he'd come for. He liked the arroyo though, with its rough channel and scrubby hillocks, and made a mental note to come back in a day or two. Who knew what would make an image...

that unexpected *chose inconnue*. A flick of ebony waxwing, the glint of a sickle of bone could transform the most barren winter landscape.

Abruptly Jess sneezed, and fished out his handkerchief from his back pocket. Dust, and there was plenty of it–even in the dead of winter. He'd tried every remedy short of a clothespin clamped on his nose, and maybe he'd try that next. He'd lost more than one still life blown off the stalk by an untimely attack of sneezing. He rubbed his nose irritably and re-pocketed his handkerchief, getting to work.

He crouched to collapse the tripod, and winced. Damn, he'd taken a hard fall. Tripped over a rut, but had the presence of mind to fall on his hip, protecting the camera. He'd knocked his head on the tripod and come upright to a sitting position, counting all five fingers...first one hand, and then the other. What a headline for his next retrospective: Famous photographer on ass in grass. He laughed out loud.

Getting to business, Jess spread out a sheet of Mylar for his camera parts. He dismantled the field Linhoff, a well-used 4 x 5 view camera, and cautiously removed the 90 mm wide-angle Rodenstock Grandagon he had brought along for this assignment. With slow and gentle movements, Jess wiped the heavy lens clean with a cloth, zipping the Rodenstock back into its protective casing. He folded the camera body flat and placed the 4 x 5 into a padded cache in the gear bag, along with the case of filters.

Jess worked efficiently, his brow furrowed in thought, attention diverted toward the slim profit of the morning: four exposed sheets of film. He knuckled his chin, suspecting he'd leaked light, prepping the last film holder. He should have preloaded the film the night before, but Catalina had stayed late.

His makeshift way of doing things reminded him of old Jigs Tattinger with his pencils and lenses, tied by strings knotted to his pack. Jigs was lucky to get a single shot in a day. But to Jess, who made his living in the field, not teaching community college students as Jigs did in Pasadena, a wasted day was a disaster. Lost dollars, no mistake; but more significantly, lost photographs. Jess considered himself a practical man, and to a degree, cheap. A want was never a need, and a solution should serve its need. The new preloaded film packs might eliminate light leaks, but the film pack itself might not marry well with his cantankerous Linhof. He'd have to ask around first; see what the others favored.

Whistling an old Chet Baker tune, *Come Rain or Come Shine*, Jess pried open the passenger door on the truck and slid his gear bag onto the bench seat. The tripod caught on a tear mended with duct tape and he cursed it. Everything he owned was old. Held together with tape and glue, fence wire and persistence. Especially persistence, what his mother used to call "country hope". Persistence, Hannah had said, filled your pockets for free.

Jess strapped the gear securely to the seat with a belt devised from short, linked bungee cords. His hands worked quickly from habit as he double-checked the tension. He couldn't afford costly lenses crashing into the metal glove box, and a '50 Ford, built on springs like chopsticks, hit the potholes of New Mexico like a sledge.

He checked his watch—already nine in the morning and he had to be in Chama by noon. Jess zipped off the field vest he wore over his heavy flannel shirt and dropped it over the gun rack. The pockets bulged with film and filters, a light meter, pencil and pad, and a crumpled pack of Marlboros, the threads parting along an unevenly mended tear ripped on barbed wire down by Ed Harker's place. He fingered the tear. He was no genius with a needle and thread. He'd have to take the vest to the tack shop.

He fished in one of the pockets and pulled out the smokes, lighting one quickly. Jess drew on the cigarette, evaluating the wasted morning. A lot of work had come back lately; unexpected problems in the prints forcing missed deadlines, too. He was ten days late on this layout for Phineas Travel Magazine, a stylish southern geezer-guide published in Georgia. His assignment editor had proven quite short-tempered, a gal aptly named Brenda Flint. Only last Wednesday she had called, and inquired coolly about a commissioned piece on seasonal changes in desert arroyos. "We do want to be *in the season*, Jess dear," she had drawled.

He scowled. He'd have to put Flint off again. He'd tried all morning, burnt several exposures, but without a doubt attained mediocrity on every one. And no amount toning or burning could turn a lifeless negative into anything better, even if, as some said, a good printer could fix mistakes made by God himself.

Jess crushed the cigarette under his heel, careful to stuff the butt under a damp rock. He'd stop smoking tomorrow. He'd been meaning to anyway—Catalina hated the smell in his clothes. He reached behind the seat of the truck and pulled out a dented thermos, pouring out a cup of coffee as he squinted at the distant bluffs. Where was that dog? He listened, catching only the rattle of dry weeds and further out, the high-pitched hunting cry of *buteo jamaicensis*, a soaring red-tailed hawk. Jess set down the thermos, cupped his hands and whistled loudly, his call carrying easily across the flats.

A muffled bark arose from beyond the far riverbank, and Jess whistled again. A black and white dog emerged from the weeds, forded the riverbed and thrashed through a knot of tumbleweed to reach Jess side. The Border Collie leapt, planting two muddy paws on Jess jeans.

"Down Ansel! Let's go, pal."

Tail wagging, the collie jumped inside the truck and Jess climbed in after, elbowing the muddy dog over as he adjusted his length behind the wheel, feeling the soreness in his hip.

Jess hit the ignition and the starter grated harshly, failing to catch. He tried again, pumping the choke hard, and this time the engine stalled. "C'mon," he cursed the truck. He never should have promised Catalina he would take her to the airport.

His thoughts turned reluctantly to their last encounter as he pumped the accelerator. She hadn't answered him. She'd let his question hang between them as she pulled her coat to her chin, her eyes large and soft in the dark.

"After all these years," she had murmured, shaking her head.

Jess had known the truth then, facing Catalina. For forty-five years photography had formed the framework of his life and he'd followed faithfully his instincts to remain anchored within its parameters. Work was the pillar of his existence. Now, everything had to do with Catalina. Something basic had shifted, and he found the realization difficult to acknowledge.

As a young soldier, Jess had been afraid of the local women. Those graceful Korean mysteries, whose dark eyes looked right through him and glanced away; women who often said "yes" with their bodies, but hid their innermost hearts. "Soldier boy," they chanted, "me make G.I. happy?"

There had been that peaceful year with Carolyn Fitch, the British war bride with twin boys and a small house in the hills, east of San Francisco. Widowed finally, after ten pointless years in which her husband, a wounded gunner, languished in a vet hospital screaming Berlitz German at the potted geraniums, Carolyn now ran a boarding house.

She was a large, comfortable woman, her hair tufted in neat rows of pin curls, dressed in a starched blouse and a dark skirt. Pretty in a plain way, as a daisy might be. She kept a clean house, drank her sherry by the television each night, and on Sundays hosted a pinochle game with her boarders. Jess rented the attic room, finding his way to Carolyn's bed as a stray cat finds the cushions. The arrangement seemed to suit his landlady as Jess took on odd jobs around the house, and on occasion, took her twelve year old sons to the ball park.

That year Jess turned twenty-one. Carolyn's pot roasts and fried chicken put weight back on his gaunt frame and he grew tanned in the summer sun. Hammering a new roof onto Carolyn's little house, he considered what he should do. There was no family left but an old aunt in Kentucky. What did he know but to shoot a camera? And the military had kept the Leica.

It was Carolyn who handed him his first camera, a medium format acquired cheap from one of the Chinese pawnbrokers in the city. She presented the bulky package to Jess his last night at the house. Unwrapping the brown paper, he had fallen silent, unable to thank her, mired in sudden uncertainty. Part of him wanted to settle with Carolyn in her little house and repair the leaky plumbing, but part of him struggled to come alive. His head was filled with foolish fantasies.

"Jessy," Carolyn said softly, for she called him that when they were alone. She stroked his wrist, her brown eyes sweet as taffy. "You got no business hanging 'round with a widow and kids. You got to cover some ground. Go on, but send me a picture or two? Remember Jessy, you're a picture maker. Don't squander the good Lord's gift."

Jess hugged Carolyn close, and wearing his army issue jacket, caught the train into the city. No plan, just a thought to look up a photographer named Minor White, who taught camera workshops at the City Art Institute. With a small savings and his camera from Carolyn in his satchel, Jess rented an upstairs apartment above a take-out restaurant. Using cardboard and discarded dishpans from the Chinese kitchens below, he converted the tiny bathroom in his apartment into a workable darkroom.

It was a strange life. Late mornings Jess worked the San Francisco flower market, unloading shipments of tulips and roses from the delivery trucks in the alleys. He took any job he could find to make rent—catering, kitchen help, and for a while, chauffeur to a blind stockbroker down in the financial district—but he liked the flower market best. The cool mornings and the vibrant color of the flowers eased the long nights.

Comely neighborhood women, with their braids and prep school accents, often agreed to be his models. He studied them, and learned the landscape of the human form. The women taught him subtlety of light and form. And what he threw away was often more important than what he kept. An image wasn't perfect until he knew it was, and it wasn't *his* until he had perfection. Until he loved the wet, glistening proof, a work more original and compelling than the sweetness of the girls themselves. His fascination grew with the particular, the unexpected and the simple. Lost in the celibacy of his solitary dark room, Jess pursued few meaningful relationships after Carolyn. Women and love were synonyms for uncertainty.

Turning thirty, Jess left California for Manhattan, drifting at the edges of the gallery scene. He learned to drink a martini and discovered jazz music like nothing he had ever heard. But in the city he suffered a flu that seemed to last the entire winter, wringing him out like the wash. He took to walking the streets, building back his strength. And on a rainy afternoon, wandering the cold halls of the city's vault-like museums, Jess felt drawn to the wild terrain in the haunting paintings of Georgia O'Keefe. In the spring he packed up his old pickup and headed west to the Sangre de Cristo Mountains.

With the last of his money, Jess bought a small rundown adobe in the olive-colored hills of Tesuque. He was selling commercial images now, living in limited fashion on sporadic magazine work. There was much to learn, and he winnowed his successes from his mistakes, working constantly, educating his eye. In the solitary hours of the darkroom the young photographer reveled in silent discovery.

Near the end of his forties, finally established in the edgy world of photography on the strength of his gallery work alone, uncertainty rose again. The girl was just a model; a struggling painter he met in a Taos bar. They'd spent the weekend in a cabin in the mountains, and it was this moment in Jess life that seemed to him most perfect. A passionate fusion of image and beauty, a truth he could touch.

The dog whined at his side and Jess shook his thoughts clear, stiff in the cold truck. How had it come to this, he wondered. Facing his beloved under the naked bulb of a porch light, trying to put into words everything that mattered. She had looked at him with those eyes that were like the eyes of an antelope, and said nothing. A silence that killed him. She'd turned and walked briskly to her Jeep at the end of the gravel driveway, reversed and pulled out, tires crunching over the frozen ruts. From the doorway Jess had watched Catalina Brezza, she with the name and nature of the breeze, drive away. His chest clamped and shaking, like a mechanism seized.

Jess' eyes watered, and he sneezed hard. His fingers still gripped the thermos lid of cooling coffee. Ansel whined, more loudly this time, and pressed a muddy nose to the window, steaming the glass. Jess reached across the cab and rolled down the dog's window, chukking the pup under the chin.

"Yep, time to go, pal."

Jess cranked the ignition once more and backed off the accelerator, careful not to flood the engine. He listened to the ignition grind again. Damned old Ford. Then the spark plugs caught, and the pickup shooped into a noisy shimmy. Smoke burst from the tailpipe and the Ford lurched down the gravel ruts toward the highway.

A small buck raised its head out of the mesquite. Dark eyes alert, the buck watched as the truck rattled past before springing lightly down the banks of the arroyo.

Jess grunted and gunned the engine. That was the picture.

Misalignment

Jean Charlot and Wife, Edward Weston, 1933

Dark complexity.
Jean Charlot draws the gentle face of his wife, Zohma, under his own, his hand pressing the dark curls at the back of her head tenderly as they embrace. Her face is hidden from view, but Jean Charlot's is exposed, asking an exquisitely poignant question of the viewer. What is this young, earnest man in wire-rimmed glasses thinking, as he embraces his wife? What lifts his eyes away from her? An embrace...but is this all the image has to say?

Note from the Daybook:
There is shape and density everywhere in life. Emotion. Not what I can describe in the landscape. The object I can accept, and perfect.

Jess dropped Ansel off at the house and changed quickly into a heavy sweater, climbing back into the truck with a second thermos and a burrito of cold cuts. He turned onto the two-lane road from Espanola and drove through the Rio Chama Valley, heading north towards Chama. Skeletons of tumbleweed raced down the highway before sticking, impaled, in the long miles of cattle fence. As he pushed the accelerator, hammering past fifty, Jess mind spooled empty of thoughts.

He arrived at Catalina's cabin, a log house sprawled alongside a dry creek under a thick sweep of Ponderosa pine. A basket of bark chips sat on the porch. Catalina collected the vanilla-scented bark from the pines, kept in baskets she scattered throughout the house, and it was this sweet woodsy aroma that lingered in Jess memory, embedded even in the smell of her hair. A bushy calico cat swished out of sight under the steps when Jess arrived and he knew where he'd find Catalina: her painting studio was a short walk back through the trees to a dilapidated barn.

She was in the studio finishing her packing, and looked up, smiling hello.

"Heh, Cappello."

"Sorry, I'm late." He bent over and kissed the top of her hair.

Jess began to load boxes and trunks in the Ford. When the task was completed, Catalina locked the barn, and together she and Jess returned to the cabin. Catalina lit a fire in the wood stove to heat the chilled rooms as Jess stood at the windows, lost in thought. The cabin faced a spreading view of open range, and below, the dark shapes of cattle roamed the empty acres clear-cut a half century earlier. March winds buffeted the Hispanic Highlands.

Their work done, and fallen into each other's arms, Jess lay wakeful, staring into the embers of the fire. Catalina relaxed in his arms, her dark hair fanned across his shoulder. Jess watched as she twirled a tequila shot glass between her thumb and forefinger. She felt good next to him, and he pulled the heavy blankets higher around their bodies. He met her upturned eyes.

"Venezuela is one hell of a long ways south of the border," Jess muttered gruffly. "Miss me?"

"More than you have a right to expect," she teased, slipping her free hand under the blankets.

"Not just *that*...although that, too," Jess flushed. "Heh! Careful, my side hurts."

"Jess, you've got a large bruise here. What happened?"

"Tripped."

"One of these days, Cappello, you will fall off a cliff, I swear."

Catalina set down her empty glass beside the bed and gave Jess a quick, fierce hug. They rested in silence.

"What will you do while I'm gone?" she whispered in an odd tone. Then almost immediately she tossed her hair, as if clearing her mind. "You know I've got someone to housesit my place? One of my students wants use of the studio for a few months so I've left most of my brushes and paints. I'm only taking the bare minimum."

"Those trunks in the pickup would be considered the 'bare minimum'?" Jess laughed lightly. He smiled wryly. "Oh, I'll be all right. Got another backcountry workshop. A trail ride thing the Arts Center roped me into."

Catalina pushed back, her narrow face interested. "When?"

"Ten days mid-June. Ten *long days*, I should say."

She tickled him between the ribs gently. "Oh, come on. Photographers do not live by inspiration alone. It's a paid gig, right?"

"It's not the teaching I mind," Jess replied, his mouth turned down at the corners. "It's the horses."

"Horses!" Catalina hooted, breaking into riffs of laughter. "You really *meant* backcountry! Oh God, you *do* have a pack leader?" Her gaze swept up Jess features, and he knew she was imagining him hunched over a saddle horn, leaky canteen and upside-down compass in hand. "But Jess," she murmured. "You have no sense of direction."

He colored. "I know. The Center's hired outfitters to run the actual expedition, provide the horses and stuff. I teach and run the workshop. Six days in the mountains, and four in the darkroom for lab critique."

Catalina patted Jess comfortingly on the pan of his belly. "You'll be fine then. Anybody helping?"

"Abe Santos. You know him—young guy working at the Center awhile. West coast style mostly, images with rocks and shapely vegetables. I think his work is good. Or will be."

"I don't know any Santos..." She shook her head. "Oh, you mean the vet? The guy missing an arm? He's not young, Jess—he's in his late forties!"

"Young to me."

She arched a brow. "I can't really fathom how he manages a camera. You sure he can manage a horse?"

"No worse than me."

Not know Santos? Of course Catalina knew the man. She'd been around when they were working in his darkroom, run into him in town. Was she feigning ignorance? Jess bit his lip, ashamed. She was preoccupied, that was all, although he might rightly suspect Catalina and almost anybody. He was painfully aware of his lover's tomcat lack of discretion, her willful refusal to heed convention or common sense.

Things were what they were, he reminded himself. He looked at Catalina almost tenderly. There was such an integrity at times in shamelessness.

"Abe's worked with me a long time," he said slowly. "He's good with a class—says the nice things I forget."

For Abe Santos, photography absorbed a life shattered by the war, much as it had for Jess a decade, and a war, earlier.

There was control in the darkroom, peace in solitude: that much both men knew. In the eighties, Abe had signed up for a number of Jess workshops, and as they worked under the orange light on their contact prints, a surprising partnership had emerged. There was a direct honesty about the other man Jess implicitly accepted, although they were as different as two men, or two veterans could be.

A native of Las Vegas, Santos lived with his wife Carly, and their three kids in a small house, west of Santa Fe. Stocky, his build bridged by broad shoulders, and the one oddly swinging arm stubbed at the elbow, Abraham Santos had a natural way with people; a generous, white-toothed smile, and, to Jess liking, a peculiar wit. The man made a point of establishing his competence and independence, proving his proficiency with a camera. He managed his lenses and film using ingenious knee holds and jerry-rigged short cuts, and was exceptionally organized in the darkroom. It had seemed logical to Jess to ask Abe to assist with the larger summer classes at the Center. But mostly, he was relieved to have someone help with the awkward, social aspect of his workshops.

"Well, all to the good then," Catalina nodded, chuckling. "Abe will keep you facing the right end of the horse."

They fell silent, the bedroom illuminated in slanted panels of the mellifluous golden twilight Jess loved best. His fingers tapped out a melancholy tune in the hollow of Catalina's spine as his thoughts circled aimlessly.

She seemed to read the sadness in his face.

"It's not forever, Jess. Just 'til whenever...." She shrugged and her voice trailed off. "I don't truthfully know how it will work with the Venezuelans, or how long it will take me to make this commission for the new museum. I mean, it's a big mural. Eight panels!" She squinted thoughtfully, her chin tucked in the crook of Jess' arm as she rimmed the circle of his navel with her free thumb absently tugging damp curls of pepper-white hair.

Jess winced, untwining her fingers.

Catalina grew pensive. "It's all new to me, this international stuff. I could make a hash of it! But as long as I've got this shot, I'm going to make it count."

An uneven cleft formed between Jess gray brows. "Of course. But why can't you paint the thing here? Ship the panels down. Why go to Caracas?"

"Risk the panels might rip? They could crack the paint when they uncrate them! My work could be damaged in shipment, or affected by the changes in humidity. They might assemble the damn thing upside down!" Her voice trembled in disbelief. "No way," she shook her head resolutely. "The museum has found me a local studio and a crew to do the installation, and that's how I'm going to do this commission. I won't chance a mistake. Caracas is going to have a *Catalina Brezza* done right. I'll see to it myself!" Her expression glowed.

Jess sighed, and his arm tightened around her waist. The bed springs creaked as he adjusted their weight against the pillows propped at his back. His eyes drifted over to the clay kiva in the corner of the cluttered bedroom. The pinon logs had crumbled into cylinders of silvery ash.

"I only wonder...wouldn't it be better to set a time limit? How long can this take? *Whenever* is, well, putting a lot of pressure on one day at a time."

"Precisely the way I like it, Jess." Catalina's lips set with a familiar stubbornness.

"Don't I know," Jess admitted, stroking a hair off her forehead. "But seriously, I know these things. Next the museum will ask you to stick around for a master class—turn you into a pampered glitterati to lure in the donor checks."

"As if!" Catalina snorted, her black eyes flashing. "Once they've got my murals I'll be banging the door down to get a check. That's a fact. Though I wouldn't turn down an offer to hang around the country some. I've never been to Venezuela. Papa says there's loads of Italians there, but our people wouldn't like the jungle. Not after hot, hilly Corsica. Maybe you'd come?"

"That would be one slow boat."

"Sooner or later you have to put your butt on a plane, Cappello."

"Not since 1953, not going to now. You ducked the issue... making the return trip."

Her gaze turned stony. He was a fool to have brought it up, not today, not ten years from now. Whatever she considered their years as lovers to be retained importance in their singularity. Catalina claimed choice made a relationship superb—the perfect blend of companionship and freedom. Work, solitude, play, she would say between kisses.

He paled. "Catalina, I–"

"I thought we put this to rest, Jess." The blankets crumpled to her waist as she drew herself upright, the lamplight casting deep shadows down the cleft of her breasts. Catalina glanced pointedly at the small alarm clock on the reading table and reached for her half-glasses, dislodging travel books on South America and gallery catalogs from New York into a tumble on the floor.

"No, we didn't," Jess said slowly. "When I asked when you would come back, you didn't answer. I want, I need things... more settled." He felt his cheeks grow hot. "You can't just leave, Cat."

The room fell entombed in lengthy silence.

"*Non avete cuore?*" Catalina rebuked softly.

Jess bent his head and said nothing.

Abruptly she folded her glasses, dropping them in her lap. "*Mio caro*, it's nearly time to leave for the airport. Let's not ruin our last afternoon?" She leaned her cheek against his shoulder, cajoling him with a smile.

Jess looked down at her, aching and hopeless. The poetic incongruity of her clouded his thoughts. Those graceful bones he photographed so often, her small body smooth as polished wood. The rare and singular, his Catalina. Jess felt his chest tighten. He reached out and touched her shoulder with his fingertip, tracing the ridge from her scapula down to the silky hollow at her throat.

Words failed. There was nothing large enough, complete enough to say to someone who might simply disappear from his life.

He tilted her chin to meet his eyes, brushing back the hair back from her cheek.

"Look at me, Catalina. Look carefully. I'm sixty-three, damn near old. Hell, I am old. I want to spend all of my life with you—and not with you in Venezuela, or anywhere else, and me here alone." He dropped his hands from her face. "We're good together, you and I. We respect each other's work...remember that idea for your *Dante* series last year? How we both knew what the theme had to be, what could be accomplished? We're good together, Catalina. We'll always be good together."

"Oh, Jess. Of course," Catalina murmured hopelessly.

Jess watched her thoughts race away, the impatience visible on her face.

"Please, baby," he cleared his throat, his voice unsteady. "Give what I'm saying a chance. I'm only asking to grow old with you." His weathered face radiated a gentle self-mockery.

"No, Jess," she turned away. "You're asking for what I can't give."

Slowly he forced out the words. "Not ever?"

"Not ever."

Back Drop

Moonrise, Hernandez, New Mexico, Ansel Adams, 1941

A landscape.
An extraordinary range of light and dark falls through the photograph. The image contains a contrast range of nearly a thousand to one: from the sunlit touched crosses and clouds in the background, to the dark mesquite foreground. But the negative, made in 1941, is limited by film capable of recording a contrast range of only a hundred to one—and paper that at best might print fifty to one. A successful print of *Moonrise* is a technical virtuosity over an imperfect negative. Each print of *Moonrise* is unlike any other; each print differs subtly, as light itself in any given moment.

Note from the Daybook:
Still some unexplained blurring in left field of recent negatives. Did I damage the Rodenstock when I fell? Need a lens element re-cemented? Finally got the arroyo shot. Needed the check!

More lonely than mere solitude would warrant. Be wary of the pathos of late light, the subject photographed.

Catalina was gone. The skies of summer and the wild things filled the empty spaces and Jess photographed them all. He burnt film, losing himself in the familiar work, comforted by discipline.

One night, old Miles Davis playing on the radio out of the University of Albuquerque, Jess paused at his worktable and surveyed his third botched mat. He turned the mat in his hands and squinted at the upper left hand corner of the cut, then examined the sharpness of his mat cutter blade. Sharp enough. Jess dropped the mat in frustration, letting his eyes drift to the landscape hanging on the wall. *Moonrise*...a heroic image really. A remarkable achievement with a "G" deep yellow filter, an exposure of f/32 for a full second, and a shimmer of moonrise—that fleeting, essential light breaking over the Chama Valley.

He walked toward the picture, musing over his beer, remembering that little Manhattan gallery, viewing *Moonrise* for the first time. He'd felt a surge of instant kinship with this man Adams, who made this image of the same elements of light and landscape that had affected Jess so deeply in Korea. Another photographer who chose to render the remarkable sparingly.

He contemplated *Moonrise*, every nuance and detail familiar as his own hand. It was a moody landscape. A bald moon floated in a dark sky above the distant Truchas Mountains, and below the town of Hernandez squatted in the desert brush, a few adobes scattered among the graveyard crosses. Moonlight brushed the old walls of the adobe church, illuminated the almost imperceptible bell tower cross, a sword raised to the limits of the known universe. The damn thing was eerie. If, as someone once said, music was the fragrance of the universe, then Ansel's image was how God must have composed the world.

Jess rubbed the back of his neck, finishing off the beer. He half-listened to Davis riff off on a cyclic third, pursuing a counterpoint harmony against the slow notes of a honey-toned bass. Every man, his friend Hunter once said, has his moment: a push toward his own small, blundering destiny. Manhattan was Jess. His first gallery sale!

He spun the empty bottle loosely in the palms of his hands as he listened, remembering what it felt like back in '66 wandering Manhattan, the frosted sidewalk under his feet, the biting smell of diesel and sauerbraten in the air.

What had it meant to be thirty years old? He never went home to Kentucky. No reason to. He'd escaped the makeshift canvas darkrooms of Seoul, the reconnaissance missions flown low over Franco's Spain, over a Cuba torn between Batista and the revolutionaries in the hills. Yet Jess still felt the familiar twist in his guts remembering the rumble of jet engines and shaking metal, the chill hours spent holding his own vomit in a paper bag. He was a ground boy, afraid of flying, the son of a Kentucky miner, for chrissakes. Not gone so far then from Kentucky, or the war.

Miles Davis on the radio had given way to Eric Dolphy, pushing a beat like the pulse of city streets and the erratic energy of that long ago afternoon. Jess savored in reflection the possibilities of youth and of synchronicity; of a time he knew both place and purpose. He saw himself, just a boy buoyant with good fortune, whistling the bars of a popular Gershwin tune on upper Fifth Avenue, pausing to dig in his pockets for a smoke. The tune a favorite learned from Hunter, a sweet fragment of song the black pilot sang because he said it reminded him of home, the wet sticks of Louisiana.

Hunter Jefferson Kincaide, so dark his skin reminded Jess of summer plums. Pilot of the T-44 Trainer the crew had christened *Marilyn's Mother.* All the Recon guys recognized his raspy bass crooning over the drone of the engines. Any tune—old jazz, delta blues, the occasional catchy show song. The second they were air borne, Jess anchored his brain on Hunter's voice to block the cold hissing through the gaps in the metal, smooth the turbulent shifts in altitude. He filled in the lyrics in his head as the light plane bounced over the seas and black continents, and back again. Hands clamped under his armpits, humming madly under his breath, Jess endured the terrifying midnight hours working surveillance on the *Mother.*

Afterwards, the habit of tunes stuck.

Jess flinched at the memory, fished in his jeans and lit a cigarette, aware of the reasons he had served to begin with, still able to flawlessly recall the flat, powdery no-color eyes of the county judge. Elmer Austin Robart. A turtle-faced old bugger who had given him a choice of Breathitt County Jail or the military service, predicting he'd not fare well in either.

"Apple didn't fall too far from the tree with you, boy," the robed magistrate had pronounced soberly, tapping his tobacco-stained forefinger on the desktop, inches from where Jess stood in scruffy jeans and undershirt, barely seventeen.

The judge surveyed Jess, his lips pursed as he considered the recently broken nose. "I'm going give you a piece of advice that I suspect you never got, son. It's pretty straight, so listen up. *If you don't like it, get out, or by God get your sorry ass into it."* The judge peered closely at Jess. "You follow me, son? Violence solves nothing. Use your brain. Now get out of my court."

Jess averted his eyes to the faded flag behind the bench of the Courthouse, folded in still decades of undisturbed dust. Small noises from his mother, the town's third grade teacher, scrubbing her nose with a hankie. Jess saw Louis yawn and shift his ponderous weight restlessly on the visitor's bench.

35

His father, Gianni "One-Two" Cappello, former middleweight boxer out of East Saint Louis was not in court. The old man lay piss-drunk somewhere in a side tunnel of Hardshell Number Two Mine.

"Yes, sir. Thank you sir."

The exact refrain of the next four years in the United States Air Force.

Jess possessed the liability of a hot temper, and thanks to Gianni, a quick right fist: hardscrabble to the core. But nothing comes easy to a Cappello, and in boot camp he drew the bellicose ire of a buck sergeant who made it his personal, obviously pleasurable mission to hike Jess ass daily the endless length of the parade grounds. Jess bought his favor by winning his fights. Off-duty, he earned a fierce reputation fighting barehanded. Chicken scratch matches mostly, country style—real easy money behind the mess.

He dumbfounded his superiors, not to mention himself, by demonstrating a good eye and patience with chemistry; scoring well on the battery of tests given raw recruits. The Air Force reluctantly assigned him a photography slot in Airborne Reconnaissance and handed Jess his first camera, a Leica, new in the box. Go figure, how utterly sick it made him to fly.

Faced with buckets of time alone, Jess concentrated on learning to become an adept field cameraman, and exactly nine years to the month he'd left his uniform neatly folded on the seat of a cross-town Bay City bus, Jess made his first Manhattan gallery sale. *Paid* for a picture of Seoul, that haunting image of burning debris and unforgiving snow. The irony was laughable. He owed that judge everything.

Jess celebrated his triumph alone. He didn't know many other photographers; back then they weren't plentiful as blondes in Camaros, not like they were now. He'd taken Minor White's workshop his second year out of the service, and oh what a whacko. Pacing ceaselessly, the slight photographer had required all the students to analyze his own photographs, insisting they write down feelings evoked from the images on paper held against the back of the student in front of them. While they scribbled, White ranted, ticking off the competing schools of photography, the pillars of achievement, the lions of the Icon. Concluding with operatic exasperation that if photographers were to forever number so few, they might well huddle together for warmth.

Back then White was right. Jess could go east or west. To California and the school of 'straight' photography, anchored in Weston and Adams; or East, to New York City and the monumental legacy of Stieglitz, Strand, and Steichen. Uncertain, he'd done both, and discovered the continental dimensions of the isolation in his profession.

Not so different today.

Jess tossed his cigarette butt in the empty beer bottle and touched the edge of the print on his wall. That first sale had gotten him this...*Moonrise*. The beginnings of a personal collection he prized beyond words. Jess searched out the small gallery on 86th Avenue, browsing the windows. Noting the Eugene Smith, some Callahan, a few High Sierra images by Adams stacked on easels. Roughly an hour later he'd marched back out–a wrapped print tucked securely under his left arm, absolutely ebullient. A singular 16 x 20 inch signed print of *Moonrise*! The print cost him seventy-five dollars: the entire worth of his small savings account, check included.

Thirty-six years and Adam's landscape still hung from a nail embedded in a stucco wall: the only image in a room where Jess Cappello archived his prints.

So damn long ago, Jess reflected, throwing away the botched mats.

Catalina's dealer in New York assured Jess this image—in fact any clean, careful printing by Ansel more than 35 years old—would fetch upwards of twenty thousand dollars at auction. Jess shook his head. What price mystery. None at all.

Leaving the Arts Center, Jess headed south toward the airport to pick up Abe Santos. As he drove, he checked over his roster of attendees, scanning down the list of ten registered names. At over two grand a pop for workshop fees and expenses, Jess surmised, most of the attendees would be doctors and scientists, along with the oddball chief executive officer or retired entrepreneur. The majority middle-aged, out of shape. He shook his head—a small fortune to go camping with mosquitoes, not to mention saddle sores.

Their schedule called for the group to check in June 3rd, bunk their gear for the night at the Sundance Motel, and gather at the Arts Center for the traditional get-together dinner and portfolio critique. Jess rapped the sheet with his pencil, mulling the schedule. As always, the critique was his least favorite part. It was all heart for most of them, although there existed an arrogant few, hot to sink their teeth into an endless technical debate. But acceptance and open-handed approval was largely what they came for.

He shrugged, thinking ahead. He wondered what this group would gravitate toward, what they would discover wandering the canyons and gullies of the high mountains. Were they an adventuresome bunch? He hoped so. They would head beyond the plateau into the steep, rugged foothills of the Carson National Forest, New Mexico's wild and gorgeous mountain lion country.

Jess pulled into the airport pickup lanes and at first he did not see Abe leaning off the curb, waving him down. He pulled the truck over at an angle between two waiting cabs and climbed out.

Abe cracked a smile. "Heard you were famous."

"No, I won't loan you five bucks."

Abe laughed. Jess grabbed his duffel bag, stowing it in the back.

"How's your mother?"

Abe shook his head. "Moved in and micro-chipped. Thank you, Pleasant Acres. They'll find her if she hitches Highway 90 again."

He climbed in beside Ansel and Jess suppressed a grin, wondering which of them would get the window. He needn't have wondered. Abe obligingly let the dog stretch out over his lap, poking his nose out the crack of opened window. Jess swung back into traffic, choosing the back road north, the Old Turquoise Trail. Well, it *had* been a back road, Jess complained sourly. Until the Albuquerque Chamber of Commerce splashed the route across big shiny brochures advertising Indian jewelry trading posts and Pueblo festivals.

Abe stretched out under the weight of the dog and Jess shot the man a quick glance as he navigated the two-lane road, keeping an eye out for the tourists double-parked along the gravel shoulder. Abe yawned and scraped his hair back from his forehead, revealing a broad tan line from his hat. Abe Santos had the kind of athletic build that loosens slightly with age, in the manner of a well broken-in mattress that stubbornly retained an essential frame and resilience.

"How're things in Nevada?"

"Nevada's fine. Don't change much. Still hot, still flat, still ugly," Abe sighed, burying his fingers in the black fur behind Ansel's ear. The dog sniffed out the window contentedly. "Moved Mother Daphne into one of those posh golf course units, though if you ask me, Mom thinks she's in France. Sang every damn song from *Gigi*, twice on the hour. Hope to Betsy when I'm seventy, there's something better in my cranium than '*Little Girls*'."

Jess navigated around a deep pothole, a recent pock from the winter melt. "Where's your son this summer?"

"Finished high school! Can't hardly believe it. Buck's headed to the Naval Academy...he'll spend the summer working Ed Harkin's ranch. Toughen him up for what awaits at Annapolis."

"Annapolis! Well done," Jess praised gently. Abe was proud, and rightly so. He was himself an Academy graduate, quietly pleased his son had chosen to follow in his footsteps.

"Peacetime, praise Jesus."

Jess eyes flickered over to the man's left shirtsleeve, neatly pinned at the elbow. Abe's gaze intercepted his, and Jess hunched over the steering wheel uncomfortably. He focused on the road.

"How's Catalina?"

"Left town in March, bud."

"You're lookin' pretty good then—for cold leftovers."

They rode for a while in silence, Abe Santos plucking at what would be a stubbly beard within the week. Jess frowned at the looming elevations of the Sangre de Cristo Mountains, and then abruptly Jess remembered the workshop and reached inside his vest, tossing Abe the roster of participants.

Next to each name and address was a brief description of what camera gear and type of photography the sign-ups had experience using. Eight men and two women. Both women were from the west coast. One, Jess recognized as the girlfriend of a famous celebrity photographer he knew in Monterey, a crusty likeable Swedish gal. The other woman had an odd sounding name, followed by a string of professional credits including "M.D." One more doc.

"Know any of 'em?" He asked offhand when Abe finished skimming the list.

"Yep. At least two are repeats. Okay guys from what I remember." Abe jabbed his forefinger into the page. "This guy here, Henry Hiller? He's the old guy from Portland, right? The geezer with the wooden Deardorf 4x5 rig? And isn't Mark Anthony—yabba dabba doo, *Cleo baby*, can't forget that name—isn't he that neurosurgeon from Atlanta, the one that does ER head repairs? Harley Specials?"

"Yep," Jess confirmed. "Had them both on the San Juan River trip. They're okay."

"But who's this Sarah Harte-Valentine? Excuse me, *Doctor* Sarah Harte-Valentine. Sounds like a soap star."

"Don't know. But that many credentials make me sweat. She's gotta own the alphabet, that one."

Abe laughed. "W.W.A."

"Say again?"

"Women...with attitude."

"Don't let your wife hear talk like that," Jess admonished, allowing a twist of smile. He had to admit he was anxious about this unknown Sarah Harte-Valentine, the name right out of a Victorian romance and the credentials to argue otherwise. Jess hoped she was serious about her photography—and close to a hundred years old. That's why Greta Hansen fit in so well: past fifty and as practical as her iron braids. He shrugged. Was it too much to hope Miss "heart valentine" might be Greta's twin?

"Hope they brought those padded bike shorts," Abe chuckled, crushing his Cowboy Club cap back on his head, tilting the brim against the slanted rays of sun. "My 'Other duties as assigned' most definitely do *not* include bandaging asses."

Portfolio

Woman behind Cobwebbed Window, Wynn Bullock, 1955

A mirage. A muse.
A small greeting card propped on the windowsill in Jess'
bedroom. On the front of the card is an ethereal black and
white image by Wynn Bullock: a woman's torso photographed
through the glazed windows of an old garden shed. Her body
presses against the glass, shoulders arched backward. As seen
through the window, her pale sickles of hipbone and breast are
shrouded by tendrils of ivy and cobweb, and seem to dissolve
in the diffuse light. A poetic, dreamlike image possessed of
yearning and refusal, the contrasts of light and shadow, vernal
beauty.

On the back of the card is a poem. A lyric from Li Ho, the
eighth century Chinese poet, in memory of a legendary girl
of perfect beauty, Hsiao-Hsiao Su. "Little Su", buried three
hundred years before the poet Li Ho stood vigil by her grave.
The poem has been hand-copied onto the vellum in a delicate
print. Restrained, artful flourishes mark the commencement
of each line.

The dew on hidden blossom
bears witness to her tears.
There is no being that finds its way to her heart.
Grasses are her cushions,
pines her protecting roof.
Wind is her rustling dress,
water her transparent veil.
I waited for her.
But the bluish light remained cold.
And on the western hill
the winds are driving the rain.

Li Ho's words carry the shape of longing, Jess thinks, the longing of Wynn Bullock's image.

Note from the daybook:

Fiddling with contact prints from a portraits project. Portraits are a frustrating paradigm! If I achieve likeness, I lose the spark of the person. If I achieve the personality, I lose likeness in the very tricks that will expose personality to the camera. Faces are so astonishingly mobile...the flux within features of expression. I'd like to try my hand at a portfolio around this concept: that there exists a physical stamp of innermost talent—a doctor's skill revealed in his hands, a dancer's musical inwardness exposed in her litheness, the teacher's patience in her face.

Poem sent by Catalina yesterday. I am at a loss to understand it.

"Take a seat, folks, and we'll get started."

Jess fingered the line of his jaw and waited. The workshop registrants had found their way to the Arts Center, a remodeled facility constructed from the iron framework of an old tortilla bakery, located a crooked block off the central Plaza of Santa Fe.

"How many of you have been down to the Plaza?" he asked curiously, looking around at the slim show of hands. "It's worth the time, folks." Centuries old, whitewashed adobe buildings once housed the Spanish administrators of the Santa Fe Territory. Evidence of the conflux of Indian, Spanish and frontier cultures could be found in the history of these haciendas and back street saloons, the sprawling pueblo markets. But these days, the Plaza peddled expensive collectibles and amusements—silver-buckled resort wear, antique basketry, Jeep excursions to the famous hot springs. New York art dealers came scouting for regional paintings and sculpture, and Jess knew that even his own images were identified with the hipness that was Santa Fe. Still, the past nested in the old city like buried seeds of lodge pole pine, patient, in abeyance. Garlands of dried chili twisted in the alleys above the heads of the Indian vendors squatting under the eaves, their brightly colored blankets of merchandize spread out to net the tourist dollar. Beyond lay the landscape of arid, hostile beauty, exposed in the paintings of Georgia O'Keefe that brought him here so long ago.

Jess took a place at one end of the gray fluorescent room with his back to an easel and marker board, his hands jammed deep in the pockets of his jeans. He glanced meaningfully at Abe, propped casually against the doorframe. Abe nodded and obligingly closed the door, taking a place near the long table backed against the wall. Leather and canvas portfolio cases cluttered the tabletop, mixed with a few presentation and archival boxes.

"Welcome to Santa Fe and the Center for the Arts workshop in Black and White Landscape," Jess began without preamble. "Most of us had a chance to get acquainted at dinner, but I see a few late stragglers have arrived. I am Jess Cappello—I live and work out of Tesuque—and this is our assistant instructor, Abe Santos, of Santa Fe. If any of you hadn't guessed from this collected gear and the shaggy beards, you're in the right place."

A ripple of laughter erupted in the room. The men looked around, smiling at the prickly stubble on Abe, and the full Jeremiah Johnsons on the few wearing pack shirts. The group closely resembled a Yukon dog sled team, less so the vacationing doctors and lawyers they actually were.

"Let's do role call," Jess suggested, pulling out his dog-eared roster. His two women registrants had yet to make their appearance. Not an auspicious show of timeliness, which irked Jess. "All right," he concluded, reaching the end of the list. "We're missing one S. Harte-Valentine, and Greta Hansen. Anyone know either of them or their whereabouts?"

A hand shot up in the back row and a bald man in his late sixties stood up, pulling a slip of stationary out of his back pocket and unfolding it carefully. "I've a note here from Greta, left at the front desk."

"Dr. Smithers—Gary, aren't you and Greta camera club buddies?" Jess inquired genially.

Gary Alsen Smithers, a retired bone surgeon, speaking in the flat broad vowels of a Midwesterner, smoothed the note out between his crooked thumbs and pushed his half-glasses midway up his nose. He sucked his teeth a minute before speaking aloud to the group. "Well, it says here that Greta is canceling..." he looked up in mild surprise, his pale eyes blinking behind his thick glasses. "Headed home to Denmark. Ah, poor thing, her mother's dead—stroke. Regrets and all that."

"So, no Greta?"

"No Greta." Gary Smithers took his seat, shaking his head.

Jess locked eyes with Abe. They were one woman down on their list, and unfortunately it was the one they knew. Would the other one show, or cancel as well? Jess scratched Greta's name off the list, making a mental note to notify the staff and place a call to Crimson Peaks Ranch in the morning with a revised head-count.

"Anyone heard from S. Harte-Valentine?" Jess scanned the group of blank faces. "Okay, I guess if Ms. Harte-Valentine from San Francisco is not on board by morning, she'll have to Pony Express up the mountain tomorrow." He grinned slightly. "Everybody bring sofa cushions for this little horseback riding adventure?"

The expression on the photographers' upturned faces mirrored a mixture of worry and dread...and they, poor idiots, had *paid* for the pleasure. Jess nodded in what he hoped was an encouraging manner, eyeing the stacked portfolios on the table. They had a long agenda ahead of them and he was anxious to press on. "Let's move ahead with portfolios. Who wants to be first?"

"Yo!" A tall man, the dome of his pink head circumscribed in tufts of blonde frizz, possessing the build of a linebacker long out to grass and grown soft in the belly, lunged out of his chair and rocked eagerly on the balls of his feet. Big feet, in ostrich boots, an enormous silver belt buckle on his jeans.

"You, Brett?" Jess waited as the Texan pulled his shiny black portfolio from the pile and turned to face the others in the room, squaring his shoulders as if blocking the offensive. Brand new box, Jess thought, eyeing the portfolio. The old boxes, with split leathers glued and strung shut, were the ones Jess looked for, indicative of time in the field. Jess sighed inaudibly. Why was it the *least* experienced were always the most eager to leap up first, set themselves up as a benchmark for the work to come?

Jess lugged the large easel forward into the semi-circle of photographers. Abe had his back to the group and tilted his head slightly in Jess' direction. The look in his eyes was pure, wry humor. "Be kind," he mouthed silently.

Brett Madison fumbled with the shiny latch of his portfolio, swiping his hands down his massive thighs repeatedly as he rifled through images protected in clear plastic sleeves. He seemed unsure where to begin, debating on the spot which images to unveil to the assembled class. Jess waited patiently, arranging his features into a neutral expression, the kind countenance of acceptance and placid receptivity.

"Okay, ready? Tell us a bit about yourself, your experience with a camera, what you use, and what you like to make images of. I'll lay your work out on the easel while you talk."

Over the next three hours, Jess worked his way to each photographer in the room, displaying selected of their works, those he could genuinely commend. Occasionally it was a clean print, successfully delivered from the negative. Or an eye for subject matter an unusual or distinct sense of composition. Often, the student work mimicked what one of Jess' journalism buddies in the service called "American Pie". It looked like a picture, was matted like a picture, featured something you might see in a picture–so it must be a picture. These banal images were the hardest of all for Jess to critique. There were not many kind ways to tell someone they had perfected the cliché.

"Yes, but *why* take this?" he somberly asked.

Sometimes the hapless photographer would instantly understand from the question that his or her image lacked, and sit down, dazed, experiencing for the first time the boundary between technique and subject matter. Jess tried to help each student see his image was in fact, an *etude*, a practice, not yet a worthy performance.

Jess wrote on the marker board. *The negative is the equivalent of a composer's score, and the print is the performance. Just as with music, the same negative can be performed in a variety of ways by the same photographer over a period of time.*

"Ansel Adams, folks."

He taught the importance and role of each leg in the process from composition to printing. He urged them to ask, What do I intend here? Like Adams and Bullock, and other gifted musicians who also turned their talents to photography, Jess believed music exemplified the same complexity found in a successful image. In the words of Gustav Mahler, he told them, "What is best in music is not to be found in the notes."

"There are no rules—only what works. Look your images. Really look," Jess urged, holding up a matted print. "What is best in photography is not how, or when, or with what the image was done, but why."

The hour grew late. When the final student sat down to a fluttering polite applause from the others, flushed and relieved the critique was over, Jess repeated instructions for the next morning. As the last of them bundled up their boxes and portfolios, offering jovial, encouraging comments to one another on their way out the door, Abe handed Jess a telephone message.

At last, word from Dr. Harte-Valentine. He read it quickly. Her plane had arrived late in Albuquerque, sincere apologies for missing the critique and dinner. She anticipated arriving in Santa Fe before midnight. Could she meet Jess that night, or first thing in the morning at her hotel, and would he please leave a message? He recognized the number of the pricey El Dorado.

Jess crumpled the note into a ball, tossing it in the can. "Well, that accounts for the good doctor, Abe. You willing to kill an hour and wait? Maybe Carly can join us for a drink."

"Sure," Abe shrugged easily. "Might give us a chance to hang out and catch up. Lemme call home." He paused, considering. "I think tonight went well. There were some images I liked. It's a lively bunch at any rate."

Abe dug his cell phone out of his shirt pocket and flipped it open, punching in the numbers with his right thumb. Jess followed slowly out the door, clicking off the lights, mulling over the message from Harte-Valentine. He worried the doctor had been late on purpose. But for what reason? Group shy? Too arrogant to stand for a review? Insecure with her talent? Why dodge his critique? He would know soon enough.

Carly, Abe's wife, arranged to meet them at the Wicked Coyote, a friendly, slightly rancid local watering hole a close walk to the El Dorado. Jess left a message at the hotel for the doctor to meet him at the bar when she arrived. It was a shade past eleven.

They took seats at an empty table under a velvet cactus painting, Abe brushing the crumbs of the last meal onto the floor with the corner of his sleeve. Jess ordered a round of Tecates from the plump, vacant-eyed teenage waitress, eyeing her curiously. Her hair was an electric purple and he counted seven earrings and one visible nose piercing. She lisped from the stud in her tongue. This girl would make an airport metal detector howl.

As the waitress plopped down their beer, the front door of the Coyote banged open and Carly Santos burst in through the door. She spotted them, and hurried over. Out of breath, she shrugged off her jean jacket and dumped her big black bag on the seat next to Abe, who steadied it as the contents shifted alarmingly.

Jess glanced at the bag. It was crammed with notebooks, breakfast bars, a Tang juice drink, a baggie of pretzels, a wad of credits cards secured with a rubber band, and a flashlight.

"What's the flashlight for, Carly?"

She squeezed in next to Abe, her cheeks dimpling like twin apples as he kissed her lightly. "See my way to the front door," she flashed her husband an exasperated look. "Porch light's sparking like the Fourth o' July. Don't suppose I want the lot of us electrocuted, do you?"

Jess looked at Carly, amused. She was looking well and very pretty. The waitress silently delivered another Tecate, flashing Jess the armadillo tattoo on her butt, peeking above the waistline of her jeans.

"How's class, Carly?" Jess asked, nursing his beer.

"A-okay. We're at midterms. I'll be done grading finals next week, I hope. One of the reasons I like teaching accounting—no essays!" She grinned and laid an earnest hand on Abe's arm. "I'm actually *glad* this yahoo is heading into the hills with you, Jess. I mean, after a week with Daphne..." She began to whistle the opening bars of *The Night They Invented Champagne* and Abe groaned and buried his head in his elbow. She giggled. "Besides, I can feed the kids junk food and finish 'Inventory Systems'."

Carly pushed her dark feathered hair back behind her ears and fixed Jess with a serious frown. "So, how 'bout you? How long did Catalina say she would be gone? I got the idea it was pretty open-ended."

Jess flashed Abe a sharp look, who went red.

"Yep." Jess answered noncommittally, staring down at his glass.

Abe flicked Carly a hot scowl and for a moment they drank their beer in strained silence. Then as if she could restrain herself no further, Carly pushed her glass to one side and leaned forward, her snub of a nose inches from Jess face.

Jess blinked and cocked his head

"So is this it?" Carly's voice thinned in disbelief, her lips pursed. "Are the two of you *never* going to settle down? I thought surely..." She ignored a second dark look from Abe.

Jess leaned back in his seat.

"I mean, come on, Jess! You've had a thing with Catalina Brezza for years—and a woman her age has got to be thinkin' of settling down. Pretty clear to me you two are the genuine thing, destined to be together and all that merry crap. What's going on? She pissed at you? One of you got a side dish?"

Jess glanced helplessly at Abe, who seemed to be drifting in the backwash at the bottom of his glass.

"No, Carly. None of that."

Jess surrendered to Carly's probing stare and briefly explained Catalina's decision to do the commemorative murals in Argentina.

"Yeah, but for how long? What about her work, and the galleries here?" Carly demanded impatiently.

Jess suspected Abe's wife was put out with Cat for reasons of her own. Both Abe and Carly harbored a secret hope that the local painter would round out their foursome.

"You know as much as I do, Carly," Jess shrugged, falling stubbornly silent.

Abe intervened, burping apologetically into his fist. "Come on, Carly. Drop it. Catalina Brezza does what Catalina Brezza wants to do. And anyway, it's their business."

Carly snorted and rolled her eyes toward the low ceiling tacked with business cards and dollar bills, then back to Jess. She assessed him flatly. "Don't look fine to me, Mr. Cappello. Look thin as a swizzle stick, and dinged as last year's tinsel. But who am I...why would I care? Don't mind me, just an interested *friend*...." She heaved her plump bottom out from behind the table and stomped off to the Little Buckarette's Room, her shoulder bag winging out behind her.

"What's eating her?" Jess exploded, feeling rather prickly. *Last year's tinsel?* He cocked a thumb at Carly's retreating back.

"Can't stand what don't add up, buddy."

Jess glared at him.

Abe pretended to yawn widely and checked his watch, a complicated digital compass-dial tacked onto a frayed green strap. "You want me to wait with you for this Harte-whatever woman?"

"No." Jess rubbed the back of his neck gloomily. "If she's late, I'm not waiting either. Tomorrow is a killer day. You take Carly—go home."

"The last bliss of a night in real sheets. Can't wait to shower from a bucket, man."

Carly returned, grousing about the lack of paper towels in the john, patting her wet hands irritably on her jeans. She broke off in mid-sentence, surprised that Abe was up and waiting for her. Jess remained seated at the table, nursing a second beer.

Carly's eyebrows rose a notch. "Don't tell...*moi* brought the party to an end?"

"Nope, just winding up a lengthy day," Jess answered with grudging graciousness. He glanced up. "Sorry if I seem prickly, Carly. Just got a lot on my mind."

"I bet," the younger woman answered, her face softening as she regarded him. "Take care then," she murmured, leaning over to kiss him goodnight. "And don't lose my guy here in the mountains. He has a terrible sense of direction, you know."

"No, I didn't," Jess laughed, glancing in Abe's direction. "But I'll keep it in mind. Might have to rope us together, like they do on those preschool outings. See you at the Sundance, Abe. Nine, sharp."

He waved them out the door. Alone, he spun the beer bottle slowly between the palms of his hands, watching the minutes tick across the cracked crystal of his field watch. Carly had really bugged him tonight. Why bring up Catalina? That was useless. Like trying to figure out that damn poem on the postcard. A goodbye? A "please wait"? *Shit.*

"Excuse me? You must be Jess Cappello—although you don't look like the guy."

Jess looked up. A plain-featured woman stepped directly in front of him, elegant in pressed camel slacks and a navy blazer. Something about her sharpness, the edges of her haircut, her blunt movements, triggered a memory.

"Excuse me?" Jess responded uncertainly.

"Are you, or are you not, Jess Cappello?" The woman demanded, exasperated.

British? Ah yes, the museum in San Francisco. The woman beside the girl with the copper hair.

"I'm looking for a photographer, who left word he would meet me here at eleven." Her flat green eyes zeroed in on Jess' beer and narrowed, disapproving. "Clearly, I'm mistaken. Never mind."

She spun to leave as Jess found his voice.

"You would be Dr. Harte-Valentine, of San Francisco? I am Jess Cappello." Jess rose to his feet awkwardly and extended his hand.

Eyeing him with equal amounts of suspicion and dismay, the English woman shook his hand coolly. Jess swallowed uncomfortably and gestured they should take seats. He waited for her to be seated first, and then took his own. He forced a cordial smile.

"I got your note at the Center. Glad you finally arrived." Oh brother, he thought, as her glance darkened. He should have omitted that "finally". He jumped in. "I meant, we missed you at the critique. But you're in time to register and join the group when we head out tomorrow."

"Yes, well. Meetings in New York delayed me—and never mind, the critique part of this thing is not that important to me, the getting away is." Her voice was still brusque but less biting than a moment ago. She made an effort to smile.

Jess examined the woman across from him, revising his earlier impression from plain to clean. The doctor possessed good skin and even features; with one small mole, like a freckle on her chin, her hair an off color of taffy. He noticed the smudge of a moustache, a likeable betrayal, above her upper lip.

She looked around her with a wide direct gaze.

Observing the radius of creases at the corner of her eyes and the softening of skin beneath her chin, Jess guessed her to be in her late forties, maybe early fifties. But it was her hands that genuinely caught his attention. They were broad in the palm, and lacking any callus he could feel in her handshake. Very unladylike, squared off at the fingertips, the nails clipped quite short. A good grip, steady. A true surgeon's hands, he decided. His gaze returned to her face, noting the composure with which she held her features, but catching a faint tic across her left eyelid. A surgeon wired tighter than a cat around a yarn ball.

"Would you like a beer?" Jess offered.

"No. I don't drink." She shifted in her seat, as though her mind were racing ahead to other matters.

Jess shrugged easily. He pulled out of his jacket a copy of the itinerary for the week, the Center release form, and the other documents required to complete her registration.

"If you'll look over this and return the forms to me in the morning—"

"Could we dispense the paperwork later? I have a request."

Jess raised an eyebrow.

"It's quite simple really. My daughter is here with me. I'd like to bring her on the trip."

Jess sat back and let a low whistle escape under his breath.

"Uh, Dr. Harte-Valentine..."

"Sarah, please," she said, her eyes focused on his face.

"Sarah, then." Sure, lose the last name, he thought. This gal was certainly no valentine–this was a thimble of gunpowder and vinegar. "Unfortunately, this is an 'adults only' curriculum. The Center never allows the participation of minor children. The reasons are obvious." He ticked off on his fingers, "First there's the risk, and the insurance, handling wilderness situations on your own..." Jess rubbed the side of his jaw, thinking quickly. "Perhaps I could recommend a camp facility for the week?"

"My daughter is not a *child*, Mr. Cappello. She is thirteen. I must take her on this trip. She needs it more than I do, to be precise. She's quite off her bean."

"Say again?" Jess squinted, startled.

"My daughter absolutely must come on this trip," Sarah Harte-Valentine clasped her hands tightly, her shoulders strained within the confines of her jacket. She seemed to swell with the visible intensity of an alarmed tree frog. "Look," she clipped her words short. "My daughter is not a raving lunatic— of course, I don't mean that she's literally *mad*. She is quite competent. Indeed, she is familiar with horses, cameras, the whole lot. She can hike and look after herself better, I daresay, than most of your pudgy old diddlers."

Jess tried hard not to gape openmouthed. The unexpected turn of conversation– or was it the Victorian 'pudgy old diddlers'–regardless, he was a good beat behind here. "That's fine, Sarah—Doctor—whatever. But the rules are very firm. No minors."

The woman rapped her fingers on the table. "Mr. Cappello, my daughter is a cello prodigy. Do you understand? A musical genius. She has been training since the age of four. Entirely her father's fault, although let's leave him out of this. But there you have it—a prodigy—which I disapprove of. She has a major audition for a music conservatory coming up and we are embattled—Zoë, her teacher, and I—on what exactly Zoë's future should be. This vacation is my last chance and I'll *not* let this opportunity go—superb venue for hashing things out, a backcountry trip. Are you following me, Mr. Cappello or are you an asthmatic? You're wheezing."

"Did you sign up for any other reason than to fight with your daughter?" Jess asked helplessly.

"Of course! Don't be a complete idiot. I am a qualified photographer. Zoë and I both attended your retrospective at the Museum last winter. I didn't think to register her in advance, the idea just occurred to me." She was speaking to Jess as though he were a slightly idiot child, exaggerating her words and pausing between sentences to let them sink in.

Jess counted slowly to ten before responding.

"I am...I am sympathetic to your desire to, ah, combine the workshop with some meaningful family time, but the answer remains no."

"Oh, Christ. Do listen. This is not some routine situation. Of course your rules are necessary, and its quite necessary to occasionally break them. This is a special circumstance. I'm *telling* you, Zoë needs to come."

Jess stiffened. "This is a field workshop, Dr. Harte-Valentine, and I'm in charge. The answer must be no. The Center will be happy to refund your deposit, I'm sure. Now, if you excuse me, I have an early morning."

Leaving a five-dollar bill to cover his beer, Jess zipped up his jacket and stood up. He nodded cordially at the English woman, who was quite visibly speechless, he noted with some satisfaction. Crossing the empty street to where he'd parked his truck, Jess put the key in the ignition and shook his head in wonder. What a conversation. He felt a twinge of empathy for the doomed daughter...but better to have clipped such insanity than endure it for ten days.

Jess sped out of town and reaching the outskirts, turned off the Tesuque exit into the shadowed trees onto a winding road. He drove another isolated mile. A single light burned in the front window of his small adobe. Leaving his keys on the table by the door, Jess fleetingly wondered if the woman's photographs were any good.

Shortly after seven the next morning, the phone rang. Ed Matthews at the Center. He listened to Matthews carefully, and then grunted. He hung up and slammed down the phone. "Fine," he muttered to himself. "Fucking damn fine."

Promptly at nine o'clock, the workshop members gathered outside the Sundance Motel and were introduced to their missing member, Dr. Harte-Valentine, and her daughter, Zoë. Jess coolly explained that the pack animals needed to carry a balanced load, and, as one member had dropped out unexpectedly, and given Dr. Harte-Valentine would be sharing her tent with her daughter, an exception had been made to allow her daughter to accompany the group. Pushing back his cap, Abe shot Jess a startled look, but the others simply shrugged and nodded, eager to get started.

Loading gear bags into the back of a Suburban, Jess threw in a backpack angrily. He resented like hell Harte-Valentine going around him to the Director of the Center. He glanced in their direction and got a better look at the daughter in question: same new penny hair. The kid was scratching Ansel behind the ears—and the little freeloader leaned in contentedly against her leg. She'd asked a good question, he remembered, about teachers. Otherwise, nothing remarkable to his way of thinking. No blazing star quality obvious there. Just a hollow-eyed, rather wispy looking girl-child with snipped red hair, wearing a T-shirt that said, "I Brake for Whole Notes". Music camp humor, no doubt.

Without acknowledging either mother or daughter, Jess finished loading the four-wheel drive vehicles and motioned people to climb in. The Harte-Valentines took seats in the first truck, driven by Abe, Sarah scrambling in after her daughter Zoë and making a show of chatting amiably with Gary Smithers. She flashed Jess a swift, slightly apologetic look.

Jess turned away. He had a workshop to run.

He whistled for Ansel, and the collie jumped into the rear of the truck with the gear. Jess glanced up, assessing the expanse of clear blue. Please God, the weather cooperate. Cramming his brim hat low on his head, he patted his gear vest for the cigarettes he knew he'd want later, quitting or not, and took the wheel of the second vehicle, softly whistling an old Johnson blues tune, *I'm a Steady Rollin' Man.* In a coil of dust, the caravan rumbled out onto the empty highway and headed for the northern end of the Sangre de Cristo Range, to a trailhead at Crimson Peaks Ranch, a three-hour drive from Santa Fe.

Format

Redding Stream, Connecticut, Paul Caponigro, 1968

L ight becomes form, form dissolves.
A winter brook reflects back twisted black branches, brittle in the half-light. The stream breaks evenly over a submerged rim of rock, and then dissolves into a flow of indistinguishable silver. Is the stream flowing to, or away from the viewer? Jess enjoyed the trick of perception, although he knows Caponigro photographed the waters facing downstream. The image is an allegory of light for Jess. Light takes liquid shape, and then transforms. *Redding Stream* is the purest invitation to close his eyes and drift. It is a restful photograph.

Note from the daybook:
Looking forward to the mountains. Might strangle that English doc, though. Tired of wrestling with thoughts of Catalina and that damn poem... "There is no being that finds its way to her heart"? I may be dense, but after twenty years together this is our truth?
Since the Retrospective, I feel like a fraud.

They were late leaving Crimson Peaks Ranch, and low in the sky, the stain of sunset washed the edges of the horizon. Jess hoped the light would linger long enough for them to make their first planned camp. He looked down, as his horse swiped its muzzle over a clump of yellow buttercups. The wilderness was patched with clumps of larkspur, forget-me-not, wild iris, and the wild greens of new grass—and this beast had been trying to inhale every bit of it since leaving the barn.

"Sharon Stone, you're a glutton," Jess remarked under his breath, jerking up on the reins, addressing the canoe of ear that swiveled his direction. Whose idea had it been to name the horses after movie stars anyway, he scoffed. His mare, a muscular, fight-scarred animal with a dirty white hide and tufts of black mane had been christened "Sharon Stone".

Ahead of him, Abe rode a ribby palomino named "Michelle Pfeiffer" alongside Kirby Mitts, the pack outfitter and a native of the empty wastes of South Dakota, riding on his own big brute "Stallone". The rest had saddled up a sorry bunch of starlets and Romeos. Dead last with the camp cook, the Harte-Valentine girl sat glumly on a chubby, half-brained pony known as "Danny Devito", chomping his own wide swath through the mountain grass.

Jess shifted in the saddle, his hands gripped tightly around the saddle horn, stretching his calves in the stirrups. His ass ached and he had nearly fallen off twice. But his face, shadowed beneath the broad brim of hat, was calm. He banished worry from his mind, handing over the logistics of the trek to Kirby and his crew. Ansel bounded easily at his side, dashing into the brush and rejoining him further down the trail, his coat matted with a new load of burrs. Jess tapped Sharon with his boot heel to get her moving and thought ahead to the evening's first camp. After tethering the horses and pitching tents, they would dine on whatever Kirby's crew had stashed in the big saddle packs on the mules.

He craned around and counted heads: fifteen riders on horses, four mules. They had already lost one participant at the Ranch. A tubby chap with a varicose nose the color of a kidney bean. What Abe unkindly pointed out as the unmistakable honker of a hard drinker. The dentist from Pennsylvania had become violently allergic to horsehair. Wiping his running eyes, he waved them off with desperate jollity, promising to reconnect for the post-ride critique at the Center and to spend his time fruitfully photographing naked hippies at Black Rock Hot Springs. Good riddance, Jess had thought. The man's portfolio had been a disaster of out of focus negatives, obsessed with body parts.

Jess surveyed the caravan with satisfaction. Each photographer carried his or her own camera gear and film in padded, dust-proof canisters strapped securely to the heavy saddles, sleeping bags and personal gear stuffed in the larger packs on the mules. The whole operation appeared impressively self-sufficient, Jess observed wryly. In reality, the outfitters had stocked line shacks near each planned camp with coolers of food and beer, cook tents, propane stoves and battery camp lights. It was a well-provisioned game of pioneer.

"Mr. Cappello."

Jess looked over his shoulder as the English woman kicked her pinto, "Mariah Carey", up alongside Sharon Stone. He whacked Sharon across the neck with the ends of the reins as the mare bared her teeth, stretching to take a toothy chunk out of Mariah's neck. He assessed the doctor silently. In trim jeans, sitting competently in the saddle, she appeared slighter and more softly rounded than his first impression of her at the bar. Her pale skin was finely coated with the billowing dust.

She leaned forward on her saddle horn and looked Jess straight in the eye. "I'd like to not get off on the wrong foot with you."

"Bit late for that."

"An apology should set things right, don't you agree." It wasn't a question.

"Can your daughter handle that pony by herself?" Jess kept his eyes ahead on the ravine. Already in shadows, the steep canyon would be dark and cool, and perhaps slippery.

"She's a musician, not a moron," the doctor responded sharply before she caught herself, visibly controlling her temper and taking a deep breath. "Yes, Zoë can handle a horse, even that hideous rodeo DNA she's mounted on. She took equestrienne lessons."

She cast a glance at Jess, and he loosened his grip on the saddle-horn, flushing. The woman's lips thinned.

"She was once a girl scout, can stake a tent, does most of the cooking at home, and knows a fair amount of Gray's Anatomy. Her favorite color is green, and despite her haircut, has no visible tattoos I am aware of. Zoë knows the entire repertoire of Bach, Bruch, Brahms, Kummer, etcetera, and at the age of thirteen does not smoke or drink. Anything else?" The sarcasm was light, but there.

So much for the right foot, Jess mused.

"No, ma'am. Just stay in line with her. She is most definitely your responsibility."

He kicked Sharon hard in the ribs, enduring the horse's disgruntled fart, and trotted ahead of the doctor. Jess swore under his breath. He wanted a peaceful camp, an uneventful workshop. Looking at the slumped silhouette on the fat pony, he wasn't sure who he felt more sorry for, himself or the little musician. A Rodgers-Hart tune popped into his head *...all you can count on is the raindrops that fall on little girl blue,* and he whistled the melancholy tune as the mare dropped to a walk and shuffled along the rocky terrain, her head in the flowers.

By nightfall Kirby was serving beans. Jess and Abe sat off to one side of the central fire, Ansel coiled at their feet, twitching and groaning his deep adventurous doggie-dreams. Abe pushed his cap back on his head and stretched his shoulders backwards with a sigh.

"Well, I never thought I'd be glad to get off the girl of my fantasies, but I am."

Jess snorted, and took a sip of coffee from his plastic mug. "Miss Pfeiffer a handful?"

"Skittish as all hell. Had me believing in boogiemen behind every rock and tree. Scrawny, too. Like riding a fence."

"Get used to it. This is day one."

He caught Abe's quick look and shrugged.

Abe raised an eyebrow. "What's with you? You've been as jolly as the last steer in the stockyard. Sore butt?"

"Yeah, and that too."

Jess stretched his boots toward the fire and surveyed the circle of faces illuminated in the light. Friendships were beginning to form, and the low murmur of voices drifted into the clear night. It pleased him that the group had hit upon a comfortable synergy. All except for the Harte-Valentines, who ate by themselves near the cook table.

Jess watched the daughter for a moment. Her face was half-shadowed by the bulk of the camp cook, WeeJun, an old Espanola Indian, washing up pans. Zoë Harte-Valentine was seated on a canvas campstool, her dinner plate balanced on one knee, her other palm supporting her chin. Her mother was talking, sawing through her food as she gestured toward the outline of the mountains black against the night. What was the girl thinking, Jess wondered, observing the faint downturn at the corners of her mouth. It was a fair bet the girl hadn't wanted to join the expedition either. Did her mother always arrange things her own way?

He looked at Abe and hooked his thumb in the direction of the two women. "What do you make of the Harte-Valentines?" He asked softly, keeping his voice low in the night.

"Haven't heard a peep from the girl," Abe frowned, casting his eyes their direction. "Seems okay on a horse. The mother hasn't mixed much. Think we need to shoehorn them into the group?"

"Maybe." He checked his watch. "C'mon. Time for Camera Bag Aesthetics."

Jess ignored Abe's groan and stood up, stopping to refill his cup at WeeJun's stove. He approached the Harte-Valentines, who looked up warily.

"Time for a bit of jawing on photography, ladies," Jess invited pleasantly. He moved on around the fire, gathering the troops. The ranch outfitters had retired to their own camp some distance from the group and the class collected in a loose circle around the low coals of the fire. In the closeness of the dark, the nicker and rustle of the animals could be heard rummaging in their feedbags. A single coyote call rose in the hills and then fell silent.

Jess faced the group, his hands in his pockets, twiddling with a matchbook. He cleared his throat. "Well, here we go—the first of my camp fire lectures. But first, butt check. Everybody doing all right, staying vertical on the horse?"

A chorus of groans and chuckles greeted this remark.

"Okay then, there are a few topics to discuss as we work together this week. The first is gear. Your camera is your third eye, as I'm sure you've heard before. What that really means is that you and your gear need to be as collaborative and comfortable together as your hand and brain are. A successful picture is a function of object, light and perception, happens in a second and is missed just as fast. There's no time to fumble with a lens, fix a sticky shutter, or adjust a tripod." He paused, surveying the mixed interest and fatigue apparent on the faces in the firelight. He felt a genuine kinship with these chasers of light.

"So know your gear thoroughly. How to put it together, solve problems, and make adjustments on the fly. The first order of business tomorrow is to check your equipment, make sure you're ready."

"Say Jess..."

Up floated the reedy voice of Henry Hiller, an eighty-something retired engineer from Portland. "My gear is nearly as old as I am. Any advice on upgrades—like when, or if?" The old man had the smile of a wry chimpanzee.

Jess liked Henry; this was their third expedition together. The old guy scrabbled like a goat in the rocks, always out early in the first light. Hiller was also characteristically modest about the still lifes he liked to arrange using natural debris—boulders, broken branches, deer scat, thistle, and the like. Jess thought his work engagingly original.

"Use what works, Henry."

"What?" A guffaw rose from the direction of Mark Anthony, the quick-spoken black neurosurgeon from Atlanta. Also a workshop regular, Anthony usually packed the latest gear, the most expensive and newest toys. He was a rabid gear nut.

"Yes, Mark. If it's new and doesn't do the job, the stuff's useless. So what if gear's ancient—as long as it gets the image you want its priceless."

"But heh," the young neurosurgeon objected, "there's a world of innovation out there."

"Oh sure, there are useful technical improvements...but in truth, the actual essence of the craft has remained unchanged from the days of the first camera obscura. Charles Sheeler put it this way—isn't amazing how photography has advanced without improving? Lemme tell you, I still botch as many negatives, and Henry and I have both been through a half-century of innovation."

Mark acquiesced the point and Jess moved on to summarize the technical shifts from Fox Talbot and fixing images in salt baths, to Steichen and photogravure printing, the arrival of the 35 mm, and the popularity of the Speed Graphic in the heyday of photojournalism in the mid-century. He briefly acknowledged the arrival of the digital age, cameras the size of a pack of cigarettes, and online computer printing.

"So Jess, do you consider digitally mastered prints to be genuine photographic art?" Mark interrupted provocatively. Jess heard Abe sigh.

"Yes, I do, but not in the same vein as a platinum print. Digital work uses chips and diodes in lieu of chemicals, but its ultimate process is identical–the capture and manipulation of image."

Abe spoke up, his face in the shadows. "I disagree, Jess. Seems to me, digital work is not art but print technology. There's no room for natural error in digital work—the surprise combination of elements that create art. It's scan technology, a digital library of cut and paste, set the tone, twist the dial."

Jess shrugged, he partly agreed with Abe. "It depends on the degree to which the machine or the man makes the print, don't you think? To get back to my original point, gear is an extension of you, the perceiver. To the degree that gets turned around, your images will miss the mark."

A voice carried over the others, a cultured mid-town accent. "Freeze frames! Obviously, things shift until you press the button! I never see a lake the way a camera does. I love to see things in a different way all over again."

A murmur of agreement swept the circle and Jess looked over the heads of Smithers and Madison at Mike Teets, the New Yorker seated beside Zoë Harte-Valentine. He nodded at Mike, hoping to draw Zoë into the conversation as well, but the girl ducked her head and focused on her boots. Her hands were twined in the thick ruff at Ansel's neck, tugging out burrs. He grunted. Had the goddamned dog adopted her? Then his gaze collided with her mother's guarded watchfulness and he remembered his goal: peace, peace at all costs.

"Mike is quite right about the transitional nature of reality–the fixed image that results when a shutter clicks. Our eyes perceive the world in shifting arrangements of light and object, but the camera captures pinpoint relationships in time. The image is a fixed thing, although perception is not. As photographers we wade between the two."

"I deal with the human visual apparatus—trying to restore the capabilities of the eye ravaged by disability or disease," interjected Zoë's mother. "From what you've just said, Mr. Cappello, one might extrapolate the camera let's us specify what we *think,* or *choose* to see."

"Well, I guess when my images are not turning out well, I know the problem is in my gear or my perception, but rarely an imperfect reality."

And back at his studio lay a pile of botched images. All executed on perfectly calibrated equipment, the implications of which were quite clear. Jess took a seat.

He let the conversation roam, interested in the play of opinions. Walking around the circle, Abe was passing out trail maps, and from somewhere a bottle of scotch. Jess was surprised to see Henry Hiller pour Sarah Harte-Valentine a shot in her coffee cup. So the doc did drink, after all. He stood up slowly.

"Well, that's it for tonight. Tomorrow we do a foot hike up that ravine we've been riding through. Kirby tells me WeeJun's got a jar of horse liniment for what aches, and if you find snakes in your tent throw a pair of socks their way. Stink'll kill 'em."

"Just park a horse in the middle!" Someone called out.

Chuckling, Jess walked off, Ansel at his heels, toward the sheltered pines. Under the moonless sky, the array of tents behind him formed a strange circus of peaked shadows in hollow tones of gray. He closed his eyes, inhaling the scent of vanilla pine, stunned by a sudden hunger for Catalina. Restless, he smoked a cigarette before returning to douse the campfire.

Ansel growled low in the throat and a voice hailed unexpectedly from the dark.

"Hope your dog doesn't bite, Cappello. Must say, you seemed surprised I was an eye surgeon."

"Not really," Jess answered warily, stepping slightly away. What he least desired at this moment was another verbal contest with the Brit. "Many participants in these workshops are doctors."

"Of course," Sarah agreed from her crossed-leg position by the glowing coals, her face a pale smudge in the dark. "Photography offers many of the same elements as medicine— intense absorption, flawless precision, and of course–hand tools. All without the element of malpractice...bad taste entirely beside the point." Her voice broke in quiet laughter, rich in its unexpected warmth.

Jess crouched by the edge of the fire pit, drizzling a pale of water over the ashes.

Sarah re-crossed her legs. "You interest me, Jess Cappello. I rather anticipated you would be a gear jock. From the precision of your work, I supposed you'd be the chap to catalog configurations of competing enlargers and paper finishes, that kind of nonsense."

"It's not nonsense, just not an excuse for a bad photograph." He frowned. "You've seen my work?"

"Of course. Would I take a workshop from an amateur?" Her voice was light, hard for him to read. "You've exhibited nearly everywhere. Personally, I own two of your images—

Snowbank, and *Black Hills.* Are these not the same hills Georgia O'Keefe immortalized in her paintings?"

"The same."

"Well, your work is flawless, clean. Quite lyrical. One might say romantic, for a man. Yes, you surprise me, Mr. Cappello."

The coals hissed as Jess emptied the bucket, avoiding Sarah's eyes.

"Indeed, a romantic, philosophical vision." Sarah mused. "But, you wouldn't like my work," she concluded, rising to her feet.

"Why is that?"

"The images are rather hard. I never photograph the simply pretty." Her tone had grown slightly defiant.

"Pretty is insipid," Jess agreed quietly. "The magnetic, attractive value of a thing lies in its merit, not pleasingness. That, however, is entirely personal."

"Right you are. The eye of the beholder."

And with that she was gone.

Methodically, Jess filled a second bucket of water and fully doused the embers, stepping back from the billowing choke of smoke and steam. It was unsettling to think Sarah owned *Snowbank.* That picture seemed to haunt him, Catalina on every wall. Above glittered a hard and brilliant sky, but Jess ignored the pinpoints of stars; no longer a heaven shared, a different constellation south of the Equator.

Camp broke early. Jess was more than glad to be off his horse for the day, and although eager to reach the stands of birch and quaking aspen in the upper elevations of Mt. Capulin, their hikes began in the lower canyon area. Zipping up his vest, he surveyed the 11,000 ft peak. Not a cloud. They had the weather on their side.

Jess dug in his vest for a cigarette and then thought better of it. He'd done pretty well so far, not even the Brits had egged him into dipping into his "emergency rations". Outside the latrine, he ran into Joe Papernello. Interesting guy, he thought, nodding hello. Papernello practiced pediatrics at Boston's Brigham & Women's Hospital, but before that, he had lived for a decade as an ordained Jesuit Priest in southern Italy. His portfolio featured soft-focus images of windows and doors—mysterious exits and openings—and Jess wondered what turn of heart brought him from Italy to the States, and into medicine. It was hard to imagine a more reserved fellow—thin and balding, the priest wore solitude like a pair of old boots softened and familiar. Papernello returned his quiet greeting, and Jess moved on to check tents and assign hiking partners, thinking as younger men, they might have been friends.

Breaking into smaller groups limited trekking in a one long dust tunnel up the trail, and until Jess had a solid feel for their individual navigational skills, he and Abe could keep a closer eye on the group. A few he knew he could count on. Old Hiller could use a compass and had a dog's uncanny nose for the way back from practically anywhere. Anthony was a fussy old lady, but useful, with his topographical and elevation maps, his red pencil noting every twist and turn he hiked. Smithers too, was steady and levelheaded.

The others—who knew? Jess had been amused by the assortment of high tech field clothes some of them wore, bearing labels from every pricey outdoor catalog and adventure gear supplier on the planet. In his own much-abused field vest and crumpled hat, he was surely the antithesis of "packaged travel".

Following a hearty breakfast of oatmeal and biscuits, Jess pulled out his roster. "Sunblock! Water canteens full! And if your boots are new, stick a band-aid in your pocket. No one wants to come down strapped over Danny Devito. Anybody seen the Harte-Valentines?"

He asked Abe to take on Sarah and her daughter, plus Hiller, Brett Madison, and Paul Sorkum. Sorkum would prove the live wire, he supposed. A sociable engineer from the Salt Lake area, Sorkum had six children and worked out of a darkroom converted from his garage—the only quiet spot in the house, he claimed. The thirty-nine year old Mormon had talked nearly nonstop from the orientation dinner–joshing, teasing and making a joke of things. With any luck, Sorkum would balance out the prickly Harte-Valentines.

He'd take Mark, Papernello the Priest, Smithers, and the patent law partners from New York, Mike Teets and Peter Winooski. The trim fifty year olds, nattily attired in pastel polo shirts and Mephisto hiking shoes, were clearly a couple, and thus far on the trek had occupied themselves nesting their tent, doling out vitamin supplements and bug lotion. Jess wondered which of them would declare the first blister, bee sting, or sprained ankle of the trip. Their portfolio was not entirely bad however, varying from campy sexual eggplants to the girders and linear architecture of New York City. But Jess had suppressed a sigh when the two confessed this was their first trip "West". Such tender hides belonged at the Santa Fe Opera sipping champagne, not mounted on the twin, pie-eyed Appy horses "Kevin Kline" and "Billy Crystal".

Jess backtracked through the tents, pausing in front of the Harte-Valentine's green dome. Their boots were still outside the flap, but Zoë's plaintive cry pierced the air.

"I don't want to go, Mum! It's stupid. Leave me here."

"Nonsense, Zoë Marie." Sarah's brusque voice contradicted. "You *will* hike with us. You need the fresh air and the exercise. I won't have you reading sheet music when you could be absorbing nature. Get suited–quickly please."

"You *never* let me do what I want. Have you looked at this group? They're old people! I hate tagging along, and I could care less for this photographic mumbo-jumbo."

"Zoë, look..." Sarah's voice sounded tired and frustrated. "Do this for me. Forget fighting about the audition and school next year. Spend some time with me away from music. That world completely absorbs you, you're like a, a–oh, I don't know–a pond fish! Bubbling along under the surface playing that bloody cello. And I don't care what Alexei says—a young girl needs more than music practice. You need adventure, some life!"

"You're always telling me what to do, Mum!" Zoë's voice was miserable and defiant. "I love cello and I'm good at it, too! *Why* can't you leave me alone? If I wanted to do something else, I would!"

I bet you would, too, Jess agreed silently. What did her mother have against music, anyway? Good lord, it wasn't as if the girl wanted to abandon school and join a grunge band. But the two weren't likely to hammer this out anytime soon...he had a hike to get underway.

"Heh there," he called, pitching his voice loudly. "Time to roust!"

Sarah immediately poked her head out, jamming her hair back under a sun visor. "Right. On our way."

The group stood under the tall pines, backpacks and camera gear checked and ready, water bottles and hats in their hands. Zoë and her mother slipped in at the back of the circle, adjusting their packs. Jess caught Abe's eye and walked over.

"Revised plan of action," Jess muttered, keeping his voice low. "I'm gonna do you a favor, Abe, and split the cat fight. You take the mother–I'll take the girl." Jess turned to the Harte-Valentine's and smiled neutrally. "Zoë, I'm going to take you in my group. We've organized the most peaceful, um, grouping possible. It seems Danny Devito just has this thing for Sharon Stone and is not very gentlemanly with Abe's mare, Michelle."

"But we're not riding today..." Sarah protested.

Jess ignored her. "Peter, you go with Abe's group. Mike stay with me."

Quickly Jess outlined the timetable for shooting pictures, reminded everyone to grab one of WeeJun's packed lunches, and discussed where to regroup for the hike back. By way of local color, he identified the genus of various trees, landmarks in the peaks to navigate by, and the waterfall attractions along the creek side trail.

"Make the most of the morning, folks, we break camp and head further up the mountain tomorrow. And make noise on the trail—whistle, talk, whatever—this is mountain lion country."

A nervous skip of glances flitted between Peter and Mike, but a slow grin of anticipation spread across Brett Madison's face, the big Texan. "Wish I'd brought my hunting rifle."

"We're not shooting anything but film," Jess grunted.

Abe smashed on his cap, already sweating under the straps of his padded backpack. A folded tripod banged against his thigh as he jiggled restlessly in place. "Let's roll! And no' gear farts', people! If your shutter sticks, draw. We have a strict 'no whining' policy."

They grinned, shouldering their packs, and Jess marked the time, eight a.m. A late start, but by week's end, the group would have found its trail rhythm. He held his group back until Abe advanced up the trail a quarter-mile or so, and then headed single file up the left side of the canyon. The gulch was cool, broad slants of morning light inching down the gray rock of the canyon walls toward the sandy creek. Ansel bounded ahead, setting a brisk pace up the trail.

That afternoon on the return trek, Zoë moved up beside Jess' elbow, Ansel beating his tail softly against her legs as she walked. Jess looked sideways at the girl. She had moped most of the morning, wandering around the creek while the others set up their shots and nosed around for things of interest. Her face was streaked with dust, and her short hair clung damply to her forehead where she had the beginnings of sunburn. She'd brought nothing along in her daypack but a lunch and water bottle, and Jess suspected she'd been bored to tears. Interesting eyes though. No wonder her favorite color was green. Hers were the color of stones in the creek.

"Tired?"

"Yeah, some."

They walked along in silence for a while, Jess noodling on an exposure he'd set on a rock fall shot. If he'd accommodated the shadows right, what he hoped were shadows and not some trick of vision, he'd have a very interesting tumble of shapes and textures in the frame, including a tuft of wildflower that dangled haplessly from the dirt above the slide.

"What were you whistling?" The girl asked suddenly.

"When?"

"Back at the beginning. This morning."

Jess thought back, trying to remember. "Oh, that. *Travelin' Light*, I think. A Chet Baker tune."

"I've heard it before."

Jess flicked her a second look, surprised. An old trumpet standard seemed a little out of a cellist's range.

She kept her eyes fixed on the trial.

"You don't believe me. My father plays trumpet in London. He's a jazz musician."

"No kidding. What's his name?"

"Red Valentine."

Jess slapped his hand against his thigh. "Not *the* Red Valentine? Of *Back Alleys and Smoke, Kiss Me Goodbye, Kensington Square*?"

"Yep. That's him."

"Well, you have a very famous father."

How could he have failed to put the Valentine in her last name with that of the famous Valentine in the London jazz world? It seemed so obvious now; especially in light of the girl's own musical gifts, and Red's notorious hair. He put this fresh fact into perspective.

"You take after your Dad—musically, I mean?" He slowed his steps and lifted a low overhanging branch for her to pass under, and as he did so, looked over his shoulder to check his lagging troops. They were all crunching along in the dust, lost in thought.

"Oh no. Not really." Zoë shook her head, amused. "I'm a classical musician. My repertoire is virtuoso, or symphony. But I know the music he plays—like what you whistled back there. I have his tapes, and memories of him practicing around the house in London."

"How long ago was that?" Jess asked curiously. He was surprised the kid was volunteering much personal information, but she probably felt lonely. Music was her thing, clearly not photography.

"Back when I was a kid. Six, I think. Before Mum moved us to the States."

Jess let that sink in. So Red remained in London and Sarah took their daughter to the United States. Sarah was clearly English—why relocate an entire continent?

Zoë took a swig off her water bottle and tucked her hands in her slim jeans. "Mum took a residency at the Stanford Medical Center and that's where we live." She shrugged. "I've spent summers in England, but not many. With this audition, it's all gonna change."

"Audition?" He asked distractedly, slapping a fly off his neck.

"Yeah. I'm auditioning for the Curtis Music Institute. You know, in Philadelphia? It's a very big thing for me, but Mum's against it."

Zoë tripped over a stone and bumped up against him. Jess reached out a hand and steadied her. The kid barely reached to his elbow. How could someone so tiny manage a huge cello?

"Attending Curtis is an honor, Mr. Cappello. It would mean master classes, a solo debut, a chance to play regularly with first class orchestras! But Mum's obsessed about me missing school." The teenager scowled.

"Even Beethoven needed to read and write, Zoë."

He was admittedly on thin ground here. He'd barely completed high school, and had the Air Force to thank for whatever knowledge he possessed of the practical world. But in forty-five years, the world had become a different place: computers the size of your hand, telephones without wires, cloned sheep. He was inclined to agree with Zoë's mother.

"Of course," she sighed crossly, as if she'd been down this road before. "I'll take regular classes outside of Curtis. I'll get my high school diploma, but then maybe a college degree or an advanced certificate in musical performance from the Institute." She flashed a hard look from her strange green eyes. "Take my word for it, it's not the school thing she really objects to. It's going into music—like my father."

"Ah." So Zoë was the shuttlecock in an international clash of wills. *Little girl blue...*

"What?" she looked up at him, her sunglasses swinging around her neck on a loose string.

Jess smiled gently—she was such a kid. Today's musical billboard was a raspberry jersey, inscribed, "Beethoven Had Octaves to Be Crabby", and as they walked, Zoë fussed unconsciously with the two plastic barrettes pinning down her cowlick. She struck Jess as a bit of dragonfly in scuffed shoes, and he tried to imagine what her music was like. He supposed something light, agile, elusive. How much melody could you expect from a teenager he bet weighed less than a hundred pounds with her backpack on? He glanced at Zoë's hands. Her fingers were limber tenacious vines.

"We'll be in camp soon."

They hiked the remainder of the trail back into the pine grove in silence and Zoë slipped off to her tent. Jess waited for the others to troop in, keeping head count. Everyone accounted for, he helped himself to a cold beer from Kirby's cooler and dropped his gear off. After a quick wash-up to rinse the dirt and sweat off his neck and hands, Jess wandered over toward the cook tent.

Abe's group was just coming in. Abe caught sight of Jess and gave him a thumbs up, but Sarah scuttled over, her denim shirt no longer crisp, grass stains on the knees of her jeans. Her eyes, darker and more deep-set than her daughter's, skimmed his face uncertainly. She halted, lifting her sun visor.

"How was your hike?" she asked, clearing her throat of dust.

"Good." What he supposed she really meant was *How was Zoë?* "And yours?"

"Satisfactory. We crossed paths with a gray fox. Large ears, quite fearless eyes."

"Lucky you. Get some good shots in the bag?"

"No," she shrugged, lifting her shirt off her chest where it clung, damp with sweat. She frowned. "Excuse me, I need to change." And she sagged over to her tent, dropping her gear, obviously exhausted, before kicking off her boots and disappearing inside.

Jess took another swig of his beer, musing about Red Valentine.

Filter and Lens

Remnants of Resonance 8, Brad Cole, 1988

T hrough the hole.
Stand on the rocks, cup your hand around your eye and stare west toward Asia through a low row of rectangular windows marching across the sea—a pier, left marooned and incomplete, *Remnants of Resonance 8*. Cole, the photographer, stands within the distinctive resonance of Edward Weston's work before him. His image is one of mimicry and device. A telescoped, compressed view: the surf in the foreground, the broken pilings, the soft line of the ocean horizon. The negative printed in a circular frame indistinct at the edges, in tonalities of silver, ash gray, wet black. An idea of shifting shapes, a lengthening puzzle. They all courted that deceit, Jess thought, the fiction of the eye.

Note from the Daybook:

Still in the foothills—made an image of a rock scrabble from a landslide. Exercising my eye really, nothing in the image. Thought of George Tice, that thing he said that a particular place provides the excuse to produce work... You see what you are ready to see, what mirrors your mind at a particular time. When I finished the shot and glanced down, that gray blur was floating on my hand.

The second day, they mounted their celebrities and embarked on the four-hour ride up the southeastern slope of Mt. Capulin. As the trail climbed above the valley floor, the lower bluffs dropped behind them in smudges of colored rock. A gusty breeze lifted the meadow grasses and badgered the tops of the trees. The day smelled like rain, Jess thought, squinting at the sky. He hoped the overcast would hold to the end of the day though. The muted light was an advantage for afternoon shots.

An hour out, Kirby Mitts brought his horse in next to Jess on the trail and tipped his Stetson back on his head. Kirby had the face of a likeable iguana, crevices and loose skin leathered from years as a ranch hand in Wyoming, followed by a stint laying rail with the Santa Fe and Topeka, and endless harsh winters in northern New Mexico. Kirby was the kind of westerner Jess trusted implicitly: a man who lived in the elements and related to the wilderness with a guarded cynicism. WeeJun told Jess the misshaped look of Kirby's right hand was the kiss of frostbite, and Jess didn't doubt it.

Kirby clapped his horse gently on the neck, slowing the big chestnut to the dawdling sway of Sharon Stone. "Catch the sky?" he asked abruptly, in a voice with the rasp of dust in it.

"Looks like a late rain, I'd guess."

"By nightfall," Kirby half-grimaced, revealing a fence line of gold and tobacco stained teeth. "Seen the tracks?"

Jess shook his head. Other than the odd trail rabbit and yesterday's fox, he'd spotted nothing but deer and elk scat along the way.

"Back there, by that spring." Kirby nodded behind them. "Cougar."

"No shit," Jess breathed. In a decade leading photography expeditions, he'd seen only the tamer wildlife, although he knew the locals hunted lion, puma, and black bear in the upper reaches of the wilderness. He'd hankered, in a mild sort of way, for a shot at one of the trophy animals himself–with his lens. He hadn't handled firearms since the service. It wasn't something you'd forget, but it came with a lot of baggage.

Kirby cracked his jaw and shrugged. "Jus' mentionin' it. No doubt long gone, especially with that collie of yours nosing about. Head's up, though. A lion's got a big territory."

"Thanks," Jess nodded. "I'll give the group a warning tonight. Of course, if the beast has any sense, he'll eat Sharon Stone first. She's tenderloin on legs–what a cow."

Kirby hooted and spurred his horse forward, resuming his place at the head of the pack line.

By afternoon the straggling expedition pulled into the next selected campsite. Kirby and WeeJun, and the wrangler named Bob—wasn't there always a wrangler named Bob, Jess thought—brought down supplies from the line shack and threw the camp together with speedy efficiency. Strange, to set an expedition up with payloads of food and gear ferried in by pickup along the forest service roads, while they themselves clunked along on horses. Better than shooting bear for breakfast, he supposed. And certainly, the ample provisions helped mealtime alone justify the hefty fee per saddle pad.

The photographers split up and set up a short distance away. Watching them grunt and groan under the weight of their bulky view cameras, Jess and Abe exchanged a smile— there was much truth in the old saw that if you couldn't drive to it, screw it. Jess caught Zoë take off with Ansel, but as long as she had the dog with her, he needn't worry. That dog always came home for a meal.

They camped by an open meadow marked on the map as Gooseberry Creek, a slender rivulet of mountain runoff. As twilight drained to a pewter gloss, the creek spawned a cloud of mosquitoes that swelled into camp. The breeze shifted directions and Jess prayed it would swing back and drive the little drillers back to the creek. But Peter and Mike were doing a pretty good job of basting the ensemble with excess supplies of Deet, and most everyone had added a long-sleeved shirt. Jess slapped a mosquito from his cheek as he flung out his bedroll, and zipped the tent flaps tight.

Dinner was juicy rib eye, and baked potato cooked in the coals. Jess ate in the curl of wood smoke, preferring the sting in his eyes to the endless mosquitoe whine.

Abe shoved Ansel over slightly with his boot, and announced, "So when in the hell are you going to tell me how to do a portrait right?"

Jess raised an eyebrow.

"I mean," Abe said, enticing a lick of flames to crawl a dry twist of mesquite and waving the smoke around his head, cursing the mosquitoes, "the kind of portrait you did of that miner. Catalina told me about it. Said it made the hair on the back of her neck stand-up, it was so *there*."

Jess hesitated, beer midway to his mouth. That portrait was Gianni Cappello, taken in prison the last time Jess had gone to tell him that Louis was dead. Less a portrait than a lump of hatred in silver emulsion.

"That what you after," he inquired cautiously. "Shop of horrors effect?"

"Wouldn't mind *any* effect, honest to God. When I take shots, people sort of flatten out. People in my pictures go dead. Ghost images."

"You might consider the aesthetic proposed by Fernand Leger, Abe. And who is Catalina?" Sarah, in a large Stanford

U sweatshirt, joined them at the edge of the fire. She was cupping a hot tea in her hand. Jess looked down.

"Fernand who?"

"Leger was referring to his experiences as a soldier in the war, Abe." Sarah's eyes barely lingered on his missing arm as she continued in a neutral voice. "He was obsessed with the details of machines, all the common objects around him. And I quote...'Here I discovered the beauty of the fragment.' I believe he meant the ability of the part to invoke the whole."

"Why credit the universe in the part...the separate whole?" Abe countered. "Think of Weston's pepper, Imogene Cunningham's shell."

"Possibly," she acknowledged, her eyes sliding Jess direction. "But photographing people might come down to a fragment. You follow me? A feature, one glance that contains the crucial element of self."

Sarah shifted to the right of the wood smoke, nodding as Henry Hiller and Joe Papernello wandered up and took chairs around the fire pit.

It looked like this might be tonight's group, Jess concluded. Mike's voice could be heard somewhere in the dark trading basting recipes with WeeJun, and Peter had turned in early complaining of a sore back. Zoë too, had long since retired to the bug-proof sanctuary of her tent.

Yards away, under the light of two lanterns, Sorkum and Madison huddled in a tight circle around Mark Anthony at the camp table, dealing a deck of cards. Gary Smithers sat to the right, passing a whiskey bottle back and forth, still arguing with Sorkum over the merits of various dot-com companies, a debate that had raged most of the day as they photographed the valley and surrounding peaks.

Joe Papernello leaned back comfortably, his hands laced loosely across his knees. He spoke up, a faint lisp of accent deepening his voice. "I read a book years ago called

Conversations with Kafka. This guy Gustav Janouch is taking Kafka's picture and they're joking about the amazing technology of things—this is 1921, yes? Janouch calls the camera a know-thyself apparatus and Kafka corrects him. No, he says, it's a mistake-thyself."

Jess and Abe chuckled.

"So Kafka argues with Janouch that the camera concentrates the eye only on the superficial and obscures the substance of the genuine. Kafka believed no lens could capture hidden life, which one had to grope for, by feeling. He felt the camera didn't multiply our eyes, but distorts true vision, rather like a fisheye lens."

"Do you agree?" Sarah asked slowly. "I'm not sure I do. I don't disagree—who hasn't seen pictures of oneself so unfamiliar as to seem alien. But I accept the premise the camera doesn't lie."

"Like old Ed." Henry Hiller chuckled. "Now there was a coot that lied about everything *but* the camera. Weston claimed the camera was an honest medium, that a photographer is more likely to approach nature in a spirit of inquiry, of communion—his word, friends—instead of fake, self-dubbed authorship." Henry huddled on a stool, unkinking the string he used to tie his gear together, shaking the dust from his black cloth.

"What do you say, Cappello?" Smithers yelled over from the poker table, apparently listening in.

"Criminey, what a bunch of 'coners'!" Paul Sorkum threw in, laughing.

"What's that?" Abe demanded.

"Learned it from my daughter—means conehead, gear head, stuffed shirt, anyone who knows who the heck Fernand Leger and Kafka are."

"You have been rather silent," Abe needled Jess with a wink.

"I'm not sure I have a worthy opinion on the matter," Jess admitted.

"Oh, come now," Sarah burst out impatiently. "You're in galleries everywhere, Cappello! You've got four books to your name, and Aperture probably has you bronzed on their masthead. What do you mean you haven't got an opinion?"

Jess bristled, deliberating as he rubbed the side of his jaw. The others remained silent, waiting. Finally he took a long draught of beer, setting the bottle down at his feet.

"I'm not dodging the question, Sarah," he clarified quietly. "But the older I get, the more I think photography *is* a kind of trick. It separates perception. Between the thing and the seeing of the thing. I believed I could measure the loss in reality, calibrate the exact dilution, and measure my own work." He shook his head. *"Caveat emptor*...what you see is what you get. Maybe reproduction possesses its own verity, I don't know, but I think the camera tells a 'what is' different from reality."

"Meaning?" Papernello unwrapped a chocolate bar, munching quietly.

"Meaning I tend to agree with Kafka, the camera captures superficialities. And also with Leger, the whole reveals itself in the fragment."

"Like an accent, huh?" Hiller muttered half-aloud. "Certain words are one sort of hint, but you can guess an awful lot about a person's locale from a mash of 'em spoken together. Like, you're Italian, Joe. Bit and whole." He grabbed for his pile of string as a gust of wind tumbled it under his feet.

Sarah stared at Henry Hiller in impatient disbelief, but Joe Papernello smiled.

"I got interested in photography restoring the Brothers' collection of old pictures of the architecture and the history of the monastery. I learned to preserve and fix old images, but you know, the photographs seemed so remote, different from what I myself could see around me, that they left more questions than answers."

"And why'd you leave Italy and become a doctor? Kid doctor, right?" Abe pumped unexpectedly.

Seemed they were all fascinated with the priest.

Papernello shrugged. "Same reason I became a priest. I want to fix things. But fixing bodies is the most practical. It is hard to reach the inside of someone when his outside is hurting. And," his smile gentled, "I like being around children."

Jess peeled the label off his empty bottle, thinking. He frowned unseen in the shadows, when he felt the first icy splatters of rain.

They looked up as the pings of rain exploded into a downpour born on a torrent of wind. Madison hollered in dismay and quickly swept the cards up in his vest as water pooled into rivulets on the canvas drop cloth above them, pouring over the edges onto the table. Jess folded the campstool, sliding it hurriedly under the cover of canvas as Ansel retreated under the shelter of the table, his nose on his paws.

"If the rain's still with us by morning, suit yourselves to a sleep-in or hike in the vicinity of camp!" Jess yelled out. "Don't wander off! Kirby's seen cat tracks and I wouldn't want the bunch of us giving a cougar a bellyache!"

Rain fisted in the rising wind and hammered hard on the canvas roofs, dinging down through the trees as the group scrambled to their tents. Pulling his hat on and turning his vest collar up against the wind, Jess took a quick look around. He secured a flapping corner of the cook canopy, and then weighted the cover cloths with iron skillets, glancing toward the makeshift corral. Hobbled a hundred yards beyond the camp, the horses had already turned back to the wind, their hides black with rain. In brief seconds the campfire coughed out under the steady downpour, and Jess retreated to his own tent. Papernello's words dogged his thoughts as he unlaced his boots. How hard it was to reach the inside, to fix anything.

Rain continued in steady sheets of cold, wind-driven misery until noon the following day. The camp remained quiet, only Henry Hiller and young Zoë wandering about under the dripping trees in their slickers. Jess used the solitary time in his tent to take apart his cameras and clean out the fine dust that crept through the canvas wraps. He'd exposed only a few sheets of film, and a quarter roll of 35mm. His new Contax 645 SLR hadn't even cracked a shutter. The others were burning through film, hoping quantity might somehow net quality, but that was the way of it: experience taught deliberation.

He unwrapped the sleek Contax, looking it over. He'd borrowed a few of the Zeiss T* lenses from the shop and was eager to put the camera through its paces. The camera was an autofocus medium format that handled like a 35mm. A studio camera really, but Jess was curious to see if he could get any decent handheld shots.

It was always a compromise, he mused, hating the idea of an autofocus. Compromises– hedging depth of field, film speed, aperture. Relying on a camera instead of his eyes. He looked up from his work as Ansel nosed against the sealed flap of the tent, whining slightly.

"Need out?"

Jess unzipped the tent flap and the collie scooted through in a rush. Jess watched as the dog bounded to the edge of the camp and disappeared into the nearby meadow. Then he heard Zoë's low voice call to the dog and realized Ansel had joined the girl out by the tethered horses.

Deciding to stretch his legs, Jess shrugged on a rain jacket and laced up his boots, stepping out into rivulets of rain crisscrossing the ground outside his tent. Overhead the clouds had broken apart into dark gray underbellies, pierced by shifting rays of sunlight. The air smelled clean, a cool green odor rising from the meadow. Jess grabbed the new Contax. Time to see if his new toy worked. The shifting light interested him. If he was lucky, he might catch the mist rising off the ground, water drops on the crowns of thistles.

Walking the general direction Ansel had taken, Jess found himself along the edge of camp near Zoë. She was standing next to a rather bedraggled Danny Devito, the pony's sand-colored coat matted wetly to his sides. The girl was drying his drooping ears with a bit of rag, chatting to him softly. At Jess' approach she looked up and then swiftly away, but not before Jess had time to observe the clear imprint of three fingers of a hand in the soft flesh of her cheek.

"What's up?" he asked gently, pushing his hat up.

"Nothing."

Jess studied the girl's averted face for a moment. "Seems the rain's let up. Going on the hike to the cave?"

"What cave?"

The teenager worked her rag in the pony's ear. Danny bumped her elbow with his whiskered nose, nibbling at the yellow toggle on her jacket.

"Cabot Cave—an old prospector's dig. Left from a silver rush around these parts in the late 1800s. Carved out of sand and limestone by water seepage. Interesting formations, and all that. You might like it."

He waited, expecting a "no", and half-turned to leave.

"Why not," Zoë shrugged.

The pony pushed his head roughly against her shoulder. She felt into her pocket and fished out a half-eaten yellow apple. Danny took the fruit in his teeth and sawed contentedly. Yipping sharply, Ansel immediately planted his muddy front feet against Zoë's jeans, begging shamelessly.

"Ansel seems to like you."

Her expression, hooded and pale, flicked across his face briefly, before returning to stare fixedly at the pony.

"He's a nice dog. I like animals."

"I can see that."

Silence.

Jess shrugged. This was not his problem. But the marks on her cheek brought back memories of Gianni's frequent fist, the lame excuses he was forced to make at school.

"Well, we're heading out at two o'clock. Hope you join us." Jess half turned, then paused, studying the side profile of the girl as she continued to swipe down the horse's face with her rag. He made an 'L' with his left forefinger and thumb, framing the two, judging the light with a slight squint. Reaching for the Contax hanging off at his side, he rapidly set the f-stop and lifted the camera to his eye. *Click.*

Zoë spun around at the whir of the shutter and glared, pointing at the black camera box. "What'd you do that for?" she demanded, a blush rising up her neck from under the collar of her yellow jacket.

"Do you mind?" Jess was honestly surprised.

Zoë bit her lip, and then returned to her task.

Jess hesitated, waiting.

Zoë suddenly spoke, her face buried in the neck of the pony.

"I had a fight with my mother, Mr. Cappello. *Again.* She hates my music." Her voice was sad, sadder than anything Jess had ever heard or seen, even the gloomy rain-soaked look of her pony.

Jess felt a surge of anger toward Sarah. The kid was hurting. On the inside *and* the outside.

"She only wants the best for you, Zoë," he offered slowly. "I'm sure of that." The sole reason Zoë was on the expedition, according to her mother. Jess looked at the fading marks on Zoë's cheek. Was this concern, or control?

"How would you know?"

"She's your mother, Zoë. Your Mom's a smart lady."

"Whose side are you on anyway?"

Zoë rubbed her nose furiously with her fingers, blinking rapidly.

"Whoa there! I'm not on anybody's side, kiddo. Me, I think musical talent is a gift—one of the greatest. But your mother cares enough to want the best for you. Her point of view might have merit in the long run."

"*Gawd*," the girl bawled out suddenly, throwing the rag in the mud. "She sent you out here! Hip hip hurray for the grown-up's side." Zoë twisted around and faced Jess dead on, her expression dark against the blazing sunlight that had broken out over the meadow. "Did my wondrous mother tell you she hit me? That she forbid me to practice for the audition? Did she?" Zoë's voice was shrill, quavering with repressed tears.

"I haven't spoken with your mother, honest. I came out for a walk with Ansel." Jess fingered his camera nervously.

"Yeah? Well, she thinks you walk on water! One of your dumb pictures hangs over her desk, and she has all four of your lousy books."

Zoë threw a final, angry glare and stomped through the wet grass toward camp. The clang and rattle of WeeJun's lunch preparations had begun, but Jess lingered by the horses, absorbing this last, surprising statement. He kicked a divot of wild oat loose from the soppy soil and then hastily pressed it back with the toe of his boot, troubled by Zoë's accusations. Clearly the girl had it in her to be cheeky. Giving Danny Devito an absent-minded pat on the nose, Jess whistled Ansel in from the direction of the creek and returned back to the circle of tents. He greeted the others and they gathered around the camp table for lunch.

Afterward, Kirby approached Jess and elbowed him slightly apart from the others. He was carrying his rifle, the nose pointed toward the ground, held close to his side.

"Me and Bob're goin'out for a bit of a look-see. That cat's still trailing us some. His tracks are all over the back end of the meadow."

"Coincidence?"

"Maybe. Maybe not." The wrangler shrugged. "Winter drives these predators down. Most likely a young tom, feeling his oats. If we get a chance to scare 'im off, we will. Just wanted you to know—in case you hear shots."

Jess frowned, thinking about the planned hike to Cabot's Cave. "We're heading up to Cabot's Cave shortly. That okay?"

Kirby chewed the tip of a toothpick. "You handle a rifle?" he asked abruptly, assessing the photographer from under the brim of his Stetson.

"Some. In the military."

"Good enough," the other man nodded, narrowing his eyes as he scanned the hip-high grasses. "There's a spare rifle in the line shack. Take it along. Might as well be alert." The wrangler tapped the nose of his rifle against his boot and mounting his horse, rode off in the direction of Gooseberry Creek. Bob, mounted on a muddy quarter horse, trailed slightly behind.

Jess watched the outfitters cut through the grass and disappear from sight. Christ, a rifle. Kirby seemed genuinely concerned about the mountain lion. He'd have to leave his camera gear behind. Sighing, Jess searched for WeeJun underneath the canvas cook shelter, emptying the ratty tarp bowed with rainwater. Jess quietly passed on Kirby's instructions. The brown-faced Mexican cook simply nodded, and pointed to his own rifle nested high in the crook of a nearby tree. "Allus ready, boss."

Jess hiked the direction WeeJun indicated to the line shack. His little workshop in the Carson National Forest had shifted rather alarmingly again, from family therapy to lion posse.

Double Exposure

Tide Pool, Wynn Bullock, 1957

A constellation of stars, fissures of a rock thrown into ice. Jess met Wynn Bullock in the early sixties, in Los Angeles. Bullock shared a whiskey with Jess, the old master and the young upstart drinking together from kitchen glasses. The old man deeply believed in a theory of opposites: that nothing exists without its equal opposite. His work delved juxapositional elements of structure, double exposure, what critics dismissed as less traditional techniques of negative print, solarization, double printing. But Jess knew better. Bullock was a genius. Jess purchased *Tide Pool* that afternoon, the image an illusion spun of salt crust, wind vapor and water ripples. Somehow these diverse elements formed an image of the Milky Way, a mirror of the universe. Another fiction of photography.

Bullock pocketed Jess' money, assuring him that seconds after the shot was taken, the surface of the tide pool shifted in the ocean winds, the image erased.

"What do you really see?" Bullock goaded the young man. "What is there, or what I have shown you?" Bullock lit up a cigarette, citing some obscure semanticist, Alfred Korzybski, his hero, who declared even the names attached to objects filter and distort perceptions of reality. "My tide pool," he chortled, enjoying the joke, "your map of the stars." And then Bullock, bent with a troubled back, took his drink to the old club Steinway in his cramped living room and began pounding the chords of a Harbach and Kern song, his eyes crinkling at the corners as he offered up the lyrics *of Smoke Gets in your Eyes...*

Note from the Daybook:

'Genus Opuntia'—prickly pear and cholla cacti, which possess sharp spines and deposit toxic calcium oxalate crystals under the skin. The 'teddy bear' cholla sends jumpers—don't hike too close. Add to the genus that kid. Had on a tee shirt yesterday, says "Sotto Voce". Had to ask what it meant. What do you think? she says, and treks off alone.

Can't complain—a single night of rain. Followed Henry Hiller into camp yesterday, amazed at the rigging he uses to tie everything to his body. Alerted everyone local lion wants to be a photo star.

The group headed to Cabot Cave shortly after two, but first Jess had a word with Abe Santos. The younger man's eyebrows shot up in surprise when he noted Jess was carrying a rifle, but he listened to him explain about the cat tracks, not too concerned. Sarah came out of her tent bundled in a bright blue polar fleece vest, her face grim and withdrawn. Avoiding Jess, she joined her fellow docs Mark Anthony and Gary Smithers on the trail. Zoë, still in her slicker despite the blazing sun, had taken off with Ansel at the front of the group.

Abe set a blistering pace up the muddy trail and Jess brought up the rear; the rifle, a serviceable, if old, Winchester saddle carbine, strapped below his rucksack. He'd packed the usual first aid kit, with extra flashlights for the cave, and the new Contax. Jess had kept his eyes peeled for cat tracks or telltale scat, but hadn't seen a thing beyond Ansel's dog prints sunk in the clay. Gathering around the entrance to the cave, set back from the trail in a bluff overgrown with brush and young saplings, the photographers assembled tripods and pooled light sources.

Cameras loaded, the group hovered around Abe Santos, peering anxiously inside the dark slit in the rock and talking amongst themselves in excitable whispers. Armed with a flashlight and an old Nikon 35mm around his neck, Abe led the group through the narrow fissure in the rock, single file, and began exploring the mouth of the cave as Abe directed the set-up of lights in the main cavern. Sarah, nearer the entrance than the rest.

Jess positioned himself a stone's throw away at the rim of the trail, with a good view of the sparse meadows below and the rocky outcroppings above. He looked up in surprise as Sarah touched him on the sleeve. She blinked out in the full sunlight, adjusting the filter on her 35mm as she spoke.

"Zoë's not going in. She hates the dark. Will you keep an eye on her?"

Jess pursed his lips, nodding reluctantly. "She's with Ansel, Sarah. Up the trail."

Sarah's eyes flickered to the conspicuous rifle strapped to Jess' pack, but she merely nodded and slipped back into the cave with the others.

A half hour passed. Jess could still hear the whispers and rustlings of the photographers poking around in the cavern behind him. The last of the rain clouds had crested the peaks and cleared east, the hot sun rapidly sucking the recent moisture from the earth. Jess removed his windbreaker, taking a slug of water from his water bottle. Ansel barked, and he spotted the blur of Zoë's yellow slicker dipping through the trees to his left. As long as the girl hung out with his dog she'd be fine. Ansel never strayed far, and possessed a more reliable sense of direction than Jess' compass, lost in the field more than once, leaving it to the dog to bring them home.

Jess unzipped his pack and reached for his camera, laying it out on his lap. He fit the necessary filters, and then the 80mm lens, examining his surroundings. Above the mouth of the cave, desert marigold and wilting white blooms of evening primrose grew between dense clumps of scarlet beardtongue. Nearer the exposed scarp, ironwood trees dominated the ponderosa, clinging tenaciously in the crevices of boulders the scale of ships. Jess sighted his camera on the mouth of the cave, but then panned to a nearby bank of blooming wildflowers, popping off a few shots. Out of habit, he jotted the names of the wildflowers down in his small notebook, along with the filters and f-stop he used.

Jess removed from his vest a torn and water-stained field guide. He indulged himself in a cigarette, cupping his hand to shelter the match as he lit up, flipping open the pages of the book searching for the curved-beak bird scratching under the mesquite. Might be a *Crissal* thrasher, but that seemed unlikely for the size, and how far north they were. He drew on the cigarette with perverse pleasure—the best damn part of quitting was starting up again. No, he read, Crissal thrashers preferred the warm Sonoran desert, nor had he spotted a russet undertail covert when the bird scuttled off. Probably a sage thrasher, he decided. That kind ground-nested all over the Colorado Plateau. But sage thrashers lacked a carved beak, didn't they?

Stiff and bored, Jess slipped the field guide back in his pocket and listened—nothing but the light whisk of wind through the pines. He picked up the Contax again. A bed of mariposa and sega lilies gleamed with rainwater pooled in the throats of their nectaries. *Calochortus*—meant beautiful grass, beds of green, broad-leafed vegetation pockmarked with potholes dug by the bears, rooting for the starchy bulbs. Hidden in the shadowed clefts of rock, weathered drifts of snow bore a pinkish hue known to the locals as 'watermelon snow'. Jess adjusted the lens. He had tasted the watermelon flavor, although warily, as the peculiar hue owed its flavor to a spring algae composed of airborne radioactive particles, abundant enough to make a Geiger counter boogie. Rumored to be dust from Los Alamos, mineral-rich rocks were the likely source of the low-levels of radioactivity. Jess switched the camera autofocus setting to manual for a single shot. If he could...

A spate of frenzied, erratic barking erupted from around the bluff and Jess rose to his feet. He knew that bark. It was Ansel's war cry. Zoë's voice—shrill and panicked—called the dog back, following another crescendo of barking fading rapidly down the trail.

Sarah emerged from the mouth of the cave, her face small in the shadows.

"Zoë?"

"I'm on it," Jess responded curtly, slipping the rifle out of its cache. "Don't panic, Sarah. Stay put. Ansel has some critter up a tree."

Jess covered the ground between the cave and the tree line quickly, fingering the safety on his rifle as he jogged around the bend in the trail, searching for Zoë's yellow slicker in the trees. He'd loaded how many shells? Two? Three? He cursed himself—he couldn't remember. Ansel was cutting loose in full bay, clearly on the hunt, Zoë yelling in pursuit through the trees. What was she thinking, idiot girl!

Jess ran up a ridge off the trail where the trees gave way to rock in the midst of a stand of chalky pine, the skeletal etchings of a lightning strike. Scanning above him, he spotted

Zoë's slicker high up in the rocks, scrambling further up the mountainside.

"Zoë! Zoë—stop!" Jess shouted, cupping his mouth with his hands, his rifle cradled in the crook of his elbows. But either she did not hear him over the racket of Ansel's furious barking, or she had chosen to ignore him. She continued to climb, disappearing over an outcropping of bare rock. Jess swore under his breath and took off in pursuit. Leaving the trail, he forked diagonally up the slide in the direction Zoë had gone, picking his way through the boulders and fallen trees.

Jess pumped up the steep incline, feeling his calve muscles buckle. As he clambered over a fallen trunk, his vest caught on a snag of broken branch. He jerked free, coming to an abrupt halt. The unmistakable sounds of an animal fight reached him. The bawling, harsh snarl of a big cat, followed by a high-pitched shriek. Zoë's.

Ansel had found the mountain lion.

Jess bolted up the rocky hill, his heart pounding in his chest. Skirting the largest of the boulders, he spotted Zoë cornered in a crevice between two up-ended slabs of granite. Twenty-five feet in front of her, the tawny blur of a lion tangled with the black and white markings of his dog. The animals twisted in the red dirt, the jaws of the lion and the dog locked at each other's throats as they rolled between the rocks. The lion easily outweighed the small collie, and with a powerful thrust of his hind paws, dragged the dog under his grip, smacking the collie sideways against the rocks that sheltered Zoë. The howls of the animals hammered in his ears, the sweet smell of blood rising in the air.

Jess crouched and swiftly released the safety on the rifle, bringing the Winchester up to his shoulder. He squinted down the barrel sight.

"Stay down, Zoë! Stay down!" he shouted hoarsely.

The animals tumbled into his field of vision; the big cat locking on the dog's quivering body the precise moment Jess squeezed the trigger and fired. The shot zinged off the rock above the cougar's rear flank. For the briefest second, the wild cat leveled his yellow eyes on Jess. Then the lion lifted his teeth from Ansel's neck, blood running down the long, hooked canines, parted his jaws and released a roar that echoed over the rocks surrounding Jess and Zoë. Fumbling, Jess expelled the spent shell casing, took aim and fired again, burying the bullet in the dirt, two feet short of its mark. Snarling, the lion leapt off the collie and bounded easily over the rocks, disappearing with a whisk of its tufted tail into the higher reaches of rock.

The pounding of hooves reached Jess from the trail below as Kirby and Bob raced in tandem out of the trees. The men drew up at the base of the rockslide and Kirby freed his rifle from his saddle scabbard.

"All right?" Kirby bellowed up the hill.

Jess waved the rifle over his head.

"Did you hit him?" the cowboy demanded, hauling his horse into a half-rear, twisting on the narrow trail.

"No!" Jess shouted forcefully.

Kirby had to know it was a lethal and dangerous lion, not a weakened, wounded one on the run. Jess gestured with the muzzle of the rifle up the hill behind him. The two ranch hands nodded and spurred their horses down the trail away from the rockslide, seeking an easier egress up the mountainside.

Jess surveyed the jumble of rocks. Had the lion really gone? His rifle was empty; the extra shells in his pack. He gritted his teeth and hefted the rifle. He sure as hell could crack a skull if he had to. Jess caught a sudden dart, as Zoë burst from behind her hiding place to crouch in the dirt.

"Jess!" she cried out desperately, looking across at him, her face drained of color. "Come quick! Ansel's really hurt."

Jess ran to where Zoë kneeled over the limp body of the dog. He nudged Zoë aside and placed one hand under the dog's head, the other feeling behind the jaw for a pulse. The collie was conscious, but barely. His neck and fur were soaked in blood, and an open gash, nearly six inches long, exposed his shoulder bone to the ribs. His flanks were raked with gashes. The dog's breathing altered, falling rapid and shallow, and the animal groaned as Jess palpitated his legs and spine for further wounds. Jess shook his head. How had the dog fought for so long? Ansel's body had been literally shredded.

"He's going into shock," Jess muttered, barely aware of the girl folded in against his side. "We've got to stop the bleeding from the neck and that shoulder wound. Get him to camp. God knows, we've got enough docs *somebody* outta be able to sew him up."

Jess shrugged off his vest and whipped his shirt over his head, ripping the cotton cloth into three long strips. One he gave to Zoë with curt instructions to press against the shoulder gash to staunch the flow of blood, the other two he padded over the deep puncture wounds in Ansel's neck and chest. He worked feverishly, drawing on as much military field training as he could recall. Ansel whimpered, only to sag in Jess' hands, unconscious.

"Zoë, grab the rifle."

Grunting under the weight of the dog, and aware of Zoë white-faced with fright beside him, Jess heaved Ansel in his arms and struggled awkwardly down the rocks, his boots slipping as he retraced his path to the trail. Zoë clung onto his belt with one hand, the Winchester clasped in her other as she stumbled after him.

Kirby and Bob had doubled back, and caught up with them, shaking their heads grimly. "That cat's long gone."

"Give us a hand?"

Kirby looked at the trembling girl, and then reached down and swung Zoë up behind him on his horse. Bob dismounted, and lifting Ansel from Jess' arms, held him as Jess mounted the wrangler's quarter horse. The gelding's nostrils flared confronted with the raw scent of blood, and Jess struggled with the jittery animal, reining him in sharply. Bob handed the limp dog up to Jess, draping the collie across his thighs.

"Meet ya back in camp," the ranch hand nodded to Kirby, and tapped his rifle calmly. "I'll hike it."

"Right." Jess and Kirby exchanged grave glances. "Hang on now, girl."

"Bob," Jess detained the ranch hand. "Stop at the cave, would you? Let them know what's happened? Zoë's mother must be frantic. Have Abe get the group back to camp—but no panic. Understand?"

The man nodded, unzipped his chaps and folded them over his arm, heading down the trail.

Kirby spurred his big gelding off the south edge of the trail, cutting through the trees toward the lower meadows. Branches raked sharply across Jess' bare back and he bent low over the saddle, clinging to Ansel. As they emerged from the trees, the horses slipped down the hillsides on their haunches, plucking their way through the swampy meadow, flooded from the night's rain.

They rode the length of Gooseberry Creek and had crossed the last meadow to camp when Jess remembered, too late, the first aid kit in his rucksack. He could feel the sticky warmth of Ansel's blood soaking through his jeans. Suddenly, the horse stumbled in a mole hole, and he grabbed for the saddle horn, concentrating on holding himself and the dog in the saddle. His eyes rested on Zoë's back as she hugged Kirby tightly, her slight body bouncing on the horse's broad rump. His collie would not have attacked unless the girl was in danger, of that, Jess was sure. And that lion would have avoided confronting the girl and the dog, but pursued out of tree cover, the spooked tom had turned to defend itself.

Jess' hands tightened in the mangled fur at the dog's neck. What a brave kid, he reflected soberly. But the strange bond between his dog and Sarah's daughter may have cost Ansel his life.

Circles of Confusion

Drizzle on 40th Street, New York, Edward Steichen, 1925

Dream of night.
40th Street, a slot canyon of sharp-edged skyscrapers, which dissolve into dark patterns of gridiron and glass. Headlights and streetlights, a solitary lamp in a tenth story window diffuse in the drizzle, become stars in the fog, points of light without reference to object or space. A city clouded with fog and rain, a city simply washed away.

Note from the Daybook:
Deepest memory is associated with simple objects—pick up a rifle to remember shooting one. In Korea I was only conscious of the job I had to do: photograph enemy territory and field actions. I never had to face another man and shoot him; I shot the world with my camera.

"I heard shots! I heard shots!" WeeJun ran up and took the horses from them as they dismounted. Kirby poured Zoë a stiff shot of whiskey, which she sipped, in a daze. She coughed, doubling over, scarlet in the face. But the crying had definitely stopped.

"Jeez, kid," Kirby muttered helplessly, taking away the shot glass. "Heh, Weejun, get the kid some milk or soda pop, would ya?" Cursing himself, Kirby took the horses to unsaddle them for the night.

Jess left the girl in the cook's care, and turned his attentions to Ansel. He laid the dog out on a ground tarp in front of the cook stove. Shaking with cold, he pulled a borrowed sweatshirt from the laundry line, and rubbing his hands together to warm them, reached for the pot of warm water simmering on the propane burner. He rummaged through the cook's supply chest and located another medical kit, dumping the contents out on the table.

"Damnation." What could he do with nail clippers, blister band-aids, and Benadryl?

Jess kneeled on the ground and undid the bandages on Ansel's neck and shoulder; relieved the bleeding had slowed to an ooze. He lifted the dog's eyelids: the eyeballs rolled up, baring dull whites. Pup was out like a light. Then Jess lifted Ansel's muzzle and examined the gums above his teeth. The tissue had paled from a normal healthy pink to purplish blue. The dog was in danger of dying from shock and blood loss, and he had no idea what to do. Grimly, Jess began to clean Ansel's wounds with a hand towel. The torn flesh simply lifted in his hands over the dog's shoulder bone, and involuntarily, Jess shuddered.

"Let me do that!" a voice commanded.

Jess glanced over his shoulder as Sarah strode across the camp with a satchel in her hands.

"Zoë's over there," Jess offered, indicating the supply tent.

"I know," Sarah panted, catching her breath. "She's fine, thanks to you and this hound of yours."

"We haven't got any decent medical supplies," Jess shook his head. "I thought I could, but I can't. Not really—"

"But I can."

Sarah shoved Jess aside and unzipped her canvas satchel. "I've got everything but the operating room in this bag. Clear off the cook's table if you please, lay out paper towels, and then lift the dog up."

Jess followed directions and moved to Ansel's other side as the surgeon gently swabbed the largest wounds with a small bottle of hydrogen peroxide.

Sarah handed the bottle and a package of cotton balls to Jess. "Here," she instructed. "Do the rest." Checking the pulse in the dog's neck, she worked silently and efficiently, staunching blood flow with a narrow, pliers-like clamp. Picking up surgical scissors, she snipped the fur from the deepest injuries, clipping the jagged tears of flesh neatly even.

"Damn good thing this pup is unconscious," Sarah sighed under her breath, briefly meeting Jess' eyes. "I don't know the first thing about canine anesthesia."

"He's in shock, isn't he?" Jess asked quietly, stroking Ansel.

"Yes," Sarah answered shortly, her mind on her task. "I'd say your dog hasn't lost a critical amount of blood. Your field assist was excellent."

Sarah began sewing up the wound on Ansel's shoulder, piecing the skin flaps together with her fingers as she worked. She squirted a thick line of antibiotic over the raw seam and knotted the thread, clipping it off. She pressed two butterfly bandages over the long gash, but the edges of the bandages immediately came detached in the dog's fur. Muttering impatiently, Sarah secured them with a full roll of ace bandage.

"Now, the wounds under his neck."

She instructed Jess to hold the dog's head up, clicking her tongue in dismay.

"Some of these wounds are quite deep, Jess. There's a puncture wound here, near the windpipe that concerns me. I'll plug these with antibiotic and take a few covering stitches, but really, your dog needs to see a veterinarian."

Jess nodded, rubbing his shoulder, numb from the kick of the Winchester. He turned around as the others trooped into camp behind Abe Santos, shooting Jess and Sarah worried glances as they dispersed around the makeshift operating table.

Abe touched Jess on the shoulder.

"Heard what happened. Sent Sarah straight on down with Bob. Jesus shit... that cat made a mess of Ansel!" He stared at the skin and fur on the table, and then at Sarah, sniping off a new suture with her scissors.

Abe lifted Jess' rucksack and camera off his shoulder. "Retrieved your stuff, pal—I'll stick it in your tent."

WeeJun scuttled over and lit two lanterns over the table, thrusting Jess a hot cup of coffee.

"Drink it," Sarah instructed tersely. "You're a ghastly color." She was poking a huge hypo under the skin at the top of Ansel's shoulder, near the spine. She depressed the plunger.

"What the hell's that?" Jess demanded, alarmed, as a balloon swelled under the dog's hide.

"I.V. fluids, Jess," Sarah reassured calmly. "Animals can be hydrated subdurally. The skin is separate from the underlying muscle and this fluid will be absorbed through the tissue." She massaged the blister of liquid. "I've only got one fluid pack, I'm afraid, to cope with the shock...but it's a start."

She laid a hand lightly on the dog's muzzle, feeling for the faint, warm exchange of breath. She sighed.

"All done. Let's move him someplace quiet now. All we can do is wait."

Jess could feel her eyes as he stroked Ansel's ear.

"Thank you, Sarah," Jess offered simply.

"No, thank you...for saving Zoë."

She packed up her satchel and watched as Jess lifted the animal off the table and headed toward his tent. "If I were you," she called after him, "I'd get one of those cowboys to radio a pickup from the ranch and transport your dog to a proper vet."

Of course! They could meet on the forest service road at first daylight. Jess looked toward the clear sky. Long purple shadows dulled the distant peak. Bob and Weejun were already crisscrossing the camp, lighting the propane lanterns. He'd work it all out somehow, if the dog made it through the night.

Inside his tent, Jess laid Ansel on a tarp and then covered the animal with a thick wool shirt and his double-sided camera cloth. He felt for the dog's pulse: faint, but steady. Changing into a shirt of his own, Jess returned to the camp circle with the borrowed sweatshirt in his hand. There'd have to be an all-hands meeting tonight on the subject of the lion. It would be up to the group if they went forward or not: they obviously knew the risks.

Zoë stood waiting in the dark. She flicked her flashlight over Jess.

"Jess, it's me," she whispered. "Can I sit with Ansel?"

Jess hesitated. She had washed the tears and dust from her face. She looked pale, but composed. He nodded and walked the teenager back to his tent.

"You're sure?" he asked quietly. "You feeling all right? Let me know if he wakens or worsens in any way. I'll bring you a dinner plate...."

The girl nodded, taking her place cross-legged at the collie's side. She stroked Ansel along the jaw.

"Your Mom's a helluva vet," Jess smiled gently, but the girl had begun to hum; a quiet, moody melody he recognized with surprise.

"*Travelin' Light?*"

She looked up. "Works for you," she smiled shyly. "Maybe what Ansel needs is some music."

Jess touched Zoë gently on the head, turning to leave.

He needed that whiskey Kirby had waiting.

The teenager did not part from the dog's side all evening, although the collie regained consciousness an hour or two after Sarah's patch-up, but then lapsed back into a weak sleep. WeeJun brought Jess a leftover pot of broth from the evening's stew, and Zoë spoon-fed the dog enough to satisfy the cook and herself that their patient would survive the night.

"Ten-four," the walkie-talkie crackled. "We'll be at the junction at 0900."

Kirby would ferry the dog across his saddle to the nearest juncture with a forest service road, four miles away, and then someone from the ranch would drive Ansel into Taos to the local veterinarian.

When she learned of the plan to transfer Ansel off the mountain, Zoë became adamant about accompanying the injured dog to the vet.

"You've got to let me go, Mum. You've got to!"

Faced with the all too familiar set of her daughter's chin, Sarah gave in, and agreed that if Jess and Kirby okayed Zoë as a ranch guest for the duration of the expedition, she could keep an eye on Ansel.

Jess consented, secretly relieved. Before dinner, Kirby had faced them squarely, pushing his Stetson back on his head.

"I'd like to assure y'all that lion's gone. Bob and me tracked him aways, and he's headed up-country. Wouldn't be surprised if ol' Ansel gave him a right good lickin' back!"

The group decided by a vote of hands to continue the workshop. Sending Zoë to the ranch solved both Jess dilemma of what to do with Ansel, and how in the hell to keep an eye on the kid if Kirby proved wrong.

Following the dinner meeting, Jess brought Zoë's sleeping bag and a thermos of hot cocoa Kirby made to his tent. Lifting his tent flap, he reached under the makeshift blankets and felt Ansel's chest, relieved the collie's breathing had deepened to a near normal rhythm. Zoë too, was sleeping, curled up next to the dog. Jess covered her with her sleeping bag and threw his own bedroll under his arm—he'd bunk under the stars tonight.

Abe approached him at the perimeter of camp.

"Heh, looks like we ought to hold a bull session tonight. You up for it? The gang's restless, uneasy after that cougar."

Jess straightened his shoulders.

"That's what we're here for."

The late night campfire delved into the mysteries of Cabot's Cave and the difficulties of lighting without a natural source. A crash course in studio lighting, Jess accepted wryly. He didn't blame the others for steering clear of the topic of the lion. They didn't know the girl, and any dog that's not your own is just a dog. Jess refilled his coffee mug, and tried to explain the ways reflected light and backlighting complimented and cancelled each other.

"The idea has a lot to do with the lens, and the so-called 'circles of confusion'."

Jess slugged back the coffee, suddenly damn sure the brew wasn't decaffeinated, and might not even be coffee. Watching from the shadows, Weejun and Kirby grinned, holding up a fifth of Jack Daniels.

"Babe, I *live* in a circle of confusion," murmured Mike Teets, zipped into some kind of full-body purple fleece cocoon.

"I've heard of that," Paul Sorkum spoke up. He twirled the end of a long twig in the coals, letting it heat up to a fiery point, and then drawing smoking circles in the air. "Points of light and their organization, if I'm not mistaken."

"Right," Jess nodded, feeling the whiskey warm his belly. "Each point of light from the subject is gathered in the lens, which builds discs of light to make up a composite image. The smaller the discs, the sharper the image."

"So...very diffuse lighting will make broad band imagery? A foggy assembly of light points?" Peter Winooski lit up a small cigar, zipping his vest against the night chill.

"Yep."

"Winooski, douse that thing," Smithers grumbled. "Smells worse than your boots."

"Um, no way. I made it from my boots."

"Think of a computer printer," Abe called over. He was stretched out on the ground, leaning back against a saddle covered with a sweat-matted horse blanket. "The closer and denser the dot matrix, the clearer the print. In a camera lens, the circles remain disorganized if they're diffuse and large, but take precise shape when narrowed down."

"Before and after," Henry tossed in, whittling a stick with his penknife. "What I see before I put on my glasses...and after I do."

They all looked up as a coyote's distant bark echoed in the hills.

"The eye works the same way," Sarah affirmed quietly.

Jess looked around in surprise. Sarah sat hunched on a campstool to the right of Abe, both hands curled in the pocket of her blue fleece. There were dark circles under her eyes.

Sarah glanced around the circle. "In the human eye, light passes through the cornea and the lens, and is reflected onto the retina–which functions like film. The light generated from an object we look at is organized in the cones and rods–remember high school biology? We rely on the large peripheral area of the retina, and the retina's most focused point, the macula."

"Ah ha!" Brett Madison grunted. "I get it. An autofocus camera does both the work of the eye and the lens!"

Jess studied the tips of his boots, listening intently.

"In ophthalmology, my specialty," Sarah continued, "we confront problems like these 'circles of confusion'. For example," she accepted the mug of coffee Weejun passed her, and after a sip, took another, deeper swallow with a comic pucker. "In macular degeneration, the fine focusing capability of the retina is lost and the eye registers only a blur. In stigmatisms, the lens and retina are out of synch. That kind of thing."

"Well, hell," Henry grunted, pouring a generous capful of whiskey into his second cup of coffee. "No wonder my pictures look generally whacked. You got a blind man taking pictures. Them circles *are* confusin'!"

Gary Smithers chuckled in agreement, his thin face sporting a peppery crust of new beard, which he plucked unconsciously. He cracked his knuckles, refusing seconds on coffee. "Say, where is that blasted 'plane of focus' anyway? It keeps moving around on me."

Abe grinned at Jess and tossed another split of pinon on the fire. Sparks spit upward into the night. "You could wear camera lenses like goggles, Henry. Imagine, life in 200mm detail."

"No, thanks," Henry shot back, stirring his whiskey toddy with his little finger. "I *like* those circles of confusion. All warm and fuzzy."

Mark Anthony, silent up to now, jiggled his feet nervously. He sat on a campstool beside Sarah, layered in a lumberman's flannel shirt and high-tech climbing vest.

"So okay, this is the brain's take on it," he said, and offered a theory about the neurology of nerves and light receptors in the brain "seeking organization at any cost". His handsome face was so serious Abe laughed.

"Not in my brain they don't."

"This is way too med school," Paul Sorkum shook his head. "It's basic engineering, guys..."

Brett and Paul began arguing the merits of digitization, and the conversation circled the fire another few minutes. The lion forgotten, the photographers speculated amongst themselves about the performance of their gear and the day's work in the cave. Jess relaxed, satisfied they had enough film in the can to make the developing sessions at the Arts Center worthwhile.

"In the morning we mount up, gang. We're looping this side of the mountain, but tomorrow, we cut through that saddleback toward Crimson Peaks Ranch. Then down through the backside meadows—less time in the pine, more wildflowers and mesquite. Still lifes, Henry."

Abe had disappeared, and suddenly returned with a large peanut butter jar cradled in his hands. "This here is WeeJun's famous butt rub—liniment for horses and their riders. If you use it, sleep with your tent open—use just the netting. Stink would be too polite a word for this stuff."

"Not for me," Peter declined, waving his cigar. "Ask Brett, I'm a regular petunia."

Brett Madison grinned uncomfortably. He fiddled with his belt buckle. Mike and Peter liked to tease him a lot.

Exchanging goodnights, the circle broke.

Unnoticed, Jess approached Sarah. He touched her on the arm. "Can I ask a question, Sarah?"

"Sure, Jess. Is it about Ansel?"

"No, no. What you said about the eyes.... Would a blur like the kind you described be occasional, or all the time?"

"Referring to the macula? Why do you ask?" She zipped her jacket to her chin, crossing her arms to keep warm.

"Just curious."

"'Just curious' gets you admission to a museum, Jess. An optical blur gets you to me." She surveyed him neutrally, tucking her hands under her armpits. "The succinct answer to your question is that any deterioration in the macula is a kind of burnout—think heat spot on celluloid film. It's permanent damage, I'm afraid. Nothing 'occasional' about it, although initially retinal damage can be hard to detect as the eye compensates."

"Thanks. That's all I wanted to know."

He started to walk away.

"And Jess?" Sarah's expression was inscrutable in the gloom. "It gets worse— much worse."

Jess swung over to the outfitters' tents and borrowed a smoke from Kirby—his vest lay somewhere up on the rockslide. He'd miss that vest. Walking back through the dark, he lifted the cigarette to his nose and smelled the rough bite of tobacco. A smoke was about the best thing in the whole damn day.

Jess lit Kirby's Marlboro. All he'd sighted down that rifle barrel was a gray hole. He'd missed that mountain lion because he hadn't seen it.

Expose for the Shadow

Sir John Herschel, Julia Margaret Cameron, 1867

The inner man. The image as mentor.

Fresh from his first success in Manhattan, his print of *Moonrise* hanging on the wall of his 500 square foot bed-let in Brooklyn, Jess caught the northbound train to Boston, a letter of introduction from Beaumont Newhall to Albert Crossman in hand. Beaumont Newhall, confidante of Stieglitz and friend of Ansel Adams, well known in New York for his knowledge of fine photography and currently curator of the collection at the George Eastman House in Rochester, insisted Jess make the journey to Boston. A stately, white-haired gentleman with a soft Yankee voice, Newhall had given Jess a personal letter of introduction to the Department Head of Photography at the Museum of Fine Art in Boston, Albert Crossman. "You must do as the great photographers before you, young man," Newhall advised Jess, after reviewing his portfolio. "Learn the pedigree of your medium. See what other, better photographers understand about their work. In this way you will learn about your own."

Jess presented his letter to the curator in Boston. Crossman, a taciturn, prune-faced fellow bent unevenly at the shoulders like tin guttering, asked to see Jess' portfolio. Silently he reviewed the contents and then pursing his lips, handed Jess off to an assistant who led him into the recesses of the archives. To his surprise, Crossman allowed Jess nearly three days in the rare archives. After his return to Brooklyn, what Jess remembered was the work of Julia Margaret Cameron.

Born in Calcutta in 1815, Cameron was the third daughter of an Englishman in the employ of the Bengal Civil Service. In the naissance of early chemistry, Cameron worked with silver nitrates, traveling between England, India and Ceylon, creating portraits of the avant-garde of her time: Longfellow, Tennyson, Carlyle, and Mrs. Leslie Stephens, the mother of Virginia Woolf. It was her stunning cameo of Sir John Herschel that Jess could not forget.

Alone in the archives, he gingerly fingered the edge of the hundred year old image through its protective slip, finally sliding it from the casing with his cloth gloves and laying the image gently on the table in the curator's workroom. He adjusted the high intensity light above his head and examined the print in detail.

Herschel's profile appeared to float out of the black. The aged man wore a dark cloth beret of the Italian style. White, unruly hair sprung thickly from his square skull. He wore a collar of fine white linen beneath a gentleman's cloak of black velvet. Gazing at the cloak, Jess could vividly imagine the feel of the heavy, sensuous velvet, the deep black richly different from the fine black of the wool beret, and the empty black of the background. What made the image unsettling was its timeless proximity. The strength of Herschel's gaze, the rigor of his set mouth, the alive and sensate impression of the man's very thought. Deep furrows lined the old philosopher's forehead. What was the great man thinking when Cameron took this portrait? How had Cameron captured the interior life in his eyes?

Delicately Jess turned the print over and discovered a slip of paper taped to the back; a note, typed on an old set of keys and yellowed at the edges, a quote by Cameron herself.

"When I have had such great men before my camera, my whole soul has endeavored to do its duty towards them in recording faithfully the greatness of the inner man as well as the features of the outer man. The photograph thus taken has been almost the embodiment of a prayer."

He slipped the image back into its sleeve. *Sir John Herschel* was more than a portrait. It was the man himself.

Note from the Daybook:
The expedition has created significance in these images. Or perhaps, just the opposite?

Returned from the wilderness, the last day of the workshop kept the class occupied in the darkroom. The Arts Center offered facilities designed to accommodate local college photography classes, and each participant found sufficient wet side and dry side opportunities to develop their film. Under the subdued orange glow of the darkroom light, Jess went from student to student, waiting with them for that moment that brought forth magic under the developer like desire struck from the heart. Even with eleven bodies in the cramped space, the group was united in mind and effort. Very little conversation occurred as Jess circulated among them: observing, answering questions, and helping with the chemistry.

Abe stationed himself at the back of the room with Mark, Paul, and Brett, exploring techniques of double exposure, so Jess wandered over to check on Henry. The last day in the meadows, Henry constructed a pinhole lens by poking a sewing needle through a piece of tin, and attached this "lens" to his camera. Henry had spent the entire day making five and ten-minute exposures of wildflowers, and now, in the gentle wash of developing solution, a soft, otherworldly image of iris leaves bloomed from the chemical bath.

"Remarkable, Henry," Jess commented quietly. "Just the light, no lens."

"Plain amazin'," the old man nodded. "This here's how they did it in my great-granddaddy's day."

Jess moved on to inspect the contact prints developed that morning. He unclipped one from the overhead wire and brought it nearer the low wall light. It was the image he had made with the Contax. The candid shot of Zoë.

"Lovely work, Jess. I'm surprised Zoë let you take that. She royally detests having her photograph taken."

Jess looked sideways at Sarah who had moved to his elbow, examining the contact print critically.

"You think she'd like a print? Sort of a memento?" Jess offered, unsure. "She was drying off that pony after the rain."

"I do," Sarah nodded.

Jess hesitated. "I had trouble with the enlarger."

Sarah shot him a quick glance.

"Where's the problem?"

Jess indicated with his finger. "There, left of center."

Sarah leaned over and took a long, hard look at the image, her expression hard to read.

"It's perfectly defined, Jess."

He clipped the image back on the line.

"You need to see an eye doctor," Sarah pronounced flatly.

He stiffened.

"Jess?" She was waiting.

"Things'll take care of themselves," Jess muttered uncomfortably.

"Think again," the doctor said sharply. "Floaters? Maybe. But not what you've described." Sarah considered his back, deliberating her choice of words. She reached out and touched his elbow, forcing him to turn and face her. "Jess? This might be quite serious. And it's your livelihood."

"Sarah, why did you ask me that question at the Retrospective in San Francisco? About those who do the work and those who teach?"

She seemed flustered at the abrupt shift. "Because *I* both practice, and teach. I am forever questioning which is more worthy."

"Why separate them at all?"

"Because we're rarely good at both." Her face grew kinder. "Or able to continue...both."

Abe wandered up behind them.

"What's the topic? Talbot wasn't the inventor of the photograph after all?"

"Dr. Harte-Valentine was just giving me a medical lecture." Jess growled.

Sarah reached up and plucked the photograph of Zoë back off the wire. She thrust it directly under Jess' nose. "What do you see, right here?" she demanded. Her finger jabbed at the center of the image. "Close your right eye and describe it, Jess."

Jess backed away, but then hesitated as he caught the look on Abe's face. He grabbed the print from Sarah. What the hell—he'd taken the damn shot. Zoë stood framed in strong backlight, the sun haloed in her hair, her arm around the neck of—a blur.

"Zoë, and that horse she was petting," he answered gruffly. "Danny Devito."

"Which way is the animal looking, Jess." Sarah pressed.

He reddened. "I don't know," he responded hoarsely. "I can't clearly see it."

"What *do* you see, Jess?" Sarah asked more gently. "Distortion? A blur? A black field?"

"A grayish blur," he shrugged. "If I shift kinda sideways, I can catch it with my peripheral vision. But dead-on— nothing."

Abe looked at Jess in alarm, but the photographer was contemplating the doctor, his face expressionless except for the tight set of his lips.

"I can't tell you the precise problem without a full examination, Jess," Sarah said slowly. "But you've told me enough to warrant a stern warning—see a doctor, *immediately.* If this 'blur' you see is a mar in the retina, at your age it might be a preliminary sign of serious, degenerative disease."

Jess looked over the heads of the students, bowed over their chemical tubs and enlargers.

Sarah spun towards Abe.

"See that your friend takes this seriously. He's too damn good to be planning a final retrospective."

Abe threw Jess a nervous glance.

Calmly, Sarah considered Jess' averted profile, still speaking to Abe Santos. "Any problem diagnosed early enough might be treatable. But if he lets it go—" she shrugged coolly. "How long has it been like this, Jess?"

He answered without thinking. "A couple of weeks, months maybe. I thought the problem was in the lens or the cameras. I was trying to ferret out the trouble." He looked at both of them awkwardly.

"When I get back I'll call for a few referrals, Jess." Sarah pursed her lips. "If you want to fly to northern California, I'll fit you into the clinic schedule. This kind of thing is our specialty."

Abe hooted, an apprehensive, nervous chuckle. "Not our boy, Sarah. Jess Cappello doesn't fly. Famous for it, in fact."

Sarah rolled her eyes in frustration. "Then I'll locate a doctor here—there must be good professionals in Albuquerque. Just do something before it's too late. Now, excuse me—I have to collect Zoë. She's at the vet."

"I'm headed there myself," Jess interjected. "Ansel's discharged today. Guess they re-stitched his shoulder and worked on his windpipe some," he nodded at Sarah. "The vet says you saved his life."

"First the dog, now the man," she grunted. "If you're coming, let's go."

"Right. I'll be back in an hour, Abe. Get these guys to wrap it up. Dinner's at six, and then show and tell time."

Jess followed Sarah out the side door, his shoulders hunched.

Once outside in the shade of a row of gnarled cottonwoods, Jess turned to Sarah, keeping his words clipped. "I didn't appreciate that 'intervention', Sarah. This is my business and I don't want it discussed publicly, especially in front of a friend."

Sarah stopped, jingling her car keys loosely in her hand. She contemplated Jess a few seconds before answering.

"You're right. It was inappropriate. But quite on purpose."

"I'm sure of that," Jess answered, exasperated. "Why?"

"Because I know your type. Yes—" she held up a hand, silencing his rebuttal. "You're a type, Jess Cappello. I wasn't kidding in there. I see patients all the time with presenting symptoms such as yours. Sadly, it's often too late to help them."

She shifted her weight to her heels as she looked up at him.

"Look, you and I didn't get off to such a great start...my fault entirely. But you were a good sport about it and kind to Zoë, which I appreciate. I'd see you myself, but..."

"I don't believe in doctors, Sarah," Jess answered flatly. "Poking at things worsens their condition."

"You surprise me, Jess," Sarah retorted. "You might be forgiven for thinking your problem was camera failure, but now you know otherwise! You have a potential medical crisis that might *destroy* your ability to make images!"

"You can't know that. You're painting a worse case scenario."

"Maybe," Sarah agreed, looking down, oddly defeated. In the bright sunshine she looked unexpectedly young in her striped cotton shirt, tiny beads of sweat forming on her upper lip. She eyed him strangely. "Does your work mean so little to you? What else do you have? I mean—" she spread her hands in confusion, "there's you, your gear, and your dog. What's left if you *can't* work?"

Jess scowled.

"You doubt my credentials as a surgeon, as an ophthalmologist?"

"Lord, no."

Sarah held her ground. "Then drive to Palo Alto and let me take a look at you myself. I'll do my level best to protect my investment."

"Your what?"

"I own some of your work, Jess. I'd like a few pieces more."

They stood beside Sarah's rental car. She climbed in and lowered the window, fanning out the heat. "Look, what would you advise Abe if this were his dilemma? And you didn't let Ansel just languish and die from his wounds.... This is life, Jess! We have to fight back when things go wrong."

Sarah turned the key in the ignition and without a second glance, backed the car out of the lot and headed towards town. Jess stood looking after her, his mind gone blank. Then an image crept in. Himself, old and bent, feeling his way with a cane...someone in *his* house all day long, putting things out for him, guiding his steps, making his meals, taking him to the toilet.

"Not me," he declared aloud.

Jess crossed the lot and climbed into his truck. He had a dog to see.

The final event of the workshop was a mini-gallery presentation of the group's work, fresh from the darkroom. Jess was genuinely impressed with the variety and uniqueness of the images made during the trail ride. They hiked the same trails, looked at the same scenery, yet every image was unique to the photographer who took it. There were wide-angle landscapes of the meadows and peaks, close-up images of wildflowers and the dark cave formations, still life tableaux of branches, creek stones, and dried mud, and even a roster of portraits taken of the camp crew. The group circulated in front of one another's work with interest, contrasting out loud the work they arrived with and the work they were taking home.

"It's been a helluva adventure," Brett Madison declared with gusto. "But I'm not gonna miss that nag, Goldie Hawn. That buckskin is one sorry excuse for a barrel with hooves, and I've got the bowed legs to prove it!"

The others laughed in agreement.

"Jess," Mike inquired, swirling his wine around the curve of his glass. "When's the next workshop? May we suggest Provence? By car? You know, picnics and vineyards...late afternoon naps?"

"And no wild animals," Peter Winooski murmured.

Jess laughed, handing out workshop evaluation forms and the schedule for next year's workshops.

"What's next for you?" Joe Papernello asked, the bald pate of his head covered by a bright yellow Big Bird cap. His brown eyes were smiling. Next to him, Henry Hiller was whacking at a cheese wheel with a Red Cross penknife extended on a long cord from his waist.

"Work–my own, some commercial. But listen up...the Center has signed me to lead a workshop down the Colorado River next spring through the Grand Canyon. Wood dories and inflatables," Jess raised his voice challengingly. "Three weeks in a rubber ducky. Any of you game? I'm hoping Abe will join me."

The group applauded raucously, Abe standing at the back of the room.

"What's a one-armed man and an oar? Spin-cycle!" Abe wisecracked, watching Henry out of the corner of his eye. The old photographer dropped a wedge of cheese off the plate and then stabbed it with the point of his knife, laying it precisely in the center of his cracker. "I'm with Mike, let's go photograph Alaska—by luxury cruise."

Jess suppressed a grin. Abe was looking a little frazzled around the edges. Carly'd been after him since their return to town with her "honey-do" list.

"That's a 'Lifestyles of the Rich and Famous' gig. We're the 'Beverly Hillbillies' crew," Jess corrected humorously. "Make a note–the Canyon trip opens for booking in late November, folks. Mark your calendars as spaces fill up fast."

He glanced around the rag-tag group, more scuffed and sunburned than when they'd first met, and substantially more bearded. Gary Smithers had won the unofficial camp award for his bristle of salty stubble ringed jaw-to-ear exactly, as Zoë pointed out, like a Who from Whoville in the Dr. Seuss classic. The bone doc was wearing his prize, a black "Cher" tee shirt, in honor of his knock-kneed mare.

Jess accepted a beer from Mark Anthony. The dapper man from Atlanta was circulating with tall necks in one hand, and a bottle of red in the other. Anthony was looking rather

"Wild Wild West" tonight, in a fancy leather vest and shiny downtown boots. Where had the tech-line vest and Mephisto hiking boots gone? Jess sighed. He'd grown fond of some of them, and there wasn't a bad egg in the bunch.

"From saddle pads to life vests," Jess quipped. "Who says photographers are wimps?"

Inadvertently his eyes collided with Abe's troubled gaze. He could tell his friend was wondering if he would lead the canyon trip at all. Unavoidably, Jess looked across the room at Sarah. Stretched out comfortably in her chair in pressed khakis, her legs crossed at the ankle, she was watching him closely. With a nod, and a half-smile, Jess lifted his beer to toast the class, missing the swift exchange of glances between Sarah and Abe.

To the clink of wine glasses and beer, Jess closed the Santa Fe workshop.

Density

Georgia O'Keeffe, Alfred Stieglitz, 1920

She surrenders to her hands.
Georgia O'Keeffe, a woman of strong bones and raw power. Photographed by Stieglitz, her lover, himself a man of shadows, secret ambitions, and cool arrogance. On a winter afternoon at the National Gallery of Art, Jess unexpectedly came upon the gelatin silver image. He stood before the small print for long moments. It was all there: Stieglitz' obsession with O'Keeffe, and in turn, the painter's absolute obsession with her art. O'Keeffe is facing sideways, and her eyes are closed. She is lifting her arms, smooth lambrequins above her head. Her hands seem to open, as if to unfurl and unleash her power. Life dances from her hands, trips through her fingers...and the mind waits. O'Keeffe holds the consciousness of the body, the destiny of being. It is all there.

Note from the Daybook:
I ask for whatever God sees, what more there is beyond the shadow and the light. They leak from me like rain—my thoughts, my visions, my knowledge of the world.

Jess rose early, before the first light, padding about the house in his bare feet, making a plate of eggs and a hot pot of coffee. Ansel lay stretched out on his blanket by the narrow pantry, watching Jess with limpid eyes, his nose wistfully sniffing the cooking smells. Jess took him the leftovers, and watched as the collie gulped it down. The dog was gaining back some of the weight he'd lost at the clinic, but was a sorry sight for sure; shaved bald across his chest and shoulder, a grid of heavy, quilted stitches. Jess scratched the dog gently behind the ears and let him curl back up to sleep. They were quite a pair, he thought wryly—lame and nearly good for nothing.

Jess dumped his breakfast plates in the sink and poured a second cup of coffee, observing the sunrise through the small kitchen window. Lifting the cup to his lips, he caught a glimpse of himself in the glass and grimacing, ran a hand through his hair. Lord almighty, he had the look of a moth-eaten toy, some kid's worn stuffed monkey, loose in the joints and stretched at the neck. When had he gotten so old? His hair, or what was left of it, had faded to the color of a bleached walnut shell, and he could no longer remember when it had been thick, and as dark as the coffee in his cup. Spiffs of wiry body hair curled over the neck of his tee shirt. No hair where he wanted it, and twice as much where it didn't matter. Some kind of ugly, he thought ruefully, taking his cup out the back door. He let the screen door bang behind him.

Behind the wing of the house he used for his darkroom and work area, the yard lay wild with weeds. Dry meadow grass, peppered with loose rocks and ruts of bare clay, converged with a tall thicket of junipers in the back that provided the house with a useful windbreak in the spring. Jess stood on the steps, taking in the clear air, the fresh bite of astringent pine. A pudgy duo of white-winged doves cobbled beneath the bushes left of the stoop, chuckling deep in their throats as they pecked for a castaway piece of dog kibble. Overhead, a Coopers Hawk swooped low, a gray dash against the coral dawn, and already the sky had begun to deepen to pottery blue, high summer clouds pulling east toward the mountains.

Jess sat down on the stoop and reluctantly pulled the envelope out of the back pocket of his jeans. A triangle of colorful bird stamps was affixed to the corner. He turned the flimsy airmail stationary over in his hands, studying the handwriting, stunned by the pang of recognition that even Catalina's handwriting could bring. The letter had arrived days ago, thrown unopened in the fruit bowl alongside a slowly desiccating grapefruit. Mail made him uneasy, he neither sent it, nor received it. He smoothed the envelope with his thumbs, finally slitting it open with a thumbnail. He unfolded the single sheet of airmail stationary inside.

Ciao Jess,

Summer in New Mexico and fall in Venezuela. Time flies! The country grapes in the hills around Colonia Tovar are gone, the leaves intense gold and claret. The sun bakes everything— Rosa's tortillas, the tiles on the roofs–light bounces off lakes like hubcaps. My borrowed studio is in an old cannery south of Caracas—you can smell sardines in the wall paint! The project goes well–after several (sigh) pointless meetings with the museum board, I completed the last of the eight panels sketched to scale, and yesterday began canvas prep (see the back of this letter!) for "The Four Seasons". Will there ever be a museum that wants something besides the weather (quattro comici!) or the entire history of man painted on its foyer? Just once to do something to make people think! Milton's "Paradise Lost"–even 'Gulliver's Travels'–would make a wild mural.

Your workshop, mio caro, did the ponies survive? Are you done now? Pay me a visit! Roberto, my 'loaner' assistant, seems to have uptown connections as well as an 'in' at the farmers' market—we do eat well. Yummy paellas, shrimp the size of a gopher snake's head. There are plenty of rooms, if you don't mind the fish smell.

Jess, do me a favor? Call up to the cabin and remind Jeff to restock the paints and things he uses I like to keep on hand...oh, and remind him to throw Jasper in the attic once in awhile to chase out the roof rats.

I miss our mornings, mio caro. Give Ansel a pat for me.

XOXO, Catalina

P.S. Did you get the poem I sent?

Jess flipped the letter over and studied the light pencil sketch of Catalina's mural on the back. She had designed a seasonal montage, beginning with a fencepost gnarled in grapevines, the luscious harvest hanging free and so realistic that you wanted to cup the fat grapes in your hand. The work was good, a fine monument to the vineyards of Venezuela—and each subsequent panel would honor a region and natural resource of the South American coastal country. He smiled sadly. He knew how much that bored her, how temped she must have been to tweak the content, embolden it with some private twist. And that's when he saw them, the tiny naked dancing Greeks in the design of the grape leaves. Catalina's little joke.

Jess folded the letter closed and slipped it back in his pocket. For a long time he sat with his coffee, lost in thought. Somewhere in the green mesquite, a hidden songbird warbled, weaving bright, wordless tunes in the air.

Sudden barking from Ansel alerted Jess to the crunch of tires in the driveway and he rose to his feet. Cautiously he skirted the side of the house. Sarah Harte-Valentine and her daughter were getting out of their rental car, approaching his front door.

Raising her hand to knock, Sarah looked right, surprised to see Jess by the far edge of the house. Her eyes swept over him, brightly friendly.

"Hi, Jess!" Zoë waved. Her grin revealed a slight gap between her front teeth Jess had not noticed before.

"Come to say goodbye to Ansel?" Jess asked, approaching the two. "You'll find him in the kitchen, Zoë."

"That's one reason," Sarah confirmed cryptically, jamming her hands into the pockets of her slacks.

Jess raised his brows, but nodded at Zoë, holding open the front door so she could slip inside and find Ansel. "I thought you'd be on your way to the west coast by now," he murmured to Sarah.

"Will be, in a few hours. But we—Zoë and I—need to speak with you. Sorry to arrive unannounced...."

Sarah preceded Jess through the narrow door, her eyes darting around the interior, taking in the Navaho rugs on the floor and the framed images on the wall, picking her way through the hapless clutter. She moved a balled-up sock aside with the toe of her shoe, and smiled. "Nice place."

Jess cleared his throat, feeling at a loss. "Coffee?"

"Only the leaded—you Americans water everything down."

Following Jess to the kitchen, Sarah plopped down at the square table, her fingers drumming on the split oak as Jess poured out coffee. He eyed his percolator warily as he refilled his own cup. The Corning ware pot had been a flea market find, but recently had begun a kind of death shimmy, a sucking and hissing sound as the 'ready light' flickered uncertainly, and that surely promised trouble. He set the pot back on the counter and placed Sarah's cup before her. Leaning back against the counter he observed the English woman. In her usual khakis and button-down shirt, Sarah looked every inch the professional. Only the tanned skin at her neck and wrists suggested recent time in the mountains.

"Can I take Ansel for a walk?" Zoë asked hopefully from the floor beside the collie. Ansel was assiduously licking her hand, his tail wiggling. "The vet did say he needs to keep his joints and muscles from stiffening."

"Sure. But put him on a leash. No cat chases—big or little."

The kitchen door banged shut behind them.

Sarah took a quick sip of coffee and nodded appreciatively.

"Um, good. Well, then...right to business, shall I? I want you to come to my clinic for evaluation, Jess."

"Your clinic is two thousand miles from here, Sarah," Jess pointed out reflexively.

She waved her hand. "I've thought about this, truly. I think you require the best consultation and care. There are experimental treatments out there, some worthwhile..."

"You sound as though you've already decided what's wrong," Jess interrupted, crossing his arms tightly.

"I've a strong suspicion," the doctor admitted, tucking a stray strand of blonde hair behind her ear.

Jess watched her through hooded eyes. "What exactly do you think is the problem?"

"I'd rather not say without an examination," Sarah prevaricated, "I might be wrong. We're not field dressing a mauled dog." She permitted herself a small smile.

"I hate doctors."

"I'll try not to take that personally."

Sarah cradled her coffee cup between her hands and leaned forward, her face withdrawn into an armored expression reminiscent of his first boot camp sergeant in Biloxi, Bolton "Bad Ass" Bronson, the only man to make the theatre of war preferable to the entire State of Louisiana.

She pushed her cup aside, her eyes, fixed and green as a lizard's. "This is my field, Cappello."

"But I live here, in New Mexico. Besides, there's Ansel to think of, and I've got assignments to fulfill."

"I've already spoken to Abe," Sarah admitted, as Jess shot her a look of purest astonishment. "And he feels exactly as I do. In any case, he immediately offered to take care of your dog." Her voice lowered, becoming more persuasive. "We're talking two weeks, Jess—max. You can rearrange your work, can't you? It's essential you not delay, and I suspect left to your own devices, you would."

Jess pivoted to face angrily out the kitchen window. Abe and Sarah in this together? First, sandbagged in the darkroom, and now in his own home!

"Look, Sarah. I—"

Zoë bounded through the screen door into the kitchen carrying Ansel's water bowl. Jess held back, waiting as the teenager ran fresh water from the sink and refilled the container. Balancing the metal dish in both hands, the girl smiled at him brightly, looking from Jess to her mother. "Did he say yes, Mum? Did he?"

"We're just discussing it now, Zoë," her mother cautioned quietly. "Well Jess, you might as well hear the whole proposal."

He faced the two of them. "Seems like it."

"Zoë and I know you don't like to fly ..." Sarah fiddled with her cuff button and then let out a small breath, pressing on. "So, why not let Abe take care of things here, and you motor west. Your vision's adequate for driving I should think. If you were to leave tomorrow, mightn't you be in California in two or three days? You'd stay with us—we have a guest room. And," she hesitated a fraction of a second, "Zoë would like to make the trip with you."

Sarah frowned at her daughter as Zoë hopped from one foot to the other, splashing water from the bowl onto the tile floor.

"Zoë's never seen the mountain west, and honestly, it hasn't been enough of a break," she lowered her voice to a conspiratorial whisper, "from the cello."

Zoë made a face, but kept silent.

Sarah folded her hands. "That's our entire proposal, Jess."

"Actually you'd sleep in my music room," Zoë giggled suddenly. "But there's a bed, and I'll clear out all my stuff."

"Zoë," Sarah turned to her daughter. "Would you give us a spot of privacy? Jess may have some, err, medical questions for me."

"Gotcha! I'll be out with Ansel. Gosh, he looks better, Jess." Zoë grinned again and ducked out the kitchen door, the water bowl balanced haphazardly in her hands, a good portion already down the front of her shirt on poor Mozart's head.

Sarah cleared her throat. "I've shocked you–I can see it on your face. But hear me out, please? You need me, and, actually, I need you." She looked down at her hands, her face tight. "Zoë and I had another disagreement last night, a right royal battle about her music audition. The thing is scheduled in less than two weeks, you see. Now, I must fly to a conference in Los Angeles tomorrow, and haven't had a chance to make any reasonable headway with her. I was hoping a few days on the road with you might convince Zoë of the realities of life as, uh, an artist."

"You are certifiable, Sarah Harte-Valentine," Jess said in awe, rubbing the back of his neck in genuine astonishment. "You want *me* to tell your daughter there's no money in the arts, that this career's a great risk, not to follow her own instincts? I can't do that! And I wouldn't anyway—I don't even *know* you people."

Sarah held her hand up, eerily composed.

"Wait! Yes, I want you to give her the benefit of your experience, but not because you do, or don't, support my desire for Zoë to go to school and get a professional degree of some kind. You see, you have a different opinion and experience than mine. Or Red's," she added under her breath.

"What difference does that make?"

"Jess, honestly? Red—Zoë's father— is a very successful and very charming, *very* erratic man. He's had little to do with Zoë since she was born. His life is centered in his music, and he made that quite clear to us both a long time ago." Sarah's eyes were troubled. "I think Zoë believes following in her father's footsteps will bring Red back into her life." Her glance slid away.

"It won't, Jess. If anything, it will drive him further from her. Zoë is a true prodigy—there is no question hers is a gift, not just an aptitude. This is bound to make Red jealous. I couldn't bear that. Not for Zoë."

"Why would Red Valentine be jealous of his own daughter? He's famous in his own right."

"Red Valentine is an immature, ego-centric, *aging* star," Sarah snapped, running her fingers through her hair. "He is terribly insecure and always has been. More so now, knowing the music world considers him a—*a standard*—not a cutting edge musician. In Red's life there is room for one—Red."

Jess fell silent, unsettled by the bluntness in Sarah's face. He didn't know Red Valentine. By reputation the trumpeter was a true success in the edgy post-Miles Davis jazz world, and still in demand in London clubs. But he could see Sarah wasn't lying.

She looked him straight in the eye.

"I want you to talk to Zoë about the realities, Jess, just the realities...the solitary hours, the constant competition for recognition, the unpredictable travel and income, especially the nomad lifestyle. You can do this with authority," her eyes flickered uncertainly. "You're a success at it yourself. If she evaluates music separate from pleasing her father, then maybe she'll make a more rational decision."

"Or not, Sarah." Jess refuted soberly. "Zoë may be more genuine than you give her credit for." He paused. "Maybe the hang-up with Red is yours...not Zoë's."

Color crept up the sides of Sarah's neck. "Be that as it may, this is a critical decision for Zoë. Her teacher is pushing her toward the Curtis School and a career as a soloist. If she somehow doesn't make the grade, she'll land in an orchestra. She won't listen to me because I'm her mother. You're the only artist we both know—and respect—that can offer a point of view she hasn't already rejected."

"I won't be your flunkey, Sarah."

"I'm not asking you to be!" The English woman burst out, struggling to regain self-control. Her voice shook as she faced him again and measured her words with care. "I am asking you as...as a friend, if you like...to talk with Zoë. Without my intervention."

"Sarah, be reasonable. I'm neither a parent nor a musician. Photography was my *only* option. I was fit for nothing else, but fortunately, fairly adept at it. You're asking me to advise Zoë, and I'm not the least qualified."

"I beg to contradict," the doctor whispered, her expression oddly unguarded, tense with hope. "She'll listen to you. I know she will."

"Sarah," Jess shook his head. "You don't even know me. Why would you trust your daughter on a road trip with the likes of me? I don't want to be responsible for any kid."

"I'm not a fool, Jess. I've asked around. Abe told me he would actually *will* you his own kids, if he thought you'd remember to feed them. And Zoë's no trouble, she's quite independent."

133

Jess made a mental note to beg, no insist, Abe to do no such thing–and to shut the hell up.

"Sarah, the fact remains, I'm a stranger."

"The Art Center recommends you as the most responsible of all their instructors. And, my friend at the Department of Motor Vehicles says you have a clean record. You certainly don't strike anyone as a pervert."

Jess let out an expletive and flung his empty cup down with a clatter on the counter behind him.

Sarah half-rose from her chair, leaning forward on her hands across the kitchen table.

"Cappello, I propose trading the fees for your treatment, and hospitalization if necessary–the very best I can do for you–for honest time with Zoë. It's a fair trade in my eyes. Is it in yours?"

"Oh, for god's sake...." At a loss for words, Jess bent down to pick up the scattered shards of broken pottery. The truth had reared its ugly head. How did she know he didn't have the money to pay for expensive hospitalization? He'd never had a need, or interest, in insurance. He could feel the weight of it like a rock in the center of his chest. He'd be forced to consult a doctor sometime. How long could he pretend otherwise?

He looked at Sarah, noticing unconsciously how the slanted light from the kitchen window gilded the outline of her hair. *Some angel.* But he could not interfere in Zoë's life—he had no right.

"Sarah, I can't." Jess shook his head, defeated. "It's not fair to Zoë."

"But she knows, Jess! We talked it out last night. Zoë has agreed to wait a week before she makes any decision, regardless of what I, or her maestro, have to say."

Jess hesitated, genuinely puzzled. "Why would she agree to that?"

Sarah smiled oddly. "She likes you."

"I won't persuade her one way or the other, Sarah."

"Just come to the clinic and let Zoë accompany you, Jess," Sarah begged simply. "I'll take a look at your eyes and we'll have you back in New Mexico in two weeks. Deal?"

A tiny twitch had appeared in the corner of Sarah's mouth, and Jess coughed into his hand, surprised at the vulnerability that tiny quiver betrayed. He admired the doctor's relentless nature, a raw determination that could press steel flat. If he ever needed a doc, and a good one at that, she'd fit the bill. As to Zoë, he suspected the die was long since cast.

"You're not getting the best end of this deal," he warned.

"Let Zoë be the judge of that."

Jess hooked his thumbs in the belt loops of his jeans.

"Well, I've got new tires on the truck. We'll see what Santos has to say. If it can be worked out…"

"Oh, hurray!" Zoë bubbled in delight, peeking around the porch door. "I'm packed and my duffel's in the car! Please, can we go by the Grand Canyon?"

Jess locked eyes with Sarah before he answered Zoë, folding his arms laconically.

"We go whichever way gets me there quickest, young lady."

F/8 and Be There

Wendy, Northern California, Jock Sturges, 1987

A summer dream.

The fallen trunk of redwood juts over the green river, sunlight dancing on the water. Indolent in the heat, a young girl lies stretched out on her back, her translucent skirt a blossom against the dark bark of broken redwood. Her small hands are clasped in repose. So much a part of the river and its silences, so deep in the dulcet light, she might not really be there, but for the shimmering drift of her hair.

Note from the Daybook:
The journey lies before me, and I've a hunch it's more than I bargained for.

Abe Santos readily confirmed his offer to care for Ansel, and to look after the place during his absence, forcing Jess to admit his last excuse was gone. Like it or not, he was headed to San Francisco with a teenager. Sarah left for the airport later that morning, leaving Zoë and her duffle, her phone numbers—home, clinic, pager, and mobile—and directions to their house, south of San Francisco.

"Head for Stanford University," she advised, writing abbreviated instructions down on a pad of paper. "The freeways loop the bay, and you want to head west, toward Palo Alto."

He had no clue what to do with Zoë, who was now following him around with as much persistence as Ansel.

"Mum drilled into you that I'm to get the starving, miserable life of an artist speech?" She chirped behind him as he readied for the trip, throwing clothes into a backpack. She stuck to his heels as he crossed the house into the studio wing, nosing around as Jess deliberated over the camera gear spread out on a worktable.

He ignored her, balancing lenses in his hand. His honest preference was to lug along the battered wooden Deardorff 8x10 field camera—but that would entail too much gear for a houseguest, he supposed. His hand strayed to the new camera. The Contax would be the logical choice. The damn box came with crutches, for godssakes, and a medium format would be nice. He hesitated. After the clinic maybe he'd spend time in the tidelands, or knock over the Santa Cruz Mountains to the coastline. He chewed the end of his field book pencil, thinking, and made a quick note to grab a tripod and dark cloth.

"I *said*–" Zoë circled in close to him, her green eyes squinting up curiously. "Say, are you going to take pictures? I thought your eyes were funny."

"So I hear," Jess grunted, zipping up his pack. "An exercise in creative use of white space—or in my case, gray."

Zoë grinned, showing that toothy gap. "You *are* funny."

"See if you think so in twenty-four hours, Sunshine."

He was not optimistic. He intended to drive directly west, right on through the heat, thunderstorms, and the inevitable, endless, teenage pleas to stop for a soda or trinkets at the reservation stands.

Zoë merely smiled, rather Sphinx-like, and wandered off with Ansel, leaving Jess to heave a quiet sigh of relief. After only a few hours, he felt as though Zoë was everywhere, diffused in the air, like lint.

"California," he muttered, throwing in his daybook for good measure. "Burn *another* set of tires..."

Abe swung by a couple of hours later and joined Jess in a late lunch on the patio. They sat on campstools under a tall cottonwood, small bits of downy seed floating loose on the breeze, flocking the spiny tumbleweed jammed in the wire fencing, getting stuck in Jess teeth.

"Can Ansel travel, do you think?" Abe asked, mouth full of burrito, wiping green chili sauce off his chin with the back of his hand. He looked sideways at the mutt in question, dozing on the porch. "Sure is damn hot."

"Can't see why not," Jess answered. What the pup needed was food and rest. Natural healing would take care of the rest. The collie was young, and as in all life, fortune favored the young.

"Well then, I'd like to take him home with me, if it's all right with you." Abe reached for the beer Jess handed over. He took it between his knees and deftly twisted the cap off with his one hand. "He'll be happier with folks around, not lying here, missing you. My kids'll baby him, same as Zoë." Abe glanced toward the girl, eating her lunch a few feet away.

"Good by me," Jess shrugged. "Carly okay with another mouth to feed?"

"Sure, what's one more in a passel," Abe chuckled. "So long as your dog isn't gonna be asking for filet mignon."

"Straight kibble, available leftovers, constitution of a garbage disposal."

"Hear anything from our Italian nomad? It's Carly wants to know."

Jess cocked his head and surveyed his friend slowly. "You talk too much, Santos," he muttered. "And, to the wrong people."

"So, have you? You know I'm only asking 'cause Carly's gonna drill me."

"A letter, and a postcard a while back," Jess admitted, throwing tidbits to the doves lurking in the bushes. "Catalina seems to like her set-up. Already starting her canvases."

"Doesn't she paint on the walls? I thought murals were done on the buildings."

"Not Catalina's, she likes them on canvas. Likes to rearrange the panels for a different look."

"When's she coming home, did she say?" Abe kept his voice low as Zoë got up and crossed the yard to give half her tortilla to Ansel.

"No. She didn't."

Abe seemed inclined to say something further, but then thought better of it. He brushed the dust off the back of his jeans.

"I gotta get back. You need anything, just call. How long, you think?"

"Sarah said two weeks. I'm planning on less."

"Well, no need to rush," Abe advised sagely. He grimaced. "Can I use your darkroom? Carly stored four bags of mulch in mine, and now I've got *maggots*, or something, to exterminate."

"No need to ask, Abe."

"Ha! Messing around in the digs of the great Jess Cappello..."

"Oh, shut up. Be my guest." He raised a finger in warning. "But stay out of my contact files. I have a way of filing things and if you screw it up, it'll take me centuries to find anything."

"Right-o, Captain Cappello." Abe saluted snappily.

"And Abe..."

"What?"

"Thanks."

"We're rootin' for ya."

Abe left in his truck, the little collie perched uneasily on the seat beside him. The dog looked behind, tail wagging sadly as Abe drove away.

Well, that was that, Jess thought. He finished up his packing, and placed a phone call to postpone a pending assignment. He did not explain his absence.

They left a few hours before sunset, planning to cross New Mexico into Arizona by the cool of night. Zoë perched in the cab of the old pickup, her feet resting on a small backpack. Her canvas duffel was stowed with Jess' things in the locker he used to keep his gear dry. She clipped tiny headphones on, and smiled as she popped her gum.

"Wanna listen?" She pulled the plugs out of her ears and extended them to Jess. Strains of classical music, some kind of symphony, buzzed the air.

"No, thanks."

Jess tuned the radio to his favorite Albuquerque blues station and opened a soda from the compact cooler on the seat between Zoë and himself.

"Help yourself."

She made a face, but pulled out a Sprite. "I prefer juice. This stuff is pure high school chemistry."

Jess cast a single look back at his adobe, closed up against the shadows of the cottonwoods.

"Road ho," he muttered. Heading west on Interstate 40, the tires hummed steadily as the truck picked up speed, Chet Baker on the radio, playing an improv of *"On Green Dolphin Street"*.

They ate sandwiches from the cooler without stopping, and eventually Zoë fell asleep in the cab, her head pillowed on her jacket. Jess tuned in another radio station to keep him company when the first one flickered out, until the static in the mountains grew too heavy and he shut the radio off, preferring silence.

He glanced over at Zoë from time to time, his thoughts wandering to a trip he'd made sometime in the '40s, a road trip to Cleveland. He supposed he must have been at least ten, younger than Zoë. His father had won a pair of tickets to a Cincinnati Reds baseball game in a company raffle, and Louis had been unable to go. It was summer and his brother had a job helping run hog pens. The plum had fallen to Jess.

He remembered his pure excitement at the prospect of the journey. He'd never left the rocky hills of Breathitt County, and Ohio was surely a universe away. He remembered the hot sun, and the thrill of the game running to extra innings, the long drive back in the old Chevy. The only good memory he had of the old man, really. Jess flicked a glance over Zoë, head cradled in the crook of her arm like a duck's wing. Whatever the kid's relationship with her father, he was sure Sarah's view was but a single cut of the onion. Still, he was inclined to put his faith in the mother. Experience had taught him that.

Funny he remembered that baseball game. He unrolled his window a crack, lighting up a Marlboro.

He drew in hard, mingling the wrench in his chest with the inescapable flood of images. There it was, what he could never forget. Like small seizures of the heart that changed life forever somehow. And that July, simmering hot as a rice steamer, had changed everything. For weeks, the heat bore down on the county, baking the trees until the very leaves furled and drooped. The sky, hazy over the river, had grown a gritty clay color from the dust off the fields.

The twelfth of July. Ten days straight. Leaving the night shift, Gianni Cappello drove to the town's roughneck tavern and drank half his paycheck by breakfast. When the black Chevy swerved into the driveway, flinging a hard spew of gravel against the porch door, it was seven in the morning.

His father dragged his mother from bed by the curlers in her hair.

"Make me a meal, godamnit! I work my ass off for you bums!"

The eggs turned runny and Gianni flung the plate against the wall, yellow yolk sliding down the peeled wallpaper. Jess woke to the crack of the plate. God knows where Louis was. Pulling on jeans, he ran into the kitchen to see Gianni, his big, scarred hands wrapped around the hunting rifle, advancing on his mother, cowering beside the refrigerator in her violet housecoat. Her shoulders hunched high to protect her face, her nose already bleeding in a trickle over a swelling lip. Her eyes darted toward Jess and she slid them toward the front door. That sick feeling grew in the pit of his stomach. Jess understood.

He couldn't hit hard enough to take down the old bastard, but he could run. Jess sprinted the two miles to the hog farm for help, returning with Wes Smith in his wife's Pontiac. But more than breakfast stained the kitchen walls. Gianni Cappello had beaten Hannah Clarke to death with the butt of his rifle, and when the rifle cracked, the backs of his hands.

Jess eased his grip on the steering wheel. He realized his eyes hurt. Glancing at the illuminated dial on his watch, he knew he'd gone as far as he could for one night. He pulled into a dimly lit rest stop, and parked in the shadow of several freightliners. He got out of the Ford and stretched, feeling the pavement vibrate under his feet from the diesel engines. He used the facilities, splashing water on his face.

"Christ almighty," he whispered to his distorted reflection in the scratched metal above the sink. "You look like the old man."

Returning to the truck, he tucked an extra sweatshirt around Zoë's shoulders. She stirred slightly without waking. Angling his own body against the cool window glass, Jess let his eyelids drop. A few hours, that was all.

By dawn, Jess was back on the road, headed toward Flagstaff. Around eight, he pulled into Brownie's Truck Palace, and nudged Zoë awake. She shifted stiffly and looked at him blankly, blinking her green cat's eyes.

"Where are we?"

"Arizona and breakfast. The truck stop has pay showers if you'd like to clean up."

She nodded, dazed, rummaging in her duffel for a change of clothes and her toothbrush. "You drive all night?" she asked, confused.

"Most of it. This old truck has to make up in time for what it lacks in speed."

"You're mental. Your eyes look like red-hots."

A shrill beep erupted from her backpack and Zoë dove for her cell phone. She flicked it open.

"Oh, hello Mum." She grimaced at Jess. "Yeah, we're fine. Stopping for breakfast. Arizona–?" She looked at Jess questioningly.

"Outside Flagstaff," Jess confirmed.

"Flagstaff, Mum. Yeah. Yeah, I will." She shoved the phone back in her bag. "She'll call all the way to California, you know."

"Doesn't surprise me."

They walked into Brownie's and Jess pointed Zoë the way to the showers. He needed black coffee first, the strongest possible, and was sitting at the counter nursing a second cup when Zoë returned, a butterfly clip holding back her wet bangs. She'd changed to a blue-striped tee shirt with the logo of the San Francisco Youth Symphony on the front and took the stool next to him, swiveling around, back and forward, as she checked out the crowded restaurant.

Jess handed her a menu.

Their waitress, a thick-waisted woman with her hair scrunched up in a frizzy topknot, placed their food on the counter with a curious grin.

"You and you daughter on the road? These plates are what the drivers order—the *big* guys!"

Zoë stared appreciatively at her plate, heaped with home fries and pancakes and a mountain of scrambled eggs. "Beats boxed cereal!"

Jess tucked into his biscuits and gravy. At least the waitress hadn't assumed he was Zoë's grandfather.

After they'd eaten, Jess left Zoë to wander around the truck stop minimart and took a fast five-minute shower. Changed to a fresh denim shirt over a clean undershirt, his hair brushed into place and stubble shaved clean, Jess felt reasonably presentable. A long day lay ahead if he reckoned to reach the border of California.

"Gotta gas up the truck, Zoë." He handed her a twenty-dollar bill. "Why don't you restock the cooler."

She refused the money politely. "I've got money and Mum's credit card. I'm supposed to help pay for things."

Jess was about to object, but she looked so serious he pocketed the bill.

Zoë returned with a bag of trail mix and fruit drinks, and watched as Jess cleaned off the outside of the windshield.

"You must be kinda broke, huh? I mean, why drive such an old truck?"

"Suits me well enough."

"Mum says artists are always hard up."

"True enough."

"Well, *you* get by."

Zoë fell silent, her face pensive. She climbed into the truck, unrolling the window.

"I got these Grand Canyon postcards. The waitress says it's about four hours up from here. Could we go?" She cast hopeful eyes on him, her small face uncertain.

Jess sighed, putting away the window scraper. "Zoë, I'm sorry. I'd like to visit the canyon...." He avoided the deflated expression on her face, "but it's just not possible. Not this trip."

Zoë said nothing, stocking the cooler carefully with the drinks and snacks. Then she folded her sweatshirt neatly on her lap, plugged in her earphones, and looked straight out toward the road.

Jess started the engine, and in silence they exited to the Interstate and headed due west.

Zoë broke her self-imposed silence half an hour later as signs for Flagstaff began to appear along the freeway.

"Jess, I have a favor to ask."

He glanced over warily. The tone of her voice reminded him of her mother just then. He turned down the radio.

"Yes?"

Zoë fiddled with her earphones, coiled in her lap. Then she unfolded a small note, smoothing it over her knee. "I borrowed the Yellow Pages at the truck stop and found a music store listed in Flagstaff. Could we stop? There's this sheet music I need. I was supposed to study it on break, but I forgot it."

Jess stared down the road dubiously.

Zoë flushed. "Mum didn't confiscate it, I just forgot it. See, I have the rest." She yanked a folder from her backpack and waved it. "Jess, please? It's off the highway."

He reached out with a free hand and took the slip of paper with the address. Kramer's, off exit 22. They were at 29 now.

"Okay," he relented. "But make it quick."

Kramer's Music was located a mile off the exit in a strip mall, squeezed between a baseball card trading shop, and a Chinese drycleaner. It was early, and the strip mall empty, but the shop appeared to be open. Jess parked, and Zoë bounced out, disappearing inside the double doors. Minutes later, tired of waiting, Jess followed her in. The store was beyond well stocked; the display windows were packed with school band instruments, towers of drums, and stacks of rock and roll synthesizers. He located Zoë at the back of the store in an animated discussion with the shopkeeper, a dour old guy with a face like a pimento and a withery paunch, his gray hair tied back with a leather string.

Zoë was pointing to a scarred, beat-up cello in the display window.

"That sun and heat will crack the wood," she lectured the shopkeeper seriously, her green eyes earnest. "You mustn't leave a string instrument unprotected in the sun that way."

"That's a school rental, missy," the old guy answered with a condescending smile. "No sun'll hurt that cello more'n ten years of hacker's orchestra."

"You shouldn't say that!" Zoë refuted. "Beginners do get better!"

The shopkeeper raised a skeptical eyebrow, and nodded amiably as Jess approached Zoë alongside the counter. He returned to his files of sheet music, thumbing through the 'R' section as he asked over his shoulder, "What was that you wanted again?"

"*Vocalise*, by Rachmaninoff. An arrangement for piano and cello, please."

The shopkeeper grunted, flipping through the section until he licked his finger and lifted a sheaf of music out and placed it before Zoë. "This it?"

She scanned the music, frowning. "Yes, but this is an *orchestral* arrangement. Do you have it for piano and cello?" she persisted.

The man tugged at his ponytail. "Well, maybe. I'd have to look in overstock. The wife handles strings and stuff, I do band equipment. Only she isn't here right now, as her mother's sick..." He broke off, aware of the growing impatience on Zoë's face. "Oh all right, I'll look. But it'll take me a moment. Storage is upstairs." Looking displeased, the old guy traipsed behind a dusty pile of clarinet cases at the back of the shop and disappeared behind a curtain.

Jess glanced at Zoë and she shrugged.

"It has to be the right arrangement. It's not like I can pretend I'm the flute." She looked grumpy.

"Fine, fine," Jess said, waving his hand. "Let's see if he even has it."

Zoë wandered the shop restlessly, plucking at a string on the rental in the window, frowning when it croaked, hopelessly out of tune. She was flexing and unflexing her hands compulsively, and Jess observed her, curious. It was almost as though she was physically warming up for a mental run at her music.

Zoë circled back around to stand by Jess.

"I really need to practice," she said sadly.

"There'll be time enough once you're home."

"Forget it!" Zoë flared, stomping her foot. "If Mum has her way, I'll *flunk* my audition! I won't be going to Curtis, and it'll be all *my* fault. Only it isn't! I know I need to prepare. I need to play! But she– "

Absurdly near to tears, Zoë broke off as the shopkeeper returned. His eyes shifted from Zoë's flushed face to Jess' stoic expression.

"Well, I found this..." he offered doubtfully, handing Zoë an aged, gray sheaf. "It's *Vocalise* all right. This what you want?"

Zoë bent over the sheet music, spreading the folded pages across the counter. Her finger traced the flow of notes across the page, and she sang several bars of the music under her breath before she looked up, beaming, clapping with delight. "It is! Thanks ever!" And to the shopkeeper's surprise, leaned across the counter and hugged him.

The man's face softened. "You want to see something?" he asked suddenly. "Something really special?"

"What do you mean?" Zoë smiled, puzzled.

"Wait here," he said, and hopped behind the curtain again. A moment later he returned, a full-size cello held awkwardly in his hands.

"You play? Thought so. We've had this beauty in for restoration work," he explained, laying the instrument on the counter in front of Zoë.

He beamed, rewarded by the sudden animation that flooded Zoë's features. She touched the wood, stroking the watermelon belly of the cello, her finger running along the worn varnish.

"We got a strings guy comes in from Sedona and takes fiddles back for repairs—name of Isaac Becker. He apprenticed in Tucson, best school in the world, you know!" the old guy boasted proudly.

"I do know," Zoë nodded, her eyes brightening. "Besides Germany and Italy, the best luthier school anywhere is here in Arizona."

The shopkeeper polished the instrument with a soft cloth, lifting rosin from under the bridge. "Becker brought this one back last night. Had it six months—neck smashed to bits in airplane baggage. The owner plays for the city orchestra, says this is 18th century or something, French. Pretty expensive."

"I would think so," Zoë agreed softly, studying the cello with interest. "The varnish *is* that chocolaty color used by the French then, and..." she ran a slim finger along the curve of the f-holes, "this is maple, the kind available in the 1800s, a true hardwood." Zoë tilted the cello slightly and examined the repair done on the neck. "I think your instrument maker did a fine job," she commended, absolutely serious. "The neck has the proper angle, and the reattachment is almost invisible. And he matched the varnish perfectly."

The shopkeeper cleared his throat, squinting at Zoë speculatively. "You seem to know an awful lot about cellos, missy," he observed, sucking his teeth.

Zoë shrugged noncommittally, coloring slightly.

Jess looked on with interest. She did seem to know an awful lot.

The shopkeeper suddenly cracked a knuckle, making Zoë jump.

"Maybe you'd do me a favor, missy, and run a bow across these strings—test the fiddle out for me? Neither my wife nor I play and this symphony guy is picky, I might say? If the thing's not right, I'd rather send it back with Becker than call the owner in. If she's not perfect, he'll have my head for sure." The shopkeeper regarded the cello with some trepidation, as though it might rupture and disassemble before his very eyes.

Zoë shot a glance at Jess. He nodded slightly, stifling a yawn. He could see she was ready to explode with her desire to pickup the old thing. He was curious to hear her play anyway. The buildup from Sarah had been daunting. If she hadn't exaggerated, the shopkeeper was in for a real surprise.

The old man shuffled around the counter and drug out a folding chair for Zoë, slapping it open on the linoleum. Then he disappeared behind the curtain and returned carrying a bow. Zoë took it in her hand, frowning slightly.

"A student bow? Too short, and way too light for me. Do you have a full size, maybe a Steiner?"

Sighing audibly, he took the small bow with him to the rear of the store and came forward carrying a leather case. He rummaged through the case before thrusting a longer bow at Zoë, and stood back, rubbing his stomach anxiously.

She hefted the bow in her hand, balancing it between her thumb and two fingers. She nodded.

The shopkeeper lifted the old cello from the counter and placed it upright on the floor, fitting the peg into a rubber stop fetched from a shelf.

The instrument looked enormous to Jess, the curved bellows of wood nearly engulfed Zoë, the scrolled neck high above her ear. "Too big?"

"Jess, I may be small, but I've been playing on a full size cello since I was eleven."

The shopkeeper grunted.

Zoë began to pluck each string, tuning the instrument by ear. She worked her way from the C string to the G, then to D and the A, adjusting tension through the small screws at the base of the bridge, not at the pegs on the neck as Jess would have expected. He'd ask Zoë about that later. Were the elaborately carved pegs just ornamentation? They looked functional enough, he thought, holding the four strings taunt over the bridge.

The instrument tuned to her satisfaction, Zoë deftly rosined the borrowed bow. She drew it lightly across the open strings, listening to each note intently. The cello had an amber-colored voice, a kind of low growl Jess felt reverberate both in his inner ear and the sternum of his chest.

The shopkeeper looked anxious. "Well?"

"I need to play to be sure," she said matter-of-factly.

The shopkeeper shrugged impatiently.

Zoë adjusted the cello against her body at a slight angle to her knees. Her left hand curved behind the slender neck of the instrument, forming a light arch between her thumb and her fingers resting on the strings. In her other hand Zoë poised the bow over the bridge of the cello with a prepared stillness of strength and delicacy. Jess absorbed the silences in Zoë's face, the shift that subtly matured her features as it drew her inward.

Zoë began to execute a series of rapid scale and bow exercises, first on the open strings, and then skipping around the major and minor scales. She ran through legato and four-note versions, arpeggios, and fifths. Her small fingers, like nimble white spiders, leapt the bridge from the midsection to near her ear, changing three octaves in one skip up the strings.

The shopkeeper and Jess exchanged glances. The old guy scratched behind his ear as he leaned his elbows against the glass counter.

"Will you play us something, Zoë?" Jess asked quietly. "We have the time, if this gentleman does."

The old shopkeeper's ponytail bobbed vigorously.

"All right. Bach, from the Third Suite."

Zoë looked down before she drew a deep breath and whooshed it out, relaxing her shoulders. On the next beat, Zoë drew the bow across the four strings, striking a long note of plaintive melancholy. The sound vibrated in the air within the closed space of the empty shop, a single note that grew in volume, suspended around Zoë before drifting away. Almost instantaneously her bow and fingers exploded into action, and the cello began to buck notes out in rapid succession; a burst of complexity in tight allegretto measures that left both the shopkeeper and Jess holding their breath as the notes piled upon one another in a tower of sound. Her head drew near her fingers as she sought the precise flats and sharps of the music. Jess watched as Zoë's bow etched the air, its length of slim wood sailed against the taut strings and then dipped and nicked, bringing the purest sound from the instrument.

The music shifted into a long second movement, descending from eighth notes to quarter, releasing a soft and haunting line of melody. Jess closed his eyes, drawn into the colors Zoë whirled about their ears. He could imagine the fat French wood singing. The old instrument sunk low into itself, trembled, and achingly released three deep tones, a tapestry of baritone overtones Jess had never heard before. Hanging in the air, there and not there. The resonance of tones layered upon one another, an aural mosaic deep in the bone of the wood.

The adagio movement spun away and Jess watched Zoë's fingers fly, her tiny hand affecting a vibrato so clean it appeared effortless, and every note true. Her face was noticeably flushed now. She played with her eyes half-closed in absolute concentration as she transformed oxygen, molecules, and the biology of heartbeats into an explosion of gorgeous sound. The bow hung in mid air and then rose like a sea bird, catching two clean notes off the high octaves before rippling out, the last leaf to tremble on the branch, a final low E flat. Zoë dropped her arm and leaned against the neck of the cello, finished.

"*Jesus,*" the shopkeeper breathed to the empty space, the lingering vibrations palpable in the air around them.

Without thinking, Jess put his hands together, clapping slowly, and the shopkeeper joined in enthusiastically. Zoë stood up and leaned the cello with great care against the counter behind her.

"Thank you," she said simply.

Picking up her sheet music from the counter, she wandered out the front door of the store in a daze, her face turned to the morning sun.

Jess covered the cost of the sheet music and waited as the shopkeeper rang up the bill.

"Well, I *never...*" the guy was muttering to himself. "I just never! That was like nothing I've ever seen. Wait 'til the Missus hears what she's missed!" He handed Jess his change, blinking rapidly. "Who are you guys, anyway? Who is that girl?"

"Zoë Harte-Valentine. You'll be hearing that name again, I suspect."

Jess and the shopkeeper shook hands, and the old man walked Jess to the door.

"Heck, I'd guess that cello's ready to go," he grunted with a half-smile.

"I'd say so," Jess agreed. Privately, he believed the old French instrument would ever forget the small girl with red hair. He knew he wouldn't.

Jess crossed the parking lot in long, rapid strides.

"Let's get a move on!" he said, suddenly exuberant, swinging himself in the cab. "We're going to the damn Grand Canyon."

Critical Focus

Baskets, Linda Butler, A/P #2, no date

Simplicity.
Three differently sized baskets, the open weave of each basket casting shadows through the others. One basket lies flat on the table, smaller than the rest, keeper of a secret, a certain indecipherable functionality. The photograph celebrates simple geometry, the play of light and line, and the clean domesticity of things.

Winnowing, change sifting through his life. The previous winter, Jess felt the first hard shake. Leaving his agent's West Side office, he walked south, absorbed in his thoughts, mulling over what he'd just been told about the surge in popularity of digital technologies. He understood what that meant for photographers like himself, the old guard, the poets of black and white. Digital defined the logical sophistication of a camera. From lens to light meter and focus, the camera could do it all. The computer chip had given the box mathematical absolutes. Well, there was a lot of art between zero and one.

On his way past 68th, Jess paused, drawn to a window displaying an antique field camera. The shop bore the sign *Kepler's Images*. Jess peered in, unfamiliar with the gallery. He would never admit to the degree which he relished discovering his own work. It was his secret pleasure, a genuine joy visiting his own images, reuniting as they made their way through the world.

Jess wandered the shop, browsing the stacks. When he discovered Linda Butler's *Baskets* stashed in a metal file drawer of contemporary photographers, he purchased the print on the spot. The image possessed what he personally valued more than any other element in visual composition— simplicity. He admired the intrinsic strength of lines and the shapes of things, believed that objects were interesting in and of themselves.

Jess brought the image back to New Mexico and framed it for Catalina in simple clean pine. He added a poem, something of Dorianne Laux he found by chance in a hippie bookshop on Arbuelo Avenue, called *Sunday*. He chose only the last stanza, printing the lines carefully on the back of the mat:

I envy everything, all of it. I know
It's a sin. I love how you can shift
In your chair, take a deep drink
Of gold beer, curl your toes under, and hum.

Catalina had taken his gift in her hands, first studying the image and then reading the words of the inscription. She kissed Jess lightly on the forehead and placed the picture on her mantel, between a black Acoma pot and a small porcelain statute. For a week the image remained above her fireplace. Then it disappeared, and Jess never possessed the heart to ask where or why.

Note from the Daybook:

Extraordinary music from a kid and an old cello. Strange, the way something extraordinary may exist in the very ordinary, how miraculous is the simple. In my mind, the image of this girl bent over that borrowed cello. If I had taken her photograph as I saw her then...

Zoë bounded up from the corrals behind Bright Angel Lodge, her face flushed in the heat, her hair matted flat against her forehead under her Giants baseball cap. She wore another of her music shirts, this with the leonine head of Beethoven barking out the words, "Symphony Rocks".

"Enjoy the mule ride?" Jess kept his eyes off his light meter. He had his Linhoff on the tripod, exposing for a wide-angle view across the canyon toward an interior cliff formation, a sandstone spiral carved by the winds. The far wall of the canyon was beginning to redden in the long afternoon light.

"Gosh, yes!" Zoë hooted joyously. "This place has got to be the biggest hunk of amazing earth I've ever seen! The mules went down a zillion switchbacks," she hopped around him. "We dismounted way down there at the edge for lunch, but there's a ranch on the river for people staying over. I wish we could..."

Jess concentrated through the loupe on his image, using his right eye to gauge the focus and ready his shot. In seconds the light would shift square into the midsection of the sandstone, drench it brilliant yellow, and the earth a glow of ruby.

Zoë chattered on. "I wouldn't want to *hike* the Bright Angel Trail. When a mule's gotta go, they all do it! That trail whooshed in a river of pee!" She tapped his shoulder. "Can I see? Can I look through the camera, Jess?"

Jess let Zoë under the dark cloth to peek through the ground glass, explaining she would be viewing the image upside down. Eagerly, she pressed her eye to the small square of glass, then pulled back and looked up at him, her face pinched in confusion.

"It's nice and all...but I don't get it."

"Get what?" Jess asked kindly, keeping an observant eye on the progression of light up the wall as the sun sank near the northwestern rim.

"The rock, the sky. I don't see where it's –" she flushed.

"Worth making an image of?" Jess filled in, smiling at Zoë's obvious embarrassment.

"Yeah, kinda."

"The magic's in the print, Zoë." Jess murmured gently, taking his place behind the camera and double-checking his light meter. *Any minute now.... Yes.* Sunlight blasted across the final foot of the canyon wall and the spiral stone leapt from the shadows, a tower of gold thrust from the earth. It was eerie, breathtaking. Jess clicked the shutter release, rapidly changed film holders, and clicked twice again. "That should be a keeper!" he exulted.

"What's that mean?"

"You see? It's already gone."

Zoë watched with Jess as the colors in the canyon darkened in lengthening bands of light. Lavenders and blues muted the warm yellow-reds on the eastern cliffs.

"It's an intuitive thing," Jess explained, dismantling the camera, "knowing when I've got things right. What the light is doing, what the camera will record, what I intend in the developing." He unscrewed the camera from the tripod, catching a glance at Zoë, her hair aglow in the slanting sun. She appeared fey and strange, a dirty pixie. "I don't see the image only through the lens, Zoë, I also imagine it in my mind." He scratched his chin, looking dubious. "Does that make any sense?"

Zoë handed over a lens wrap and steadied the tripod as he lowered the legs. "Yeah, kind of. Like music. Notes are itty-bitty tracks on paper. I express them, right? I hear them first in my head. So it kinda works out different every time."

"Exactly," Jess nodded, stuffing the padded black bags. "Ansel Adams—you know who he is? The guy that photographed Yosemite? He said that film negatives are like a composer's score, and each print a new performance."

"Cool!" She shoved her hat back on her head, fine sweat glistening on the bridge of her nose. "But why photograph? Why not just look, *really look* at things?"

"If you can listen Zoë, why play?" Jess countered lightly.

"To be that thing..." she said slowly, "that special happening."

"Exactly." Jess wiped his forehead with a bandanna extracted from the pocket of his jeans. "Let's go to the lodge and get some lemonade."

They lugged gear back to the parking lot and stowed it in the rear of his pickup.

"Hadn't you better call your mother?" Jess suggested as they climbed the wide flagstone porch and entered the open-air rooms of the Lodge. Constructed of beams of rough-hewn lumber and colored stone, the lodge perched high above the canyon floor at Bright Angel Point. "You can let her know where we are. I snagged two cancellations for the night–pretty simple rooms, but it beats the truck for another night."

"I'll say."

Zoë suddenly looked worried. "Has coming here made you terribly late?"

Jess stretched out his shoulder muscles, grinning slightly. "Does it matter? Nope. I made a good image this afternoon."

The waitress seated them on the outdoor patio overlooking the dark yaw of the canyon and returned with two frosted glasses of lemonade. Jess drained half of his in one gulp, Zoë sipping noisily through a straw.

"Tell me about this music school you're interested in."

"What's the point?" Zoë's mood shifted. She shrugged angrily. "Mum will never allow it."

"Why Zoë?"

She leaned inward, her voice lowered to a stage whisper. "Because all her life she's been told to do the practical thing, the *right* thing. Bad for her, she married my Dad, who *never* did the practical or right thing, and Mum was left to keep us going." She took an agitated breath. "Mum's afraid I'll grow up selfish and flaky like my Dad, and that in the end, music will disappoint me."

"I'm not sure I follow." Jess was puzzled. How could such a talent disappoint?

"Because," the teen quoted," 'you can love music, but music doesn't love you back.' And after the concert career is over, which will be, like, *overnight*, I'll be just an old, lonely lady, living with a cat." Zoë's eyes flashed.

"I believe that is something Sarah would say."

"It's not funny, Jess!" Zoë protested. "So what, if that's my choice?"

Jess shrugged tolerantly. Zoë was a constant surprise. In some ways, the girl was the most levelheaded person he'd met. She was ready to look at the facts it seemed to him, to make her own choices.

Jess remembered Sarah's face in his kitchen.

"That sounds very grown-up, Zoë. However, you're giving away a future you're too young to fully imagine." He cleared his throat. "What about competition? What if you give everything up and you're not quite good enough? And family? Don't you want that someday?"

Zoë sat back, twiddling with her straw. "Why give up anything? As for *good enough*, well, isn't that the deal anyway? Measuring up?" Her green eyes fixed on him.

"Sure. But life has a way of offering exact opposites, my dear. One-way choices, some last forever."

Zoë flipped her bangs off her forehead. "I'll make the choices when I have to. Mum thinks if I go to college, get a good degree, I'll end up in a corporation somewhere, marry and be happier than she is. *I'm sure.*"

Jess ran a hand over his cropped scalp.

"Truth?" Zoë snapped. "Mum doesn't *want* to be happy. It's too late. She just wants to prove she made the right choices for herself, by making me do the same." She paused, her eyes large. "Mum left Dad, not the other way around. She couldn't stand his unpredictability."

Jess hunched over his elbows on the table. Zoë was so confident of herself. Jess caught a fleeting glimpse of himself echoed in the young girl, recalling the precise moment he picked up a camera and recognized *the thing he could do.*

"Your mother only wants the best for you, Zoë."

"Yeah," agreed Zoë flatly. "Only it's not her choice, is it? I'm not a baby anymore."

"Think carefully," he cautioned. "I'm a living example, Zoë. Check it out–I live alone, I'm usually broke, and I've no family besides a dog," his lip twitched faintly. "And honestly, my career is only as good as my next print. If my eyesight *is* ruined, well, I will no longer be able to do this work and there is nothing else I *can* do."

Again, the echo in his mind of Sarah words in the kitchen... *just tell her about the solitary hours working alone, the constant competition for recognition...the nomad lifestyle.*

"Your mother wants more for you."

"Would *you*? Want more than that?"

"I never did."

"I didn't think so," she smiled.

They left the south rim of the Grand Canyon under a bright enamel sky, the light so hard it skipped like a disk over the desert horizon. They left early to evade the heat, Zoë as navigator, watching road signs as they backtracked over the Coconino flats, then directly west again. At the California state line, Jess had marked off the exits to State Route 58 north to Bakersfield, and then the short cut over to Interstate 5, and north to San Francisco.

"We're looking at a lot of road, kiddo."

"How long?" Zoë asked, fishing in her duffel for her headphones and a new CD. Not the expected classical, but some pop boy group.

"Well, round it all off at, say, 700 miles—or all of today, driving. I'm hoping to roll into your place before midnight."

Zoë's face clouded.

"She is expecting us tonight?"

Zoë nodded glumly.

"Okay, then. Let's stock the cooler in Flagstaff, and stop only for bladder emergencies. Steady on, agreed?"

"Steady on," Zoë echoed, causing Jess to glance at her averted face. She had plugged the earphones into her ears, and was staring out the dirt-streaked windows, her fingers tapping her bare knees.

What was the kid so down about? Something in the inwardness of her distraction made Jess suspect she might be thinking ahead to the reunion with her mother...or, the audition. Jess fiddled with the radio dial until he found a suitable blues station out of Vegas. Sad, but the kid would have to work her way through it, he thought fatalistically. That was part of the deal.

He fell into humming an old Delta blues tune, his mind turning with the rhythm of the tires, hissing on the burning cement. What Robert Johnson knew. *Don't nobody seem to know me, babe, seem everybody pass me by....*

By noon, the desert heat blistered on the inside of the cab, the hot winds needling their faces through the open windows as they hurtled down the road. Jess pulled over outside of Barstow in a town by the name of Newberry Springs, entering a Mom 'n Pop store for sandwiches while Zoë used the restroom. The town was a narrow crosshatch of dusty streets and squat buildings that faced a shallow basin marked Troy Lake, one of the dry lakes of the Mojave Desert. They crouched on the scratchy sand-grass, the roar of the Interstate behind them as they gulped sandwiches, swatting at the persistent black flies.

"Why don't you like airplanes?" Zoë asked, her mouth full of French bread.

Jess uncapped a soda and took a long drink before he answered. "Makes me sick," he admitted.

"Oh," Zoë looked hugely sympathetic. "That's how I feel on boats. Hurl City."

Jess grinned, amused. He hadn't spent much time around kids, but as teenagers went, this one was a hoot.

Jess finished his lunch, his thoughts elsewhere.

"You don't talk much." Zoë observed, leaning back under her shade tree. Her eyes were quizzical beneath their fringe of blond lashes.

It occurred to him, listening to the hum of the insects beating their wings in the heat, that from Zoë's point of view he must seem genuinely eccentric. In her world music was a social experience, shared with community and performed in community. But a photographer approached his work alone, and was rarely there when, or if ever, someone viewed the results. Was he a social stump? He suspected so.

Jess tossed his wrappers in the bag at his feet. "Ansel's not much on conversation either."

Zoë grew pensive. "I hope he's gonna be okay, Jess. He's a really brave dog."

"He'll be fine. Abe's family will spoil him." He watched her trace lazy arcs in the loose sand with her sandals. "What else do you do with your life besides cello?"

"Read," she answered, shredding a dry leaf between her fingers. "Mostly fantasy stuff, like Terry Brooks, Tolkien. I like imaginary worlds."

Jess clobbered a fly lumbering up his wrist, nodding in surprise. He'd read J. R. Tolkien in Korea at night in the barracks, unable to sleep. Caught up in the quest for Middle Earth with the Hobbits, Tolkien's philosophy of darkness shadowed the very war he was assigned to photograph. The memory of those stories came back to him with startling freshness.

"Does your music school have real school—classes in algebra and stuff?"

Zoë folded her arms behind her head. Today's shirt offered a single note of music, the venerable eighth note, with the caption "Hit it!". She perused Jess with a slight frown, a look that reminded him of her mother.

"You can get a degree in composition, teaching, that sort of stuff. But kids under eighteen, like me, have to study with a tutor, or go to regular school in Philadelphia." She pouted. "And live with a parent or guardian."

Jess raised his eyebrows. Sarah had an established practice in Northern California. Did Zoë expect her mother to move to Philadelphia for this school?

"What makes this place so special?"

"Everything!" Zoë's eyes sparkled. "Master classes with real greats, like Natalia Gutman, and YoYo Ma! Students perform concerts, study theory, and history—and ohmigosh,

Orlando Cole, do you know him? And Peter Wiley? They teach the cello. Even the Guarneri Quartet guest teaches at Curtis. But mostly, I want to go because of Daniel Lee."

"Daniel who?" Jess repeated, lost in the unfamiliar names. He was amazed. Such a formal performance education did not exist for photographers, relegated as they were to the odd extension course, and private workshop. Nowadays the Fine Arts degree had become popular, what was that but organized play for the underemployed? He doubted he could handle such an immersion experience. But for Zoë, it seemed to represent the world.

"Daniel Lee, Jess! He studied with Mstislav Rostropovich." She spoke the famous Russian's name with audible reverence, her eyebrows rising over each syllable like a Coney Island coaster.

Jess nodded. At least he knew that name.

"Rostropovich asked Orlando Cole to take Daniel Lee on as a student—saying Daniel could be the greatest cellist in the world! He actually said that, Rostropovich did." Zoë blinked, her voice hushed. "Daniel Lee has been a student at Curtis since he was eleven, and that's only two years younger than me. He's eighteen now, and already debuted in London, at Wigmore Hall. My Dad heard him play and sent me the playbill." Zoë tilted her head sideways, looking at Jess dreamily, her eyes sleepy green ovals of glass. "That's what I want. That's what I want for *me*."

To play in Wigmore Hall, or for your father, Jess wondered.

He cleared his throat. "It sounds impressive, Zoë. Is it fantastically expensive?"

Certainly Sarah could afford it, he reminded himself. Still, the idea of a school devoted to the creation of exceptional musicians seemed fantastic, surreal. Cosseting new young prodigies like pets, or was it all cutthroat competitiveness and outlandish egos, youngsters crucified on the concert tour? Jess knew all about critics, and he doubted those in music were kinder than his own species.

Elbow propped against his left knee, he cupped his palm under his chin, studying Zoë thoughtfully. Was the kid up to a real grinder, or would this school shuck her of her own dreams? Sarah might be right. Sure, Zoë was good, more than good. But how good was *good enough,* and how much sheer luck did it take?

"The school's free, Jess! Curtis is a foundation, everything's free," Zoë beamed. "And check this! The pianists get their own Steinways to practice on—delivered where they live."

"Wow," Jess blinked. It was hard not to feel a pang of envy, remembering his years in drafty apartments, double-shift jobs.

"I want to live with my aunt in Philadelphia. She's near the school, on Rittenhouse Square." Zoë 's face screwed up. "But that's part of the problem."

"Your aunt? How so?"

"Aunt Sylvia is *Dad's* sis. Their parents are dead, way before me. She and Uncle Howie have no kids, so he always visits them at Christmastime, and then me in California, if he can swing it. Mum's afraid I'll see more of Dad and them, and not her."

Jess considered this, Zoë's sophisticated assessment of her cross-Atlantic family politics. He steered back to the subject of school. "How many apply to Curtis every year, Zoë? What are your odds?"

She balled up a little bit of cling wrap and shot it into the grass. "Over seven hundred and fifty students auditioned last year...and only forty were accepted."

Jess whistled, looking out over the dry lake where salts shimmered in the heat. Such odds were astoundingly against even this spunky kid from California. "Are there any other choices? In case—?"

"Yeah, but not for me."

Jess changed the subject.

"Do you have free time, Zoë? Doesn't a kid need time to well, hang?"

She scoffed. "Free time? Jeez, between school, lessons and practice, what would I do, anyway? Shop the mall for lip gloss?" Zoë lifted her face, resting her head against the trunk of the tree.

As she closed her eyes, sunlight, dappled through the leaves, washed her features in pale, dusty patterns of light. This slight girl-child appeared years older to Jess, hardened with the unmistakable signature of ambition. And discipline.

He admired the discipline.

At her age, he had wasted days shooting beer bottles with a BB gun—the beer swiped from his Dad's stash, the empties lined up on the fence in the back fields. He'd been a pro at skipping school, too, hitching into town and hanging out at the pool hall, swimming at the quarry with his pals. What did he know of ambition then, beyond devouring a sticky wrapped Goo-Goo Cluster, a chocolate, nut, and marshmallow heaven purchased for just ten cents at the Rexall Five and Dime? It took Judge Robart and the United States Air Force to teach Jess Cappello to pocket his anger, how to outlast the opposition.

His gaze swept over Sarah's daughter. This girl's backbone came from raw talent, he reminded himself. Discipline hammered from her deepest, secret knowledge, the inner voice that told her this, *this* was what she could do. And then it occurred to him he might be guilty of the very envy Sarah accused her ex-husband of. How could they *not* ache in the presence of the favored young?

"Jess?" Zoë was watching him with lazy awareness.

He stood up and dusted down his jeans. "Just thinking about the miles ahead, young lady."

Miles of life, miles of uncertain terrain. And he hoped, for Zoë's sake, a genuine adventure, the likes of which no other road would provide.

He stuck out his hand and helped the girl to her feet. They gathered up the remnants of lunch and tossed the garbage in a dented can. A crow lit on the rim of the can and immediately began picking apart the sack. Beyond them, the heat of the Mojave layered in the air, distorting the distances beneath the pale, cloudless sky.

Trouble Shooting

Untitled, Kathleen Barrows, 1989

Perfection.

The hour was late. Jess followed Zoë in the front door of the small stucco cottage on Tennyson Lane, dropped his duffle at his feet, and yawned. The teen flicked on the lights and Jess recoiled, squinting painfully as Zoë bolted down the hall to let her mother know they'd arrived.

Jess hung out awkwardly, waiting in the Harte-Valentine's living room. The family furnishings were simple mission style pieces, solid and comfortable. He drifted toward a sofa and then came to a standstill, staring at an unbelievable black and white photograph displayed prominently on the dining room wall.

Framed in glossy black and basking under its own directed light, the image was of a trio of white calla lilies, velvety throats open, petals holding court against a background foil of deep ebony and dark foliage. Crisp white edges delineated the furl of the leaves.

Jess tread cautiously across Sarah's dark orientals, coming close to peer at the signature on the image, holding one hand over his troublesome left eye and scrutinizing the print solely with his right. Kathleen somebody—he couldn't quite read the signature, but a photographer he was not immediately familiar with.

Jess scratched his chin, forgetting his fatigue. He seemed to be looking at a perfect print. Not a single, visible imperfection. No dents, divots, or distortions visible to the naked eye. He canvassed the grain of the print, examining the smooth, dense pattern of points. Flawless.

He stepped back.

"Perfect, isn't it."

Sarah, in gray sweatpants and a pale peach shirt, appeared beside him. Her pale eyes were sleepy.

"A digital print?"

"Indeed. The work of Kathleen Barrows, printed at Nash Editions in Los Angeles. Bit odd, when you think of it. Graham Nash was a rocker way back when...but rather into digital technology these days."

"Where did you come across this?"

"At auction. I like calla lilies."

"It's exceptional, Sarah."

"But it isn't *real*. That's what you're thinking, aren't you?"

Jess flinched. He was goddamned tired, and besides, he didn't know what he thought. Such a print was in a different category altogether: a computer-generated print of a good negative. Perfect, to be sure. Possibly the wave of the future.

Jess shielded his eyes from the painful glare of the spotlight and reconsidered the bold image. If technology eliminated the margins of a photographer's judgment and risk, eliminated the experimental chemical explorations, and thus the occasional error of grandeur, then what remained but chill perfection? It was all about art, in the end.

"It's a stunning image, Sarah."

Sarah sighed, placing a hand on his arm as she guided him toward the back of the house. "Bull. Zoë's making sandwiches... and then you two should get to bed."

Jess heaved his duffle onto his shoulder.

Note from the Daybook:
What trust do I possess, what ambition that is not likewise kin of fear?

White light baked hot on his face. Jess opened his eyes, acutely aware of a stabbing pain in the middle of his back, and an unsettling disorientation. Dust motes drifted in the cross rays of sunlight and he lay still, listening to the faint street noises outside. Rolling to one side, he rubbed the tender spot on his spine, taking in the unfamiliar surroundings.

Palo Alto, he realized. And a small bedroom cluttered with two music stands, and piles of sheet music shoved untidily against the walls. He was camped out on a foldout couch, the pain in his back courtesy of the metal support bar thrusting through the thin mattress. To his right, a tall bookcase listed backward against the wall, jammed with medical texts. The middle shelf however, was stacked with leather-bound folders embossed in an odd alphabet. Jess squinted. The Cyrillic alphabet? Russian? He reached over and lifted one of the red leather volumes off the shelf and opened it.

Beethoven. He recognized the Austrian composer's name transcribed into the Russian. An interesting madness, he mused. Although one must suppose a musical note was the same note in any language.

Jess swung his feet into the narrow clearance between the foldout couch and the bookshelf, considering his boxers and tee shirt. Where was his duffel? He located his bag under the far edge of the couch and quickly rifled its contents for something clean to wear, shaking out a crumpled shirt. Toothbrush in hand, he poked his head into the hallway. The house was eerily silent. He looked at his watch.

Christ, no wonder—10:15. Sarah had said she left early for the clinic, and Zoë, if he had to guess, had made a beeline for her maestro.

Jess located the bathroom off the hall, and helped himself to a long shower, restored by the jets of hot water, feeling the knots in his back easing. As he soaped up, he thought about the night's fragmented dream. He'd dreamed of gravel cutting into his bare feet, a dark, tree-tangled road. And then there had been that strange circle of blue, steel-colored, like the mouth of a pipe. And then vertigo...falling...but neither up nor down. Toweling off, Jess frowned. He shrugged off the dream, scraping at his chin with a razor in front of the Victorian mirror.

Jess slung the guest towel over the doorknob and balled his dirty clothes back in the duffle before wandering downstairs to Sarah's kitchen. The house seemed full of sun, the oak floors and open beams a warm polished honey, and everywhere the clutter of a teenager. But notably, rare, well-worn rugs and the exceptional prints on the wall gave the house a personable, lived-in feel.

In the kitchen, Jess found a note pinned to the table with a house key.

Jess,

Call the clinic at 537-1800 to confirm your preliminary exam this afternoon— 2 o'clock. The basics: help yourself to anything edible. If nothing appeals, there's a bagel shop a few blocks up on University. Street map on the table, washing machine located in the back hall closet, the nearest ATMs on University or behind us on Middlefield.

Abe left a message for you yesterday. Wants to know whether he should forward the mail, particularly a letter from a Cappellina (?).

Remember! 2:00 pm–sharp.

Sarah

Jess folded the note and slipped it into his pocket, helping himself to a cup of strong coffee from the Mr. Coffee pot on the spotless counter. He pushed open the back door, stepping into a tiny garden shoehorned into the narrow slot behind the cottage. Tangles of roses, snapdragons, and impatiens in dense profusion bloomed along a high wood fence separating Sarah's yard from her neighbors. Flop-petal poppies bordered a path of flagstones curving through the shrubbery toward a neat, white potting shed.

Someone was quite the gardener.

Jess inhaled the fresh green, so recently watered the fragrance of roses hit with an intensity that made him sneeze, twice.

He'd bet this mini botanical wonder wasn't young Zoë's doing, but Sarah a green thumb? It didn't fit with that surgical personality...more likely this splendor was the extravagant signature of a hired gardener. Still, someone spent their time here, for an empty mug sat on the table under the arbor of yellow roses. Jess took a seat at the iron table and stretched his legs out, mulling over Sarah's note.

His guts churned, simple hunger and nerves. He was embarrassed to admit how long it had been since he'd seen a doctor. He usually relied on a field kit of over-the-counter remedies, and a few pueblo herbs, to get by. He drilled his fingers against Sarah's ceramic mug. He had no idea what to expect this afternoon, and there was the matter of his deal with the English doctor. He hadn't changed Zoë's mind about her audition. How angry would Sarah be?

Jess slugged back his coffee, grimacing as his stomach flipped. He thought about the message from Abe. Another letter from Catalina. He pondered the mystery, restlessly shoving the letter into the recesses of his mind. It could wait.

He wished to hell he knew what lay ahead.

Zoë showed up at the house around one o'clock, her music under one arm, and offered to accompany Jess to the Sequoia Vision Clinic. He was glad she did, as he wholly relied on her directions to navigate the confusion of narrow streets and congested traffic clogging the compact university town. He concentrated on driving, maneuvering the pickup around double-parked cars, twice nearly turning the wrong way on a one-way street. Not a mile from Sarah's house, and his nerves were already jangled.

"This is the capitol of engineering supremacy? This mess? How do you people stand this?" He fumed, hitting the brakes.

The pickup lurched into the clinic parking lot.

Zoë laughed and climbed out, waiting patiently as Jess lifted her bike from the back, and steadied it before her. Her face had grown more freckled after the Grand Canyon, sweet and carefree.

"You wouldn't complain if you'd been on that mule ride! At least traffic doesn't stink." Her nose wrinkled expressively. "Mum's inside, Suite 106. And I'll be late tonight...a lesson with Maestro Mikavlov, plus a run-through with an accompanist. Tell her for me, would you?"

Their eyes locked, until Zoë's melted into a pure look of pleading.

"All right. I'll mention it."

"Thanks!"

She slipped her thin arms around Jess in a quick hug.

He waved her off and watched as the teenager pedaled her bike down the shady street. As she rounded the corner, Zoë shouted something back at him, her yellow shirt passing behind a parked car.

"What?" Jess yelled, straining to hear.

"I *said*–good luck!"

Zoë disappeared around the corner.

Fighting a surge of nerves, Jess checked his watch. Five minutes. He pulled his hat out of the truck and uncertainly faced the imposing three-story building, surveying the faux Italianate roof and the impressive palm entrance court.

Why rush?

Reaching into the dash compartment of the Ford, Jess located a stale package of crumpled Marlboros. He lit one up, and began to hack so badly he over-inhaled again. Hunched against the bumper of the truck, he smoked not one, but two cigarettes. His head spun with rushes of nicotine.

Still coughing, Jess covered his good eye with one hand and focused on the sign over the clinic door. The gray blur swam smack over the middle of the word *Sequoia,* and the words *Vision Clinic* dipped and folded in odd perambulations.

Stubbing out the last cigarette with the heel of his boot, Jess tucked his shirt in neatly. He'd faced worse. Judge Robart and that damn flying stuff in Korea, not to mention the first, totally serious criticism of his work. He wished he could rid himself of a hamster-sized hairball lodged in his throat though, and thought longingly of his camera, secure in the back of the truck. What would he give to hit the road right now, to set his tripod on the beaches of Point Lobos and wait for Weston's ghost?

But for that unshakeable gray erasure.

Popping a piece of Wriggly Spearmint into his mouth and chewing like a locomotive, Jess marched toward the clinic door, his buckled, threadbare hat pulled low over his brow.

They were waiting for him. He was shown directly into an exam room, reluctantly surrendering his hat to the white-toothed Jamaican receptionist with rainbow hair.

Alone in the room, he checked out the equipment, fiddling with the white metallic machines, tilting the chin rests, flipping lenses. He glared at the ubiquitous eye chart on the wall, squinting at the lowest letters. Were they still the same? He gave up, unable to distinguish even the middle lines clearly. His eyes never were what you'd call crack sharp. Forty years ago Hunter had slipped him the chart to memorize, so he wouldn't flunk recon training. But he was damned if he could remember any letters now.

"Good morning, Jess," Sarah announced smoothly, entering the examination room and shutting the door firmly behind her. "Shall we get started?"

Jess faced Sarah silently, unsettled by the English woman's brusque professionalism. She approached him in her white jacket, her hands clasping a spiral notebook and slim file folder. Her smile seemed genuine enough. He forced himself to relax.

"Right," he agreed, taking the seat indicated.

Sarah took the low stool to his left, crossing her legs crisply. "To begin, your basic family history–" and she read off a long list of diseases and illnesses. "Any of these present in your family to your knowledge?"

Jess shook his head, appalled. There was everything on her list from angina and epilepsy to venereal warts.

"Parents living?"

Again, Jess shook his head.

"Cause of death?"

He hesitated. "Accidental."

"*Both* your mother and father?" Sarah expressed surprise, her eyebrows lifting.

Jess shrugged, refusing to elaborate.

"All right then," Sarah murmured, frowning at her chart. "We need a preliminary eye exam and then drops to dilate—that is relax–your pupils. This will allow an accurate reading and a closer look at your retinas."

Sarah took Jess through a routine set of diagnostics, checking his inner eye pressure on a little machine that blew puffs of air into his eyes, and another that produced lines with green and red patterns, asking him to identify any pattern clearer than the others. She had him tilt his head back, and put a drop from a brown vial into each eye. The drops stung and Jess blinked, his vision clouded, as though swimming underwater.

Sarah continued her exam, raising differing lens monocles in front of his eyes in alternate order.

"Clearer one...or two?" She asked quietly, clicking the varying lenses in place and waiting for his response.

The exam seemed to take forever and Jess eyes ached with the strain, until finally, he was unable to see anything at all. Sarah directed a small beam of light into the backs of his eyes, examining each retina at length, her breath feathery and warm against his cheek.

She sighed. Not at all a happy sound.

"I'll be right back, Jess. Relax."

Sarah left the examining room, her starched jacket rustling as she moved, and Jess became aware of traces of her perfume, a light, green scent. He considered this as he waited. Dr. Harte-Valentine hadn't struck him as the kind of woman to wear perfume. Or sip coffee in a garden, either.

She returned, proffering a Styrofoam cup.

"Coffee? You're more than a smidge near-sighted. Any trouble reading?"

Jess tasted the coffee. Stale but hot.

"Wouldn't notice, to be honest," he joked. "My camera lenses and enlargers make these puppies look like toys."

Sarah relented, permitting a small smile. "Indeed. Well, the near-sightedness is likely age-related, you're losing reading vision as you age. We all do to some extent, but a pair of reading glasses is definitely in order."

She paused, nibbling at her lower lip as she scrutinized her notes. She looked up briskly.

"I want to do an Amsler Grid, Jess. I found a definite scattering of drusen deposits on your retinas. That's an unfamiliar term? Shall I explain?"

Jess braced himself.

"Drusen are like age spots, and are not in themselves responsible for much change in your vision. But they *can* lead to a thinning of the macula—the bulls-eye at the center of your retina." She pointed to the detailed wall print of the human eye hanging behind the door. "The macula is that small area there, at the center of the retina, hundreds of times more sensitive to detail than the rest of the retina. The macula allows us to see detail—to read fine print, recognize faces, thread a needle, appreciate color—actually, quite important."

Jess nodded. Bulls-eye all right. Fine detail was the problem, and therefore, he suspected, so was his macula.

"Have you problems with blurry or fuzzy vision in your left or right eye?' she asked carefully.

"Some. Mostly my left," Jess replied.

"Sensitive to light?"

He nodded again.

"Do straight lines, such as sentences on a page, the sides of buildings, telephone poles–that kind of thing–appear wavy to you?"

Jess shrugged, unsure.

"A dark or empty area near the center of your vision?"

"Yep."

"Both eyes?"

"Just the left."

Sarah made a quick note on his chart and then flashed her light in his eyes unexpectedly. Jess head jerked back, his pupils constricting at the sudden flash.

"Excellent, your pupils are responsive again. Let's do the Amsler."

She handed Jess a cardboard placard about 5 x 7 inches in size, with black and white graphed lines. Engineer's paper, but with a black dot placed in the exact center of the grid. She instructed him to block his left eye, and focusing with his right on the center dot, report if the lines of the graph were straight, the squares even, and if there was any distortion, blurring, or waviness in the pattern of the grid.

He shook his head.

"Very good," she responded encouragingly. "Now, the other eye."

Jess covered his right eye and again, concentrated on the placard. He squinted at the center, or where he thought the center dot might be. Try as he might, the lines would not assemble themselves properly. Worse yet, the gray blur entirely masked the center dot, extending slightly left.

"Problem here," he muttered.

Sarah handed Jess a pencil.

"Mark the area of the distortion as best you can. Focus on the center dot."

With one hand Jess shaded in an area on the grid that seemed pinched and bent, as though a tennis ball, hitting a net, caved everything backwards in space. The effect was weird, and the struggle to retain his focus made him slightly nauseous.

Sarah removed the placard from his hand. "Rest your eyes, Jess."

He felt Sarah's hip brush his shoulder as she slipped behind his chair to her wall of reference books. He waited for that waft of perfume, becoming aware the English doctor was speaking to herself as she searched her textbooks. Her voice exuded a soft, deliberate modality that blended with the hum of the overhead fluorescents, indistinct again from the murmur of muffled voices beyond the closed door. Sarah's presence was unexpectedly soothing. It didn't take a genius to figure his left eye was doing things his right eye wasn't.

Tucking a stray hair back impatiently, Sarah handed Jess a hefty medical text, opened to a drawing of an eyeball, a dissection on the plane of retinal curve. He peered at the drawing, looking for the macula. Under a layer of tissue that resembled thick, fogged glass was another layer; laced with what appeared to Jess to be twisted, bumpy red vines. The branching vines displaced the upper tissue layer, like tree roots up-lifting a sidewalk.

Sarah tapped the diagram, her expression grave.

"Here come the big words, Jess. Those extra blood vessels, or what is known as subretinal neovascularization, appear in a specific form of macular degeneration that is fairly rare. Less than ten percent of all cases involve the growth of blood vessels in the retina." She shook her head soberly. "I must tell you, this condition exists in your left retina, and there are the beginnings of a problem in your right."

Jess reached backwards and pinched the taut muscles at the back of his neck. Weren't blood vessels standard plumbing in the body human? His were bad? He handed back the book, his expression strained.

"Say again?"

She smiled gently.

"These fragmented blood vessels are not normal to your retina. They displace the retina from underneath–think of a lump under a rug–distorting the eye's focus. If left untreated they will continue their growth unchecked, until your central vision is effectively destroyed."

Sarah tapped her notebook with the end of her pencil.

"There's about a one in ten chance that if these blood vessels occur in one eye, they will occur in the other. There are signs of progression in your right, I'm afraid."

Jess twirled the empty Styrofoam cup in his hands, absorbing the medical terms, striving for the gist of Sarah's diagnosis. His tongue felt thick and cakey.

"You're telling me all this blood vessel growth is the reason I can't see right?"

"Yes. The distortion you marked on the Amsler Grid is the approximate location of the vessels and leakage."

"How did this happen, Sarah? I should have had my Wheaties?"

Sarah closed the reference text, hugging it to her chest. "Bad luck, really. Research suggests damage to the Bruch's membrane might be linked to those drusen deposits, which stimulates the growth of blood vessels. Regrettably, these tufts of neovascularization are terribly fragile, with a propensity to leak and bleed, resulting in scarring and irreversible vision loss."

"In plain English, Sarah?"

"Who knows."

She grew thoughtful, obviously troubled. "Macular degeneration is usually age-related, Jess, occurring primarily in the population over fifty. Possible hereditary links, chronic smoking, and certain vitamin deficiencies have been linked to this disease, but the type of degeneration I see here is by far the more damaging and difficult to treat. And it progresses quite rapidly."

Jess drew a sharp breath, aware he was sweating slightly. Where was the end zone here?

"When did you first notice your vision blur, Jess?"

"Six months back, on assignment. I couldn't get a print to satisfy me."

"Indeed. Well, I'm afraid your right eye will also begin to exhibit symptoms by year's end." She leaned toward him, hard and direct. "This kind of blindness is permanent, Jess. And the scarring might encroach the remainder of the retina, affecting your peripheral vision as well."

Jess pressed the palms of both hands down his thighs and slowly uncrossed his boots. Somewhere deep in his chest he felt the pressure of an expanding vacuum of space. He thought of his lady, of *Triangles*, the mystery in the shadows.

"There are treatments, Jess."

"New eye balls? Sign me up!"

Sarah pinched the bridge of her nose as if she were diving. She dropped her hand, sighing audibly, and leaned against the counter, pushing the massive reference text to one side.

"Laser is the standard treatment, generally prescribed as a kind of prophylactic," she muttered, almost angrily. "We cauterize the excess blood vessels to prevent further damage and vision loss. But a thermal laser leaves a permanent scar—its own blind spot on the macula. And existing damage remains permanent."

"You docs point a hot light at these blood vessels, dry 'em up, but leave me with the blindness I've got?"

"You might say."

"Does it reoccur?"

"The problem may develop elsewhere in the macula."

"Christ almighty, anything else?"

"Yes. But until now, strictly experimental."

Sarah handed Jess a small pamphlet from inside her jacket pocket.

"Photo dynamic therapy. A new, directed treatment, Jess. The activating drug was FDA approved this year, based on successful clinical trials. In fact, colleagues of mine were involved at the University of Iowa and the Universite Louis Pasteur, in France—I know the research."

Jess sat silently, folding and unfolding the brochure in his hands.

Sarah touched him gently on the shoulder. "I happen to think PDT is a significant break-through, Jess."

She shoved her hands back in the pockets of her jacket.

"This treatment involves no heat damage to the eye. Simply put, a non-thermal laser light activates the drug, which destroys—by clotting—all the abnormal blood vessels. There is no evidence of damage to the retina, even after multiple treatments." She paused, clearing her throat. "While nothing can reverse scarring that already exists, this approach does seem to prevent *further* vision loss and can be repeated without any adverse side affects."

"How do you know you've done one damn bit of good?"

"A routine diagnostic, before and after. Each retina is photographed following the administration of a fluorescein dye injected into your arm. The dye gives us a map of where damage has occurred, and afterwards, where treatment has been successful."

"Piss-load of chemicals up the arm, Sarah."

"I can't promise you won't glow in the dark," she admitted.

Jess eyebrows shot up. A joke!

Sarah tapped the brochure. "Read this carefully tonight. I recommend you evaluate both the routine laser treatment *and* the new PDT therapy. Either choice, we need a fluorescein angiography to know where we're working in the retina. I've blocked the procedure for tomorrow morning. Eight sharp."

"I got this thing about needles, Sarah."

"I'll add it your list. Planes *and* needles."

He grunted.

"And Jess? I tell you this as a friend—don't mistake the seriousness of this diagnosis. Don't evade treatment."

Jess rose to his feet, rotating his shoulders stiffly. He stood in silence, gazing through the slatted blinds, thinking of his scrubby backyard, the empty spaces of Tesuque.

Sarah handed him what he mistook to be a roll of film. Puzzled, he unwound the flexible plastic and discovered it was some form of frameless eye wrap. He looked at her questioningly.

"Disposable eye protectors. Wear them until your pupils are less sensitive to daylight."

Jess positioned the dark plastic over his eyes. "Film. How apropos."

"And stop smoking, Jess," Sarah scolded softly. "I saw you light up in the lot before you came in."

Jess pocketed the brochure.

"By the way," Sarah added with a slight, rushed awkwardness, "I'm taking us to dinner tonight." She evaded his gaze, rubbing a slender finger the length of one eyebrow, back and forth, as she walked him to the door. "Can we talk about the trip?"

"All right...and I forgot, Zoë said she'd be out," Jess offered apologetically. "Music."

"I see," Sarah said slowly, her lips tightening. "We'll collect her afterwards then, shall we?"

At the entrance to the clinic, Jess unexpectedly reached out and shook Sarah's hand, the formality of the gesture startling both of them. She peered up quizzically.

"Thanks...a lot," Jess mumbled softly. "It's always better to know what you're lookin' at. Or in my case, not."

Sarah laughed out loud. "Oh, I admire your pictures far too much to settle for Jess Cappello leftovers." Her face glowed, warm and genuine, and oddly enough, he believed her.

She extricated her hand. "You know the way to the house from here?"

"Yep. Follow traffic left, buck it to the right, and dive for home at the first driveway without a Jetta, Beamer, or Jag stacked at the curb. Look for a Volvo the color of a biscuit, with a flat tire and a Ralph Nader sticker. This is some town you got here, Dr. HV."

Sarah noted the abbreviation of her name with one, slightly raised eyebrow.

"Later then." Jess pushed out the door.

Sunlight ricocheted off the glass of parked cars and office buildings and Jess ducked his head, grateful for the dark plastic hugging his eyes. He jerked open the door of his pickup and leaned across the seat, shaking another stale cigarette out of the pack in the glove box. Propped against the rear fender, hat pulled low, Jess lit up. The hot metal of the tailgate burned through the back of his denim shirt as he inhaled, feeling Sarah's eyes watching from behind her office blinds.

No sense smoking this stick of shit, he admitted, tossing the butt and climbing in behind the wheel. He was going to need a fresh pack.

Image of Truth

Le Violon de Ingres, Man Ray, 1924

Double entendre.

The odalisque. The image is a silver print with soft black and silver tonal variations. The nude sits with her back to the viewer, her head and hips swathed in turbans of silk. Her chin is tucked intimately in to her left shoulder, letting the viewer glimpse a hint of youth, and definite beauty. Her back dips smoothly in at the waist and swells widely at the buttocks into a familiar and sensuous hourglass form. But behold the unexpected: two perfectly matched f-holes, that pair of delicate cursive letters that emit the sound of the violin, painted upon her back. Ingres the woman, Ingres the violin.

Note from the Daybook:

My eyes have been playing tricks all week. When I close them I see abstracts in leaves, stories on faces, the bending of light. Nothing appears the way I once understood things. Depth of field seems amiss...am I looking through things, or not far enough? Yesterday I thought I saw a rose petal dematerialize—the color swelled to a stain and the shape dissolved. What is seeing?

Sarah pulled into the driveway just before seven that evening in a gray, late model station wagon. Jess was sitting on the porch, thumbing through a newspaper. He folded the paper and came down the steps.

He nodded at the car.

"What?" Sarah asked curiously as she gathered her briefcase and jacket from the front seat.

"You drive a Volvo."

"So? It's reliable—and Zoë's cello fits in the back."

"I've just noticed people tend to reflect their cars, or is it vice versa?"

Sarah rolled her eyes, looking pointedly at his dilapidated truck parked at the curb, baked in bug guts and road grime.

His lip twitched. "Like I said."

Sarah disappeared inside, and a few moments later, returned carrying a sweater, her purse slung over one shoulder.

"Let's walk downtown."

Jess nodded, glad to stretch his legs.

They strolled for several blocks beneath the entwined limbs of old shade trees that dwarfed the quiet street; past small cottages and newer, burgeoning mansions squeezed onto the postage-sized lots. The smell of bay leaf and lemon scented the air. Jess walked easily, enjoying the soft play of last light through the leaves.

Finally Sarah spoke.

"Did you and Zoë have a chance to...um...talk?"

Jess glanced over at the doctor and shrugged.

"And?"

"To be honest, Sarah, Zoë has a pretty good grasp of the consequences." He hesitated. "I had a chance to hear her play at a music store in Arizona. She's remarkable."

"You stopped at a music store?" Sarah halted, shocked. "That isn't exactly discouraging her!"

"Sarah."

"Her audition is the day after tomorrow.... I guess I can't really prevent this."

"Sarah, what gives? It's not the Dad thing. Zoë's pretty clear-headed about Red."

Jess stopped to light a cigarette, ignoring Sarah who gasped in disbelief; struck speechless by either the cigarette or his remark, he didn't know and didn't care. He was making a point.

"Dear God, if you're going to smoke that thing, then stand away from me," she snapped.

They continued down the street. Sarah slowly began to speak.

"My parents were both doctors, Jess. Mum was a pediatrician, and Dad an infectious disease specialist with the World Health Organization. They were gone a lot when I was small...trips to war zones, to Africa. I lived with my Aunt Carlotta in London. They both died in a car wreck in Nairobi."

Jess listened without comment.

"Later I became a physician. To feel connected to my parents in some way, I suppose. All I really had was the legacy of their work." Sarah glanced down at her feet. "When I met Red, well...he was larger than my small life, boisterous really, and always on the move. Surrounded by these astonishing music people. With Red, I felt part of something."

Jess drew on the cigarette, waving the smoke behind him, seeing in the pinch of Sarah's face the lonely little girl she must have been.

Sarah lifted her head.

"A short-lived fantasy, indeed. Red was continually absent, on the road. I spent my time alone in our flat, surrounded by medical texts and trying to study, while Carlotta watched Zoë." Her voice grew quiet as she plucked at the sleeve of her sweater. "One day I realized I was giving to Zoë the exact world I had growing up, and I didn't want that. I didn't want her to grow up...empty."

Unexpectedly she laughed, a short, harsh laugh devoid of humor.

"Then Red had an affair, or should I say the first affair I was aware of." Her voice cool, contained. "I began looking for a residency, and when the Massachusetts Eye and Ear Infirmary in Boston offered one, I took it. Zoë and I left London and moved to the States."

"Tough?"

"We adjusted. Later I joined the Stanford medical research staff, and after some time, this practice."

Jess looked west over the tops of the trees. A surge of white fog tumbled slowly over the long ridges of the Santa Cruz Mountains. "Absolutely amazing," he muttered.

Sarah followed his glance.

"The coastal fog? Yes, I suppose you're right. I don't really notice it anymore."

"How did Zoë discover the cello?" Jess asked off-handedly, continuing to watch as the fog blanketed the entire ridge of mountains. Long shadows seeped through the streets, staining the neighborhoods blue-gray. A light came on in a living room window.

"She met Alexei Mikavlov. I'm not sure how, although he lives a few blocks away. One day she just lugged home this half-size cello. I let her keep it, never thinking it would go this far. I mean at the time, it solved my biggest problem, what Zoë would do after school while I was at the clinic."

She looked oddly at Jess. "She's going to end up alone."

"Zoë's happy, Sarah."

"You think so? Why do you say that?"

"She told me so."

Sarah squinted at him in the gloomy twilight.

"But she thinks *you're* unhappy, Sarah. She believes you attack her music to defend the choices *you've* made."

Sarah's mouth fell open, but then she bent her head. "Perhaps she's right. I do think in terms of the future. Of security."

"There's nothing wrong with that," Jess remarked gently. "Although there's plenty of risk, she's sure this is what she wants to do. More than I ever was," he added.

Sarah fidgeted with her handbag, shifting it to her other shoulder. "I don't want Zoë to go away, Jess."

"Then go with her."

"I can't do that! Leave the practice I've built? This is where I live now."

"Then take a leave of absence. Be with Zoë her first year. Have you ever taken time off, Sarah?"

She shrugged irritably, digging her shoe into the cracks between the broken, uneven slabs of concrete on the sidewalk. "Your workshop was the first vacation I've taken in three years."

Jess digested this. "Then perhaps you should let Zoë live with her aunt in Philadelphia."

"Zoë told you about her aunt?"

"Yes."

"Oh Christ, Jess!" Sarah exploded. "The last damn thing I need is for Red's family to poach my daughter right out from under me! He hasn't bothered with her all these years, but it would be just like him to claim her now she's a prodigy he can take credit for!" She was visibly shaking.

"I thought you were worried Red would reject Zoë."

189

Jess lit a second cigarette. Silently he offered it to Sarah. She looked at him in disbelief, but then her hand darted out and she tugged it from his fingers. The doctor took a long, wobbly draw, her face scrunched up like a child's. She choked, bending double.

"Hell bells," she swore, surrendering to another hacking cough before stomping out the cigarette with her foot. "Damn long time before I do anything that stupid again."

The streets had grown dark in the comforting glow of city lights. At the edge of the business district, Sarah led Jess toward a small Thai restaurant she liked.

"I suppose I sound like I'm clinging to Zoë," she ventured hesitantly.

Jess smiled. He wasn't sure why, but the doctor's outburst somehow softened her. The Englishwoman seemed more human, finally. He touched her lightly on the elbow.

"You're her world, Sarah, as much as her music. Don't build walls she can't surmount. If you ask her to split herself in two, both halves will suffer."

A kind of shiver seemed to shake the English woman's shoulders. She jammed her hands in the pockets of her slacks.

"Let's eat. I need to go over tomorrow's procedure with you."

After a hotly spiced meal more venturesome than those he was accustomed to, yet oddly pleasing, like the village cooking he could remember from Korea, Jess felt his body relax into a pleasant weariness. He let his mind detach from the prickly medical details Sarah conscientiously described throughout the Pad Thai noodles and the chicken on skewers.

"Oh, my God," Sarah muttered in alarm, "it's nearly nine o'clock. I told Zoë eight-thirty."

There was an awkward tussle over the dinner check, but Jess resolutely refused to pick up the two twenties he laid on the table. Unwilling to pay for the meal twice, Sarah jammed her wallet back in her shoulder bag, and puffed with frustration, headed briskly in the direction of Alexei Mikavlov's house. As they turned up the walk of a modest gray house, the sounds of strings and piano drifted through an opened window. Pools of yellow light spilled from the house onto the dark grass.

Sarah knocked firmly on the front door. The music abruptly ceased and a slight, older man in a sagging green sweater peered out at them. He frowned at the interruption before recognizing Sarah and ushering them in.

"Hello, Alexei. Is Zoë ready?"

"Sit, please. A few moments more, yes?" the maestro pleaded. "We are not quite through with the Foss."

Sarah sighed impatiently.

Jess relaxed on a worn green corduroy sofa, and looked about the room with interest. A black Yamaha baby grand piano loomed in the center of the tiny room, flanked to one side by a pair of folding wooden chairs and a music stand.

Zoë waited in one of the wooden chairs, her cello held loosely between her bare knees as she thumbed through the pages of her music. Seeing Jess, she smiled. At the piano, a tall Asian woman with Oxford glasses waited patiently. Behind the piano hung a glossy black and white photo, of an obviously much younger Alexei Mikavlov beside a bespectacled cellist Jess presumed might be none other than Rostropovich.

Mikavlov wasn't much of a housekeeper, or better yet, needed one. A pair of wall scones, their dusty globes filled with dead moths, threw wavering pools of dim light across the worn rugs. Worn yellowed scores of music occupied every available surface, including the top of an ancient turntable perched on a small shelf of classical LPs. In front of Jess, the low coffee table held a crockery teapot and several half-empty mugs on stacks of a glossy strings magazine, *The Strad*.

"Hello Wendy, hello Alexei," Sarah greeted tiredly. "This is a friend of ours, Jess Cappello."

Jess nodded politely. Alexei Mikavlov indicated the teapot and seconds later hurried from the back of the house with two clean cups. "Please," he insisted with a quick smile, handing them the cups. Then he spun around on his heel and took his place in the chair next to Zoë, taking up his cello from the floor.

"Again, the bar 12. Watch intonation. It is important. You see? A modern sound, playful like so." He fingered a few measures of the Foss *Capriccio*.

Zoë nodded, and the pianist looked back at her music, finding the place to begin.

The trio launched into the piece, Mikavlov and Zoë playing against the rapid arpeggio chords of the piano. Jess listened, while Sarah thumbed through an old Stanford Lively Arts playbill.

He observed Zoë's teacher carefully. Mikavlov was of modest height, with a wiry, supple build, and he guessed somewhere in his sixties. The Russian possessed a prominent aquiline nose; tight curls of iron gray hair worn longish on the collar. His deep-set eyes, lively and observant, darted beneath dramatic concourses of thick eyebrow. The cellist's upper lip slightly hooded the lower, lending to his face an expression of habitual brooding, but as they played, his expression assumed a detached sternness, his head thrown back in a posture of intense listening. The hands that gripped the narrow neck of the cello and bow had strong, evenly shaped fingers, oddly squared at the tips.

The man exuded a strange, captivating grace, the innate balance in his movements reminding Jess of Balanchine, the dancer. His way of moving was subtle, in discreet physical shifts—*diminuendo,* or *forte.* And when he spoke, the maestro's accent possessed the rough richness of water pushing stones.

The small feet, in loafers, marking the beat. In fact, each musical note found expression through the maestro's body. His hands skipped through the air, seemed to dance with the notes, cup and toss them free. Mikavlov held his bow suspended between his thumb and first three fingers, his hand arched as though within, a small bird were imprisoned by his fingertips.

The cellists bent themselves to the complicated score, their shared expression animated with concentration. When Jess glanced at Zoë, her whole body bent to a rising arpeggio.

Jess frowned. The chaos of sound in his ears beat like hail on the roof, but then he found himself thinking of oceans, watching the movements of the musicians draw into close, enveloping harmonies. The music gathered in an exuberant plunge, sweeping everything into the mad tempo of the *Capriccio.*

The practice ended after the Foss. Mikavlov, weary and rumpled, conferred with Zoë and Wendy before the three agreed to reconvene the following afternoon. The two girls hugged quickly, Zoë reaching up to the slightly taller pianist to giggle something in her ear. The young woman slipped her music back into her satchel, found her car keys, and made a hasty departure.

Zoë packed up her cello.

"Goot, Zoë," the Russian nodded somberly. "Tomorrow. Your solo, and again the *Capriccio.*"

"Yep," Zoë nodded agreeably. Her eyes flicked nervously toward her mother standing by the door. "Goodnight, maestro."

The walk back to the cottage took only a few minutes, Zoë pulling her cello case behind her on two sturdy wheels. Inside the house, the teenager dashed upstairs, casting wary glances over her shoulder. But Sarah remained strangely withdrawn as she wished her daughter goodnight.

"Coffee, Jess?" Sarah asked quietly.

"A beer? No? Coffee then."

Jess waited at the table as Sarah brewed a pot of coffee and arranged a few biscotti on a plate between them. His mind continued to churn restlessly. Listening to the rehearsal, he had almost believed it possible to *see* music. Not the script of notes, but the aural shape of the whole, the interior color of musical emotion.

He had toyed with this thought on the walk home. Could someone cross the senses and "see" a story, or touch the colors in a painting, possibly hear a sculpture? Say the eyes could absorb more from a novel in the shape of the words on the page, in the length of a particular sentence, the hanging punctuation on a page? He imagined poets must believe so. And perhaps a person *could* touch a painting in a similar way, or feel with fingertips the purpose of the painter in the thickness of the gobs of paint projected across a canvas. And sculpture, he learned from Catalina, is not deaf. A stone talks from the shape assumed; the echo of the artist is in the bronze.

Granted, he perceived his own world visually, reduced every aspect of sense and form into a two dimensional record. But sitting on Mikavlov's sofa, mentally framing Zoë and Mikavlov into photographic arrangements as they played, gauging the moment their heads would duck in complimentary alignment, or when their hands found balance before their cellos, their images imperceptibly transformed into sound. The music itself became the image, a strange alchemy he could not yet satisfactorily explain. What if there was a tangible way to portray this?

"Jess?" Sarah handed him a mug of black coffee, looking at him humorously. "Where were you, on Mars?"

He cleared his throat, embarrassed to have so thoroughly lost track of his surroundings. He took a scalding sip, wincing.

"Good coffee."

"Sleepy?"

He broke a hard biscuit with his fingers. "Just thinking."

"Worried about tomorrow?" Sarah asked, studying him over the rim of her cup, her eyes unreadable. They could hear the sounds of Zoë upstairs, preparing for bed.

"That might be fair to say."

She leaned back in her chair. "You know, I was just thinking of Georgia O'Keefe, the painter from Santa Fe? She had severe macular degeneration in her eighties, but she painted right into her nineties with her assistant's help."

"You're suggesting creative ways to compensate," Jess said wryly.

"No, I'm just.... Oh Jess, be realistic."

"That I'm going blind?"

"We won't know *anything* until after the angiography, especially the extent of the problem. It might be less—"

"Or more."

The doctor set her cup down, impatient. "If the vision you have is the vision you keep, that's a positive outcome with this disease, Jess. If you were to rely on your equipment for accuracy in your images, you should be able to continue making photographs—good ones."

"Gear breaks all the time," Jess murmured, pushing crumbs of biscotti around the table with the tip of his index finger. "Light meters off-set, shutters fail, film holders leak. The real bugaboo is developing. I rely on my eyes to judge tone, the accuracy of the enlargement, dodging, spotting...all of it. You know that, Sarah—you're a photographer. I can't fake printing."

Sarah's face flushed. "Well, actually I don't, Jess. I've never developed my own work. I don't know how. I use a lab downtown."

He stared at her. "How can you grasp the fundamentals of photography if you don't actually do it?"

"I know that!" she snapped defensively. "But I don't have the time. With my practice, and Zoë's schedule, when am I going to find time for a dark room class?"

Jess looked up towards the collection of wicker baskets gathering dust on the cabinet ledges. She'd spent thousands on his workshop, and yet wouldn't, or couldn't, make the time to learn the basics.

"Why *do* you photograph, Sarah?" He asked finally, genuinely puzzled.

"I like the medium," she responded, lifting her chin. "I like the process of examining the world from the inside out, the way elements of light and form create object. Yet the best images are the ones that hit you between the eyes emotionally. How is that?"

"If you'd develop your own work, you'd know why. Printing determines everything, even mood." A platinum or sepia finish gave an image a certain sensibility; a tone feeling that interpreted the image for the viewer. "I'd be happy to show you the basics. It's the least I can do, a kind of thanks, you know, for treating me."

Sarah refilled her cup and Jess, before taking her seat again at the oak table.

"I don't even have a dark room. But someday."

They lapsed into silence.

There would likely never be a 'someday' for either of them, Jess thought. His failing vision, Sarah's consuming work.

"I liked Mikavlov."

"Quite the character. Bloody genius I'm told," Sarah admitted. "Illustrious career in Leningrad and Paris. He's been good for Zoë, I suppose."

"Why so grudging?"

Sarah looked at Jess sharply.

"He and Zoë spend a lot of time together. I think she looks to him for guidance I expect I should provide, that's all."

"She's lucky to have a mentor. We're not born with very good directions on how to grow talent, or find voice, Doc. It's not easy, living with one's own ambition and ignorance." He hesitated, unexpectedly serious. "How *not* to screw up. I learned my way around photography by trial and error, Sarah."

Sarah studied the bottom of her cup, saying nothing.

"Your daughter's gift may be bigger than she is. Mikavlov will help Zoë learn to hold herself whole. She trusts him."

Sarah flashed Jess a daunting look. "Tell me what I don't know!"

"You're jealous?"

"What could you possibly know of this?" she demanded, clearly angry. "You, who've never had anything more remotely complex than a *dog* in your life, stand there and tell me what's best for Zoë! Jess Cappello, don't you dare tell me how to raise my own child!" She struck the table, hard.

"Sarah, I—"

"What can you possibly know!"

Jess pushed back his chair and quietly left the kitchen, more sorry than he could ever say.

Reading the Light

Light Abstraction No. 36, Francis Bruguiere, 1927

Cut-outs, black and white.

In the late twenties, the photographer Francis Bruguiere, a colleague of Steiglitz and member of the *Photo-Secession,* as well as painter and poet, declared light the quintessence of photography. Employing an artist's playfulness, the Frenchman created unique silhouettes of light using paper cut-outs, and experimenting with multiple exposures, staged his own visual world of make-believe.

Light Abstraction No. 36, a silver print, possesses the anxious depth of a dream. A multitude of spear-like shapes conjoin chaotically, to suggest but never identify, forms that seem natural but are not. Bruguiere's photograph, *Abstraction,* drifts in search of realism.

Note from the Daybook:

Sarah suggested last night that I 'work with what I've got'. What the hell is that supposed to mean? What I have is a problem! This is pointless.

Jess rose early, threw his things into his duffel and let himself out of the house. The neighborhood streets were empty, cool and shrouded in gray mist. He debated whether to leave a note, but decided Sarah could explain his departure to Zoë however it suited her. He lugged out his stuff, and was leaning over the side of the truck, packing down the storage box, when Sarah came out of the cottage in her bathrobe. She walked up to the side of the truck and stood there wordlessly, hugging her robe close.

"Where are you going, Jess?" she asked finally, her face rough with sleep.

"It's best if I head out," Jess responded evenly, checking the latches. "I'm sorry I butted in, Sarah. I had no business. You and Zoë have been swell."

The doctor examined her feet. "Look, don't go. Things were said--"

Jess edged around her toward the door of the cab.

"Well, thanks for everything," he muttered, sliding in behind the wheel and lowering the window. "Tell Zoë goodbye."

"God damn it, Jess!" Sarah stomped her foot, her plain English face screwed up in frustration and confusion. "Is this it? Just jump in your truck and drive off? I am your doctor, and I have every intention of treating you to the best of my ability." Sarah drew a deep breath and pressed a hand to her cheek in frustration. "Please.... Come into the house and have breakfast."

Jess stared out the windshield, silent.

Sarah put a hand on his arm. "Jess, if you leave, you jeopardize your future. Don't let *other things* get in the way of that."

His knuckles gripped the steering wheel.

"Jess, look at me."

Sarah held up the back of her hand.

"Close your right eye, and tell me what you see."

He shook his head.

"Let's get down to business," she said calmly. "We need to be at the clinic by eight."

"I'd like to call Abe first."

Jess followed Sarah back inside, and dialed the Santos' residence. Abe picked up on the first ring.

"Jess! Get my message, man?"

"Sarah passed it on. Just calling to tell you to hang on to the mail."

"Jeez, I already sent it."

"Well then, don't worry about it."

"Jess, you all right? You don't sound so good."

"About as good as a human pin cushion can be." He described for Abe what Sarah had outlined for the day. His friend whistled on the other end.

"Holy crap. Well hang in there. Sarah's the best. Your dog is fine by the way, sleeping with Carly."

"Thought that was your job."

"I don't smell as good."

Sarah insisted on toasting bagels, and whipped up three orange-banana smoothies. She downed hers in a gulp and disappeared upstairs to dress and collect her files. Jess, still facing his second cup of coffee, shoved his untouched breakfast down the disposal.

He was waiting in the downstairs hallway when Zoë darted past on her way out the door. Her hair was pinned back with sparkly barrettes, her pink skin freshly scrubbed, and she sported one of her tee shirts, *"Cellists do it with a bow"*. Her feet were bare, beaded sandals dangling from one hand. She breezed by Jess, and then paused, shifting her backpack onto her other shoulder.

"Heh, why'd you stick up for me last night?"

"You heard?"

"Hard not to! So how come?"

"Talent, Zoë. Yours."

The girl bent over and slipped on her sandals. "You're an odd duck, Jess Cappello," she tossed back over her shoulder. "But I like you."

Jess stood outside on front steps and lit a cigarette, considering his truck. Still time to hop in and head down the coast, still time. He slipped his hand into his pocket, feeling for his keys.

"Let's go!" Sarah announced, coming out of the house with her briefcase clamped under one arm, and Jess had the distinct impression that fate, his at least, was certainly out of his hands.

Jess was introduced to the clinic's technical assistant, Moses Rupa. They shook hands. Rupa, a stocky Indian with a rounded face, had eyes so soft they reminded Jess of antler down.

"Moses will be taking the images of your retina once the fluorescein is injected," Sarah explained. She indicated the cricket-legged apparatus squatting in the center of the examining room. A camera was mounted to one end and the other end appeared to be a microscope, with calibrating knobs for tilt and focus. Moses seated Jess facing the camera and adjusted a frontal brace for his shoulders and his head. Then he flipped up an armrest and laid out the I.V. apparatus and a tube of reddish-yellow liquid.

"Put your arm up on the rest, sir," the technician instructed, tying a tourniquet around his forearm, watching for a vein to plump.

"Did I mention a horrific fear of needles?" Jess croaked, as the Indian swabbed his skin clean.

Sarah glanced up from her chart. "Relax! We're not going to heave you into a cactus field."

"Nice image, Doc," Moses laughed, and deftly slipped the needle into Jess arm. He strapped his forearm securely to the pad, and started the I.V. The technician smiled from the corner of his eye. "Now you're going to glow in the dark."

Jess swallowed, his mouth parched as ash. The dye flowed quickly, a sensation chill as ice, pumping steadily up his arm. He felt his breathing tighten, the boom of his heartbeat echoing in his inner ear. He willed himself to relax, reaching for anything, a memory, a snippet of blues.

A hand touched his shoulder.

"All right, Jess?"

"Not exactly the most pleasant sensation," he answered tersely.

"No, I don't suppose it would be."

"It takes some time for the dye to reach your retinas, Mr. Cappello," Moses remarked quietly. "Try and relax."

Moses took the chair opposite Jess and fiddled with the height and angle of his instrument. He tilted the camera lens up. "You're a tall fellow," he murmured approvingly. "This'll be like shooting stars."

Jess leaned against the head brace as Moses strapped in his head, and adjusted the chin rest. He couldn't help but think of Old Sparky, that any moment now, they would throw the switch.

"Don't I get a choir? Any witnesses?" he joked uneasily.

"We need you to be still, Mr. Cappello. No blurry images."

The technician leaned over Jess, and the smell of lemon hair oil and a spice, perhaps curry, blended with the man's musky body odor, and a memory seeped back of a San Francisco morning. He was in Carolyn's kitchen when he kissed her, remembering the gleam and smell of floor wax, the ripe citrus of red persimmons in the tree outside the window.

His arm hurt. Already the back of his shirt was clinging to his shoulder blades.

Concentrating, he dredged up a few piano bars, humming the Shelley Manne version of *With a Little Bit of Luck*. Sarah looked over at him sharply, her brows drawn to a perfect line over her narrow nose.

Moses slid sideways from behind the microscope and Sarah stooped to peer into the viewfinder. She adjusted the focus a few turns and nodded. "We've got a beautiful view of the inside of your left eye, Jess. The dye is dispersed as it should be."

Moses resumed his place behind the camera. He addressed Jess again, this time sternly. "Try not to jerk when the light flashes blue. This won't take long."

The technician squinted into the viewfinder. They were eyeball to eyeball, two kids peering through a pipe.

"Don't spit," Jess joked.

Moses pressed a button on the control panel near his chin, waited, and then pressed a button below. A flash of light hit Jess retinas and a clicking, whirring sound rumbled from the machinery. Several times the technician triggered the flash.

Jess forced his eye wide open, holding his head motionless in its strapped cage. He hummed every tune off the *My Fair Lady* LP he could remember. God, he'd loved that album.... Recorded by Shelley Manne and his Friends in 1956, the LP was a Christmas gift from Louis, the first and last contact with his brother in a two-year silence. Louis skipped the funeral, and the trial, for that matter. Then a package arrived from the UN Forces stationed near Seoul, addressed to Jess in Photo Recon.

Jess had shared the LP with Hunter in the barracks, drinking beer as they listened to the cool jazz hissing on the portable turntable, as gunfire split the darkness beyond. In his head he could perfectly replay the languid, moody piano, tap out the complicated drum rhythms. Another late flight beside Hunter in the cockpit, far below them the wide sargasso plain, and Jess was radioed news that three days before, his brother's convoy hit the remains of an active mine field near Panmunjom, patrolling the site of the '53 Armistice.

"As long as you're prepped, I'd like an image of the other eye," Sarah instructed, jerking him back into the present moment. "We need a benchmark for future examinations."

The entire procedure was repeated on the right eye. Straining to cooperate, Jess felt himself quiver from the effort: his eyes ached with dryness and muscle-fatigue. He took several steadying breaths, unable to quite remember the last track on the LP.

Moses pushed back.

"That's a wrap!" he pronounced. The technician released Jess from his cradle of straps, and as Jess rubbed the back of his neck with his free hand, Moses removed the I.V. and placed a small bandage over the puncture wound.

"There are minor side effects from the dye, Jess," Sarah reassured him. "Wear sunglasses outdoors today. You might experience a slight headache, so take acetaminophen if you wish. And, your skin and urine might have a reddish tint for a day or two. Questions?"

"When do we get prints?"

Moses laughed. "This is a digital camera, Mr. Cappello. It produces a computer-enhanced image. The Doc should have analyzed some big beautiful pics of your retina by this afternoon."

Sarah tilted her head toward Moses. "He keeps the best framed on his desk."

Jess chuckled, standing up. He bent over slightly and gripped the back of the chair for support. Nothing, not even ass-kicking dizziness, was going to keep him in this room a second longer.

Sarah watched him closely.

"There's a cab out front to take you back to the house, Jess. Call if you feel unwell, or your eyesight becomes even slightly blurry. I'll bring your films home with me tonight, but based on what I saw–" she pressed her palms together, "I'm scheduling a PDT procedure on your left eye first thing tomorrow morning."

"You sure are a morning person, Dr. Harte-Valentine," he drawled, rolling down his shirtsleeve.

"Night is not a good time to do anything right."

"Not *everything*, Doc," Moses corrected with a smirk, shuffling down the hall.

The cab dropped Jess back at the house on Tennyson Lane. Wearing his plastic goggles, he moved slowly up the sidewalk. Outside the front door, a FedEx package propped against the screen. He picked it up, pried open the mailer, and pulled out an airmail letter postmarked Venezuela.

Jess entered the house and dropped down into one of the chairs in the living room, resting his eyes in the muted light. He felt queerly unwell, but his eyes seemed all right, despite the fact he'd been pumped full of neon and photographed from the inside out.

Jess picked up Catalina's letter, turning it over in his hands. Two letters in three weeks, he mused. More news of the project, updates on the mural installation, raptures over Venezuelan nightlife, he speculated. Nothing personal.

Jess leaned his head sideways in his hand, listening to the clock chime the hour. Neither love nor regret would suit La Brezza. This had been their way, had always been their way. The years had changed him, but not Cat. She was gone. And Jess understood that he was done. He was just too damn raw to be easy.

Jess set the letter face down on the chair and headed to the kitchen, rummaging through Sarah's cupboards. He fixed a cup of coffee, adding a generous pour of whiskey he found buried back behind the vinegars, and drank the hot toddy down. He poured another, and released a long, shuddering breath. How exhausted he was. How damn tired of being alone.

The man and the woman came together once the blue night deepened to indigo, and the sliver of moon crested the pines on the black ridge. They came alone to the cabin: a room of rough plank with a simple bed, covered in a white duvet, a wooden chair, and a table. On the table lay an old camera and tripod, and in the corner, two studio lights bent in darkness. A single light burned by the bed.

In the woman's hand, a lime.

Small, and wrapped in a white robe, the woman sliced the lime in two, and gave half to the man. He handed her a shot glass and poured each of them a finger of tequila. The woman raised her drink to her lips, her eyes intent on the face of the man.

She had remarkable eyes. The man almost felt as if there was someone within her, different at all times, as though her brown body was a chalice of many spirits, and she alone, the keeper. He slipped into her gaze, wondering who she was this night. He felt his thighs tense.

The woman lifted a hand and dribbled the limejuice onto the tip of her tongue. Then she smiled, a slow hungry smile, the sucking gravity of low tide, the invisible collapse of space. She kissed the man on the lips and they clung together, the bitter wildness on their tongues before the woman broke away. She drained her tequila, the glass flashing in the lamplight.

The man reached out and stroked the black copper sheen of her hair, felt the silk like the flow of heavy water cross his hand. He drank his tequila then, memorizing the feel of a river.

The young woman walked over to the cabin window and stood a moment, looking out at the brilliance of the stars, the infinity of so many points of light in the fabric of night. The moonlight was modest, the narrow crescent in the sky no more than one naked shoulder on a new bride. But this woman was no bride. She was a painter, her world created from the expanse of her mind.

She glanced over her shoulder. The man stood working with his camera in the half-light of the small lamp, his long legs in jeans, chest bare, swirls of dark hair on the pale plain of his body as he bent under the light. He shifted, revealed by the movements of his square hands as not a lover, but a photographer, observing her through glass. Seeing not the woman, but the shape of her.

The woman shrugged, and turning away, opened the window. A draft of cold air slipped through her fingers and stirred the room, and the man looked up, startled. Abruptly she threw the sash high and swung her legs over, sitting on the ledge. Beyond her, snowfields stretched to the reach of the moon, a dusting of ice, a brilliant phosphorescence of light. Snowbank. The man lifted his camera to his eye.

Oblivious to the cold, the woman dropped her robe to her hips. The man marked the image, appraising the weight of her hip curved to the window frame, the contrast in the drape of white cloth. His gaze traveled the long comma of her back. Ah, he had pressed the pad of his own thumb from that nape to buttocks, stroking the terrace of fragile bone. Carefully he gauged the angle of her jaw behind the dark hair, the face lifted to the light of bodies in flight, the new stars and the swollen great ones, blown into scarves of hot gas and ash.

The woman stretched a hand out the window and closed her fingers as if to catch a star. Gently, the photographer pressed the trigger of his old camera, listening for the whir of the aperture.

When Jess awoke, it was to the rapid octaves of a D Major scale played on the cello. The notes vibrated in the closed confines of the still house; harmonious sounds, drifting up the stairs. The fragrance of honeysuckle, sweetish green, swelled through the window near Jess head.

He twisted upright onto the edge of the foldout sofa, as downstairs, Zoë began what he dimly recognized as Rachmaninoff's *Vocalise*. Disoriented, his thoughts drifted back to the music store in Flagstaff. Zoë's own cello had a different tone, brighter, more mid-range in its voice. An English make she said. Not so old, but finely made. As she practiced, her playing sounded intuitive, familiar.

He pulled on his boots and went downstairs.

"Good evening," Zoë looked up. She grinned. "Hard day?"

"Just lazy," Jess confessed.

Zoë rested her bow across the music stand. "How did that sound to you? I practiced the whole thing with Wendy this afternoon, but I'm just not satisfied. My solo stuff is fine, the maestro has seen to that, but this piece—is it good enough?"

Jess scratched his chin.

"What did Mikavlov say?"

"He says it's fine, that I'm ready. Even the Bach, a good four of the Six Solo Suites. But I don't know!"

She lifted her bow, straightening her cello between her knees. "Listen—"

Jess put a hand on Zoë's shoulder. "Stop, my dear. Have a lemonade."

The girl hesitated, her elfin face screwed into dark worry. Finally, she laid the cello on its side by her practice chair. "Maybe you're right."

They took two glasses into the small garden. The last afternoon sunlight enveloped the tea table in a pool of gold.

"When is the audition?" Jess smiled gently.

"Tomorrow at five, at the Methodist Church on Hamilton. They rent the space for the day and schedule us in."

"They come out here, is that unusual?"

Zoë nodded. She began to pick at the callus on the tip of her left index finger. "Guess they used to only request audition tapes, or you'd have to fly out there. But they like a conference with the teacher, too, before they even take an application. There's an audition once a year, the cities vary."

Jess drank his lemonade.

"Who comes and listens?"

"Faculty from the school orchestra, and the strings department. Mikavlov thinks somebody from chamber music will be there, as he knows some of the other applicants. Maybe one of the Guarneri Quartet! That would be so cool! I'd love to meet David Soyer." Her small face beamed.

"The quartet is part of the school?"

Jess was impressed. He was familiar with the quartet from his visits to New York City with Catalina, and a lucky evening or two at Carnegie Hall. He'd seriously underestimated the prestige of this kid's classical education. What would his own work have been like, learned in the ambient circle of, say, Adams, Callahan, or Weston, instead of a cockroach-infested bathroom converted to a makeshift darkroom?

"One of many. The school invites famous soloists to give classes. Last year Curtis held master classes with YoYo Ma! I met him once, after a performance in San Jose. His hand was still sweaty!"

Zoë's ebullient enthusiasm had returned, banishing those few black moments of self-doubt.

Jess hesitated. "Did your Mom...? When did Sarah agree to the audition?"

"I've told the maestro it's all set, and asked him to take me to the audition." Zoë stared straight through him, waiting.

"She doesn't know?"

"No."

"Zoë?"

The teenager scrambled to her feet and scooping up her glass, hopped up the stairs through the kitchen door. She leaned back, holding the screen door open. "Do me a favor? I'm going to the movies with Beth tonight. Mum knows, but remind her. I'll be back by curfew."

"I'll pass it on...about the movies," Jess agreed uneasily.

When Sarah came home she found Jess reading the paper in the kitchen. She walked over and placed a photographer's light box on the table in front of him.

"Ready?"

From her briefcase she withdrew a series of digital negatives and pinned them to the surface of the box, flicking on the light. The mapping of an eye was exposed to view–a strange orb, less an eye than a globe, resting on its side. Forks of lightning, fingers of brittle white corral, and what appeared to be a squirrel's nest, blotted the heart of the globe. His finger touched the clot of blood vessels near the dark center of the negative.

"That is the subretinal neovascularization," Sarah nodded. "Here is your macula," she pointed, "and these are normal blood vessels. Compare this image to your right eye." The doctor indicated the negatives tacked on the bottom row of the light box. "You can see the macula area is clear here, unobstructed by blood vessels."

Jess turned. "What are you telling me?"

She straightened up, clicking off the light box.

"The right eye is fine, Jess. We'll have to watch, but at least we have a healthy retinal map. The left eye is a bigger mess than I anticipated. That clump under the macula is probably the angiogenesis site—where the abnormal vessels are interfering with each other and blood is leaking beneath the retina. I can only guess at the rate of disciform maculopathy."

"Sarah! What does this mean?"

She bit the edge of one nail, searching for words.

"I don't know the actual degree of scarring that has occurred—what is permanent damage, Jess. From these images, I might hope the choroidal vessels are rather new, just fast growing, and the retina has simply been displaced, bumped up as it were, a shoe under the rug. We can hope that no fibrovascular scarring has occurred. That would be irreversible."

She squeezed his arm encouragingly.

"We won't know anything for sure until after the procedure and the follow-up angiography." She smiled. "I do believe you have reason to be optimistic! Let's go with the photodynamic therapy. The PDT procedure has very low risk, and statistically, a high degree of success."

Jess flicked on the light box and stared again at the oddness of his own eyes, rendered in black and white. Blood vessels splintered like winter branches against the mysterious retina, a cloth of black. Surreal images that reminded him of solarizations. A biology wholly unrecognizable, yet as necessary to him as film to a camera.

He straightened up, his eyes hooded deep in their sockets.

"I can't *not* see, Sarah. My eyes tell me everything."

"Jess? Jess!"

But she was alone in the kitchen. The front door stood ajar. From the doorway she could see Jess striding down the street, head down into the darkness of the trees.

She watched him go, on her face a look of bewildered, not quite tender, worry.

Liquid Sunshine

White Line, Oak Bluffs, Massachusetts, David Fokos, 1996

The line wavers.

An Atlantic pier juts into the dense, coastal fog. A chalk-white railing edges the boardwalk; it too, disappears where the sea melts into cloud. A choppy, hand-painted line runs down the center of the salt-stained planks. The stripe of paint is weathered and chipped, and wavers the length of the pier until this line too, is swallowed at the horizon.

White Line. Fokos' platinum images, 8x10s printed from the negative, remained true in contrast to the finest detail; the small aperture required for extreme depth of field balanced with long exposures. The resulting ethereal quality pleased Jess.

That is, until a year ago.

On assignment for *Senior Leisure*, Jess spent two weeks in August photographing the rocky Atlantic coast, near the summer town of Ogunquit, Maine. Waiting for the inland fog to clear, he ran across Mark Haley in a dank bar on the working side of the wharf, far from the tourist boutiques and fancy oyster places. The middle-aged man sat alone, straw hat on his lap, an iced drink pressed against his forehead. The balding editor worked for *View Camera* magazine, and had once handled a feature on Jess.

"Cappello! Sit down, sit down, you old dog!" The editor exclaimed jovially, waving Jess toward the empty stool at his side. "What's hangin'? Photographing the tourists?" He winked broadly. "I'm up with the family down at The Misty Duck, bed and breakfast on Magnolia. Good enough place..."

The editor wiped his face meticulously with a white handkerchief folded in squares clutched in one freckled hand. The heat was heavy; even the sea rocked in sullen, indolent latitudes beneath the weathered pier.

Jess ordered a beer, half-listening to Haley gossip. In passing, the editor mentioned an exhibit of David Fokos' work.

"Saw him on the Vineyard, at the Granary Gallery. New stuff, you know, this digital printing." Haley nodded. "He's left platinum work in favor of this modern techno-stuff."

Like many younger photographers, Fokos had experimented with a digital printer and worked exclusively now on a costly wonder named the LightJet *5000*. The machine used lasers to generate larger prints than the typical 8x10 large format negative, and permitted a photographer to fix prints on the computer.

"What do you say to that?" Haley squinted over his handkerchief.

Jess sipped his beer.

"Don't know. Must be something to it."

"Fokos swears he's not totally abandoned the platinum image," Haley amended. "Develops digital black and whites on color paper. Claims he gets richer tones, warm platinum-like blacks."

"Then why do it? Why not just make a platinum? "

"These guys like their images *big*, my boy! Think of it! 36x36! Even 48x96 is possible!" Haley slurped down his oysters in lemon juice. His marble-blue eyes bulged in their sockets as his mouth opened.

"No mistakes with a laser! You old boys and your 'liquid sunshine', by any other name it's still a bottle blonde. Still the same artifice! Why *not* let a computer do the technical stuff? Takes hours out of the darkroom. That's efficiency!"

"There's a difference between *create* and generate, Mark."

"Bah! Success depends on the right exposure and careful composition, always. The game's in the mind, Cappello."

Jess thought about that conversation with Mark Haley a great deal, unable, or unwilling to embrace the editor's point of view. Art was constantly achieved and failed, but aesthetics aside, he liked his niche in the medium. In accord with Stieglitz, who famously declared platinum the "prince of photographic processes," Jess upheld the beauty in the actual chemistry.

Leave digital to this generation, he thought. To Barrows and her *Iris* technology prints, Fokos and his images the width of walls. He did not doubt the marvel of the LightJet 5000. But, there seemed to Jess, a certain lack of heart.

Note from the Daybook:
The irony is inescapable. What I create with brain and hand, the computer laser will repair. I am the Luddite, taken in my own time, witness to my own eclipse.

Jess walked, letting the movement of his legs calm his thoughts. He hadn't realized until that exact moment in Sarah's kitchen, that in the back of his mind, he gauged his future on either blindness or treatment. He was unprepared to contemplate a lingering disability, an existence floundering in between. He kicked a rotted tennis ball into the gutter.

Jess strode on, his thoughts darker than the darkened streets.

Across from him he saw a gray house that struck him as faintly familiar, and then realized he had made his way past Coleridge. The house belonged to Alexei Mikavlov.

Should he offer to escort Zoë home? That must be her cello he heard, good old Bach drifting out the window. Jess sighed, crossed the street and rang the doorbell. The door cracked open and Zoë's maestro poked his head out.

"Yes?"

"Mr. Mikavlov? Jess Cappello."

"Ah, yes! Come in! Come in, please."

Mikavlov opened the door wider to admit Jess. Despite the summer heat, the maestro was attired in dark corduroy slacks and a heavy brown cardigan, the sleeves pushed up past his elbows. The odor of onions and bacon permeated the front rooms of the house, with enough bite to make Jess eyes water.

"I was just wondering if Zoë needed an escort home."

The older man tilted his head. "Zoë? But she is not here."

Jess colored, remembering too late Zoë had gone with Beth to the movies. He had forgotten to tell Sarah as well. It had been Mikavlov at the cello.

"I heard the cello.... Sorry to interrupt."

He turned.

Mikavlov reached out, his hand touching Jess' elbow.

"Zoë is not home?" the Russian inquired anxiously. "Tomorrow is audition! I would not want to think..." his voice trailed off, in his dark eyes the worry Zoë had unwisely gone out, or misplaced herself, and behind that, a puzzled surprise her own family could not keep track of her.

"She's okay. I forgot she had plans with a friend." He took a step down the stairs before looking strangely back at Mikavlov. "Tell me, do you believe in Zoë? Her talent?"

215

The maestro's face froze, as if Jess had just sworn the world was flat, or the Earth had two suns. He crossed his arms, burying his fingers in the rolled knit at his elbows.

"Best student I have since conservatory," Mikavlov admitted slowly. "Rostropovich, he describe Jacqueline du Pre as 'perhaps better, even, than me'. This is Zoë."

Mikavlov scrutinized Jess suspiciously.

"You are friend of mother's?"

"I barely know them," Jess answered truthfully, "but I hope Zoë succeeds tomorrow."

The maestro sighed gazing at the treetops, languorous emerald fans, swaying in the evening breeze. He considered Jess, his gaze prosaic. "Please, come in. No good drink alone."

Jess followed the small Russian back into his house.

Mikavlov uncorked a bottle of pinot noir amongst the piles of music on the coffee table, and handed Jess a glass. They faced each other, Mikavlov on his stool, and Jess on the sagging sofa.

"Tell me, please, who are you," Mikavlov invited cordially. "I do not remember names so well since Sasha died."

It was hard not to like the courtly fellow. He supposed the Russian was only a few years older than himself, but there was something classically nineteenth century about Alexei Mikavlov that reminded Jess of delicate, hand-painted photographic portraits. The small-rimmed glasses pushed up on his nose, perhaps, or the tatty cardigan, the jumble of everything musical about the room, including the bow resting across the windowsill.

"So you are photographer?"

"I've done my share of bread and butter assignment work for travel magazines, but my serious work is in galleries." Jess winced slightly. Who was he trying to impress? He lapsed into silence.

Mikavlov merely nodded, and drank deeply from his wine, placing his crumple-heeled loafers atop Yehudi Menuhin on the cover of *Strad* magazine.

The Russian studied Jess, his gaze skeptical but mostly curious. "How you know Zoë?"

"I met Zoë and her mother in one of my photography workshops."

The Russian nodded.

Inexplicably, Jess found himself retelling the story of Ansel and the cougar, the details of his failed vision and Sarah's intervention, and especially, how Zoë had bowled him over at the music store. The maestro said nothing during Jess' long-winded narration, but his eyes seemed to grow ever more melancholy and thoughtful.

"You do not dissuade Zoë," he stated gently.

Jess shook his head. "Nope. Didn't want to. Nor, as it turns out, did she."

Mikavlov chuckled. "Yes, Zoë is quite sure in the mind."

The Russian's expression grew heavy.

"This is absolutely how must be. A musician, such a person must be very committed, the mind strong." Mikavlov studied the piano absently, stroking the side of his cheek with his fingertips. Finally, he pinched the bridge of his nose, as if to rid troublesome thoughts.

"The mother..."

Jess had noticed how the maestro always said "the mother", never Sarah, or Dr. Harte-Valentine, but a matriarchal address, this stiff titular recognition.

"The mother," Mikavlov expressed evenly, "does not support this idea." He shrugged, forgetful of his wine, which rocked in the glass. "So many times I tell her of this daughter's great talent, what rapid progress, what future she might have..." His face puckered sadly.

"She must believe at some level, Mikavlov. I mean, Zoë continues to study with you."

Mikavlov shot Jess a wry glance.

"Some time ago the mother comes to me. Cancel lesson, she says. Zoë need real career she says. To me!" He shook his head in disbelief.

"But the lessons?"

"Zoë." He nodded firmly. "She refuse to quit! Even when mother not pay. She beg me to continue, anything to continue." Alexei Mikavlov permitted a small smile at the memory. "So! We make deal. Zoë clean my little house after school, I give cello lesson."

Jess absorbed the maestro's words, stunned at how far Sarah had gone to wedge a knife between Zoë and her music, and equally surprised at the plucky stubbornness of the girl. He looked around, humorously acknowledging the general ruin of the house.

"You're not getting much on your side of the deal, Maestro."

The maestro bowed his head with dignity. "I would give for free."

Jess lifted his glass in a silent toast. Mikavlov's unwavering support must have been the final straw for Sarah, and certainly explained her hostility toward the gentle musician.

He shook his head, but Mikavlov apparently read his mind.

" Zoë find a way," he muttered philosophically.

"The audition you mean?"

"Sure. Curtis School important school of music, place to meet many celli, play with orchestra to grow. Zoë, maybe best." His eyes shone behind the deep claret of his wine.

Jess hesitated. "Is she a bit old for a child prodigy?"

Mikavlov snorted, nearly choking on his drink. Nimbly he leaped to his feet and pulled down a scrapbook from the top of a bookcase crammed with cellophane-taped, dog-eared scores. He opened the book and thrust it into Jess' lap.

"Look!" He pointed proudly to the pages.

Jess thumbed through the thick book. Photographs, newspaper stories, programs. Zoë, taking a bow at Davies Hall in San Francisco after performing at eleven, the Double Bach Concerto; Zoë and the pianist Vladimir Viardo at Villa Montalvo; Zoë at the Aspen Summer Music Festival playing with a familiar looking Chinese pianist; Zoë on stage at the Dorothy Chandler Pavilion with the London Symphony Orchestra in a youth summer fest. There were more, many more pages of newspaper articles, critical reviews, glossy programs and ticket stubs. Jess closed the book silently and set it carefully on the coffee table.

"I had no idea," he confessed.

"Only beginning," Mikavlov shrugged, dismissing the scrapbook with a flick of his hand. "She so young! The *bel canto,* how you say *the true voice,* will bloom. But," he glared fiercely, "Zoë must grow, try her bow for most demanding of conductors."

He settled back in his folding chair, brooding.

"I cannot take her further," he shook his leonine head regretfully. "She is ready for *big lights.*"

The maestro's eyes had misted, so great seemed to be his affection for Zoë, and Jess sensed Mikavlov could literally see the jeweled glimmer of her future but said nothing, drinking from his glass.

My god. The teenager already had the bit in her teeth. Jess squinted at his boots uneasily, disturbed Sarah would fight so ruthlessly in the face of what, even to her, must be demonstrable talent. What could make the stakes so high the English woman would cut her own daughter off at the knees? Jess had a flashback of Sarah's face across the table, and suddenly, he knew. Sarah was afraid to be alone.

Mikavlov interrupted his thoughts, handing Jess a plate of stale cookies. "You will be fine with your eyes, my friend," the Russian nodded sagely.

Jess stared at him blankly, his thoughts still tangled around Zoë and Sarah.

The Russian crunched noisily on a vanilla cream. "Music, picture making, all same. What we do with this," he tapped his head, "and this," he pounded his chest.

The maestro's eyes twinkled.

"Take me. Perfect pitch I had. Now, not so goot, and pitch for cellist absolute necessity." He tapped his ear lightly and shrugged fatalistically. "Everything must be *in tune.* Cannot find this like keys of piano," he rippled his fingers in the air, playing an imaginary keyboard. "Violin, viola, celli...musician must *make* tune, know in ear, in the hands before play."

"I'm sorry. Your playing is remarkable."

"So what do I do, now I not hear so well?" Mikavlov grinned faintly, his face mischievous and light. "These fingers, they know! No longer need just ears. I know students correct by vibration." He reached over and picked up his well-used cello, plucking swiftly along the open strings.

"You see?" His eyes burned brightly, joyously. "These fingers know!"

Alexei Mikavlov set his cello down, peering up at Jess. "Your eyes not so good? Too bad. Yes, too bad! But brain all there," he poked his scalp. "More places than eyes to see."

Jess frowned abruptly, leaning forward from the sofa. "Mikavlov, have you ever *touched* music, the sound of it, or, or felt like you tasted it? Experienced music in some other way?"

The Russian seemed unsurprised by the strange question. He shrugged, and ran his hands randomly through his hair.

"Sometimes taste sound like, like electricity in the teeth." He thought a moment, pursing his lips. "Sibelius, the composer?

Eleven stoves in his home in Finland, each one different color! Yes, is true. He 'hear' colors. Green the F major, the red is for him the C major, the yellow, D major. Sibelius compose in absolute silence! For me, silence not so good. But I know the *vibrato* of note. Is physics, no?"

Jess leaned back, sighing audibly.

"My friend, Cappello," the musician from the Ukraine murmured, generous in his sympathy. "You will make pictures. How can you not? So the body *gets old*," he pinched his own cheek, the lined flesh reddening across his prominent bones. "So! Spirit not stop."

Jess wished he were as sure, but raised his wine glass anyway. He and Mikavlov toasted, to the opportunity that is youth, and the journey that is age. The old cellist smiled.

Sarah was sitting at the table, wrapped in her faded blue bathrobe nursing a late cup of coffee when Jess made his way back to the house.

Sarah said nothing at the lateness of the hour, but handed him a letter.

"I found this in the living room. Zoë and I don't get much mail from Venezuela."

Jess took the letter without looking and stuffed it in his shirt pocket.

"You don't read your mail?" Sarah pestered nosily, making Jess wonder, fleetingly, if she had. The suspicion made him fluster, and Sarah watched with that strange cat's expression all women wear when they seem to know exactly what you don't say. Too drunk on the Russian's good wine to engage her, Jess said nothing and Sarah's expression shifted. He understood, reading the bitterness on her face.

Tomorrow's audition.

Unexpectedly, he felt a little sorry for the fine doctor from London.

He put a hand on her shoulder. "Good night, Sarah."

Jess made his way up the stairs. Alone in the confines of the guest room, he threw open the window to admit the cool air and stood at the sill, taken aback by the raucous chorus of night birds calling from the trees. He felt a pang of homesickness. Tesuque nights were silent, broken only by the occasional coyote and the soft pad of running paws, a rustle in the bush.

He supposed Sarah blamed him for tomorrow's audition. He shrugged. Zoë was drawn to music like moth to flame. In the end, what could either of them do?

Jess yawned and undressed. He fell asleep to the sound of Sarah's footsteps, crossing back and forth the length of her rooms.

Magic Lantern

Mr. Bennett, Vermont, Paul Strand, 1944

The particular.

Mr. Bennett is a Yankee. Even to the bit of string, looped through the collar of his cloth coat. He stands before the rough planks of a barn, his cap perched squarely above homely ears, creased with age. Sparse white stubble pebbles his blunt chin, and watchful, melancholy eyes look you dead-on. There is the soft, regretful mouth, nonetheless set to endure. The photograph is a horizontal frame of the vertical human figure, unusual and odd.

Jess thinks of Mr. Bennett. *That,* he understands, is *me.*

Note from the Daybook:

Writers, painters, musicians—they carry across foreign borders the fundamental essence of what makes their art. The easel, the pen, the brush. They journey into new territory without loss of voice. But the image maker, in our obsession with the glance of life, our first love of the surface of things—we wander and are lost. We cannot be found, but in the particular.

My god, I need to go home.

Moses led Jess to a strange looking device.

"This is it, Mr. Cappello. This new baby delivers low-level, nonthermal, 689 nm light, exactly what's required to activate the therapy drug."

Sarah appeared in the doorway, carrying a green liquid I.V. in her hands.

"That the drug?"

Sarah nodded.

"Take a seat, Jess. I'll have Moses start the intravenous. The whole procedure shouldn't take more than an hour."

She was pale this morning, half-moons like smudges of soot under her eyes. But her tone remained clipped, and distant.

Jess eyed the I.V. solution as Moses searched for a vein. "How's it know where to go?"

Moses Rupa laughed. "You want the scientific spin? I guess you photographers like the technical stuff! Okay, this drug is a photosensitizer. You know what that means, it reacts to light. Once in the bloodstream, this green stuff attaches to molecules called lipoproteins. Why? Well, cells undergoing rapid proliferation produce more lipoproteins than normal cells do, so the drug moves quickly, in higher concentrations, to these bad boy cells."

Sarah settled behind the laser, tucking her hair behind her ears. Small diamond earrings winked beneath the overhead lights and Jess wondered that he had never seen the doctor wear jewelry before. Sarah looked right through him, obviously preoccupied.

Moses continued his monologue, the soothing flow of unintelligible terminology soothing Jess nerves.

"As soon as the drug collects in your retinas, Mr. Cappello, we'll activate it using the laser light in precise, calculated doses.

No heat, not with this laser–so no damage. Activated, the drug causes targeted cell death by disrupting normal cell functions. That's how we clot and eliminate the leaking vessels, without harming the good ones."

Sarah adjusted the chin rest for Jess, her hands cool on his cheek as she positioned his head. "It's quite innovative, really–a highly selective treatment. One that allows for re-treatment, if need be."

Sarah pinned Jess' digital images to the light box on the wall, studying the left macula.

"That's all I need to know, guys." Jess offered a wobbly grin. "First red, now green? You'll have me peeing a rainbow."

Moses chuckled, adjusting the flow of the I.V. "Say, what's that you're whistling? George Thorogood? I figured you for a blues man."

"Quiet now," Sarah warned.

Sarah was efficient behind the laser. At last, she released a long breath, pushing back from the machine and stretching. She glanced at Jess over the chin rest with a slight smile.

"That should do it. I've done my part for Jess Cappello fans the world over. Now, I've got to run."

She provided Moses with post-op instructions, collected her files and headed for a surgery scheduled at Stanford Medical. Minutes later, Jess was back at Sarah's cottage, sitting alone in the living room, the drapes drawn.

Light steps bounded up the porch, followed by the heavy thunk of something bumping the front door. Zoë slipped into the house, lugging her cello case. She looked at him in surprise.

"Back already? Whoa, you look like crap...though the eye patch is rather dashing."

"Last practice?"

"Yeah, but Mikavlov sent me home early," Zoë responded glumly, hauling her case to the living room. " Told me to play a game of tennis or something."

"Not a bad idea." Jess agreed, pulling a vial of medication out of his shirt pocket. "Do me a great favor and get a glass of water? I think I'll take these horse-sized Tylenol your Mom gave me. My head's killing me."

Zoë bounded into the kitchen and came back with a tall glass of water and a handful of biscuits. "Take these first," she ordered, handing him the biscuits. "Those pills are murder on an empty stomach."

Jess lip twitched, she sounded exactly like her mother.

Zoë watched as Jess bit into a biscuit, and downed two capsules.

"Everything go okay?"

"All I saw was stars. Now we wait."

Zoë grunted. "I hate waiting."

The teen wandered over to the end table and picked up a video, and then set it back down and picked up a paperback novel, and then set that down, too. She paced around the living room, pausing in front of the big window by Jess chair to push back a fold of drape and peer down the street. The only sound in the room was the soft ticking of the mantle clock.

"Jess?" Zoë turned around and faced him, her shoulders hunched. "I can't do it."

"What, Zoë?"

"This. The audition. I just can't." She clasped her hands together to stop their trembling and stared at him, ghastly white.

"Of course you can," Jess retorted immediately, taken aback. "You've played bigger audiences than this!" He was thinking of Davies Hall, the Dorothy Chandler Pavilion, all the mementos in Mikavlov's scrapbook. What was one private audition?

"No," she shook her head, her voice falling to a whisper. "Those were performances. This is an audition. I'm being judged, Jess."

He rubbed his temples, trying to think coherently under the thickening haze of painkillers. Okay, yes, there *was* a difference. It was hard taking your performance public, harder still to have it critiqued, thrashed by experts to exact degrees of dismemberment.

Jess held out a hand, pulling her nearer his chair.

"Make it just another performance," Jess soothed her gently. "Only this time, you're playing before an informed audience, musicians like yourself who will appreciate, truly, what you've learned, and know how hard what you're doing is! Not duffers like myself, buying tickets." He caught the flicker of a smile in her eyes, and nodded encouragingly. "Seriously, Zoë. These people *want* what you have to give. Just play your heart out for them!"

"But what if I don't make it, Jess? What if I'm not good enough? I don't know what Ill do if I don't make it." Her eyes were bright with unshed tears.

"Mikavlov thinks you're good enough."

Her fingers plucked at her shirt, twisting the rolled curls of J.S. Bach. Agitated, she brushed apart the drapes, flooding the room with harsh light.

Jess winced.

"Believe, Zoë. It's the thing you were meant to do."

"But Mum doesn't believe in me. She's furious, you know." She glanced over her shoulder, her face troubled. "Do you? Believe in me?"

"Absolutely, but it hardly matters, Zoë." For it was the truth. "You have to believe in yourself. Go after what feels important to *you*. We all do, even your mother."

Zoë sniffed.

"I'll tell you what, you make some kind of magic with that big fiddle of yours, kid. Enough to make a confirmed blues man like myself tune into a little Rock–whatever his name is."

Zoë giggled. "Rachmaninoff."

She perched on the arm of his chair and touched the edge of his eye patch worriedly. "If you feel all right, will you come, Jess? I mean, would you be at the audition for me?"

"Since you ask, wouldn't miss it for the world."

Zoë popped off the chair, her face a burst of sunshine.

"Maestro is picking me up at four-thirty. You can ride with us. But right now, I'm gotta bike over to the mall! I need a barrette to match my dress." She turned and dashed up the stairs, disappearing into her bedroom. "Get some rest!" she yelled downstairs, as from the recesses of her closet first one sandal, and then another, came flying into the hall.

The auditions were held in the large church on the corner of Hamilton and University. Afraid of arriving late, Mikavlov drove far too rapidly for Jess comfort. He wasn't at all used to navigating the world through one eye and everything came at him too suddenly, without depth of field, sending his brain in a spin. Jess grabbed the door handle of the little black Toyota as Mikavlov gunned through another yellow light.

Pulling up at the curb in front of the church, Mikavlov assisted Zoë, maneuvering her cello case out of his small trunk and handing out her satchel of music. Nervously the maestro ran his fingers through his unruly mane and glared at Zoë intently.

"Everything? You have everything?"

Zoë nodded, her face translucent, pale as a moth wing. She wore a long dress with a slim fitting bodice, supported by tiny straps in green nubby silk the color of new leaves. The dress belled wide enough to accommodate her cello. Jess thought she looked lovely. Grown up and yet sweet.

"Goot," Mikavlov nodded. He kissed her on the cheek. "I go and meet panel, make hellos and give them music. Let us see who they send to hear greatest young protégé of Alexei Mikavlov!"

Zoë turned the color of her dress, smiling weakly. Obediently she followed Mikavlov into the sanctuary, clutching her cello, refusing Jess offer to carry it for her. At the threshold, sunlight streamed through the patterned glass panels high in the triangular eaves. Rainbows of light spilled from every apex of the ceiling, washing the entire sanctuary in prismatic hues. The steel chandeliers reflected the pinpoint brilliance into yet more color, split into patterns, like pond ice cracking in the spring.

Jess and Zoë looked at each other in wonder.

Mikavlov hustled forward toward the center of the church, leaving the two of them waiting in the aisle. A young woman dressed in black slacks and a white blouse, bearing a clipboard in her arms, approached them, smiling brightly at Zoë.

"You must be Miss Harte-Valentine?"

The young woman introduced herself as Yvonne Carruthers, the audition secretary.

"I need a few things to complete your application, and then I'll show you to a practice room behind the sanctuary. You have ten minutes to warm up. The audition will be held out here, on that dais where the acoustics are best." She pointed toward the raised platform at the head of the sanctuary, and then to the panel of men sitting at a long table to the right. "You will be evaluated today by our school Head of Strings, the orchestra conductor, a member of the cello department, and a guest from the Guarneri Quartet, on tour this week in San Francisco."

The secretary seemed oblivious to the way Zoë shrunk at the word "evaluated". And the naming of individuals seemed to send the young musician further into the floor.

Yvonne Carruthers patted Zoë firmly on the shoulder. "You are a lucky young woman to command such an audition!"

Wordlessly Zoë turned to Jess, her eyes huge with fright.

He leaned near and whispered in her ear. "Heh, play for me. Remember the music store in Arizona? Make this beautiful light dance!"

Zoë trembled as the young assistant led her toward the back of the church. Her silk skirts swished against the sides of the pews as Jess watched her leave.

Sarah's painkillers had effectively banished the headache, but Jess felt oddly untethered, drifting in a disconnected haze that threatened to bury him if he didn't sit down. He chose a pew about four rows back. He hoped Zoë would see him there, but that he discreetly blended into the room. Other than themselves and the panelists, the church was empty.

Far back, behind closed doors, Jess could hear the faint sounds of Zoë running scales.

Mikavlov had stepped up on the dais, chatting with four men attired in dark shirts and sports coats despite the summer heat. The Russian laughed, and leaned across to clasp one of the men, a tall English looking fellow with a head shaped like a helmet, his silver hair cut in a bowl about the ears. Mikavlov grasped him in both arms, kissing him on the cheeks.

The Russian hustled back to Jess, pleased.

"Is goot for Zoë!" he exclaimed in a hush. "Best panel! I know head of section, I play concert with him many times, and also, cellist from Guarneri. And they, they know me," he beamed with modest pride, eyes sparkling. "Know my students."

He leaned closer to Jess. "Already sixteen heard today. Zoë last." His brows knitted conspiratorially. "Must be celli opening in school orchestra, or why would he--," Mikavlov thumbed in the direction of a portly bearded man, unwrapping a toffee, "why would he be here? Aschel Ruben is head of orchestra. I meet in Israel, 1982."

Mikavlov slipped off to spend a few minutes alone with Zoë, leaving Jess to ponder the panel of men arranging themselves and their papers, drinking water from small paper cups and restlessly plucking lint off their sleeves. So this was the inner circle, the monoliths who would, or would not, grant Zoë her wings. He fingered his eye patch. The judges looked worn from a full day of auditions.

In exactly ten minutes, Zoë and Mikavlov came forward into the luminous light, the maestro's hand resting on the shoulder of his pupil. He walked Zoë onto the platform, where she laid her cello on its side next to a wooden chair, and placed her bow and sheet music on the black metal music stand. Mikavlov accompanied Zoë to the judges' table, where she was introduced, and solemnly shook hands with each member of the panel.

Mikavlov gravely informed the panel of the solo selections Zoë had prepared, and the Foss Capriccio she would play with Wendy, whom Jess had not noticed arrive but was already poised at the keys of a black Yamaha grand piano, polishing her glasses. Jess overheard a member of the panel request a brief, sight-reading test of a section of a Saint Saens concerto, to which Zoë agreed nervously. And lastly, Mikavlov handed the panel the tape of Zoë playing in string quartet, yet another required competency.

All eyes turned toward Zoë.

Holding herself quite erect, she took her seat, arranging her skirts at her feet. She organized her music on the metal stand, but did not draw it close, and Jess realized she planned to play entirely from memory.

He held his breath, his stomach in knots. The kid had everything on the line, absolutely everything. And for the first time, Jess felt the full significance of Sarah's absence, the gulf between mother and daughter evidenced in the empty pews of the church. Zoë walked alone into her future, one Sarah should have shared. The doctor might not choose to let her daughter go, but go she would.

Zoë lifted her cello from the floor, slipped the peg into the stop and tucked the instrument deep into the silks of her skirt. Mikavlov bowed slightly, first to Zoë, and then to the panel, before he took the empty seat next to the farthest judge, his strong aquiline face stilled and confident.

One of the panelists looked up from his folder, and in a deep voice queried the room. "And who is the parent, or legal guardian for Miss Zoë Harte-Valentine? The Institute requires the signature of a parent or legal guardian on the audition record and release form."

He looked out into the empty church, and finally focused in on Jess.

"You, are you here to sign for this student?"

Alone at the center of the dais, Zoë froze in stunned dismay, her fingers clenched around her bow. She glanced in panic at Mikavlov, who half-rising from his chair, locked eyes with Jess. Neither of them was Zoë's legal guardian. They had not known, and were not prepared for this stupendous technicality.

Facing the panel, Jess reluctantly shook his head, fearing to look at Zoë.

The man cleared his throat with a slight, impatient growl that boded neither Zoë, nor Mikavlov well.

"No one is here for this student?" he demanded in disbelief, fingering his slim van Dyke. He frowned, before looking at Zoë and shrugging. "If no one is here to give permission, then I regret this audition is---"

"I'm here!"

A figure in a dark suit hustled forward through the empty pews. "*I*, Sarah Harte-Valentine, give permission for this audition."

Zoë, Mikavlov, and Jess swung around in complete astonishment, their eyes fixed on the flushed face of the woman at the foot of the dais, her cell phone and briefcase clutched to the front of her suit jacket. Sarah brushed the wind-tangled hair from her face, and addressed the panel of judges.

"I'm terribly sorry I'm late, I am. I had a complication in surgery, and traffic was horrendous across town. I am Dr. Sarah Harte-Valentine, Zoë Harte-Valentine's mother. *Please* let me sign these forms. I'll not delay the audition a moment further."

The panel looked solemnly at each other and nodded. One of them slid the clipboard over for Sarah's scribbled signature, and looked at Mikavlov with a satisfied nod. Sarah scrambled into the row of pews nearest Jess, slid in, and chucked her jacket and briefcase under her feet.

Zoë still did not seem to comprehend what had transpired. She squinted into the lights, staring in disbelief at Sarah, her bow pointed aimlessly toward the ceiling, the cello listing to the left. Making a soft sound of dismay, Sarah leaned forward over the back of the pew, and catching Zoë's eye, held up her index and middle fingers, tightly crossed.

The girl stirred in her chair, and then crossed her own two fingers secretly behind the neck of her cello. Mother and daughter shared a poignant, private smile.

"That's for luck," Sarah hissed, turning to Jess. "It was our sign when *Zoë* was little." Sarah's face burned with intensity, before she abruptly turned away and faced forward.

From across the room, the old Russian winked.

Zoë lifted her bow to the first notes of the Bach Suite, and Jess gave his faith to the artist up there alone, for all

233

he believed she could do. Almost as though lifting on small wings, Zoë wove into the prisms of light, filling the sanctuary with something sharp, pure, distinctive.

Apples. Jess smelled apples. Crisp, orchard apples, green in a yellow sun.

Diffraction

Siphnos, Greece, Henri Cartier-Bresson, 1961

L ine of sight.
The white heat of the Mediterranean sun blisters the village on the hill. A young girl races through the heat, darting through the shadows. She runs up the crumbling steps, her arms akimbo, dress flying from her knees. The image is a singular, arresting contradiction: the village, somnolent in the midday heat, and the wild, determined child plunging through the silence.

Henri Cartier-Bresson: *For me, photography is to place head, heart, and eye along the same line of sight --- it is a way of life.*

You find what you photograph.

Note from the Daybook:
Diffraction is the change in the path of light rays when they pass close to an opaque edge. Possibility...that any art based on light is less than truthful, entirely relative to space and object.

Light reveals object, or perhaps simply obstruction, and the degree to which light rays glance off the edges of things and bend around them, like minds to an idea, tells me the margin between object and perception.

Yesterday in the church I remembered the image by Bresson--the one of the village girl dashing up the stone steps. Such was my impression of Zoë on the audition stage, imprisoned by the most wondrous light, playing her cello as if nothing else mattered.

Is she not that girl on the stairs? Plunging through the alley, racing to a mysterious door? If Bresson had not made this image, I would have. We chase down life.

Still flushed with the exuberance of the Foss, Zoë shook hands with the panelists, alongside her maestro. She backed away as Mikavlov tarried behind to handle final details with the Curtis School judges. She was packing up her instrument when Wendy, closing the lid on the grand piano, came over to give the young teenager a fierce hug.

"Bravo, Zoë!" Wendy whispered with a soft twinkle in her eye. "And good luck!" She waved to Mikavlov and slipped quietly out the back.

Immediately, the efficient Miss Carruthers escorted the panelists from the sanctuary.

Sarah waited awkwardly at the end of the pew as Zoë trundled forward, pulling her cello case on its wheels, strangely bemused, her gaze dreamlike, content. The Maestro joined them, beaming proudly.

"I'll make pasta!" Sarah abruptly announced, wrapping her arm tightly around Zoë. "How about I pick up some of those yummy little cakes you like from the bakery on California Street?" She smiled bravely at her daughter. "Win, lose or draw, this calls for a celebration!"

Mikavlov shrugged genially. "Sure. Okay! You hungry, Zoë?"

She nodded.

Zoë rode with Alexei and Jess, while Sarah sped away in her Volvo for groceries. In the back of the car Zoë reclined against the headrest, subdued. Even Mikavlov seemed quiet.

When Sarah arrived back at the house, her arms loaded with vegetables and a pastry box tied with cotton string, she surveyed the three of them clustered tiredly at the kitchen table.

"Haven't lost your appetites, have you?" she demanded brightly. "This is a party, chums! Our Zoë finished her audition!"

The Russian patted the tired girl on the shoulder, and their eyes touched in acknowledgement. More than a year of work for a single, majestic moment on stage.

"I'm gonna change, Mum," Zoë sighed. "This dress is scratchy."

She climbed the stairs up to her room slowly, holding her skirt up high in her hand.

Sarah unloaded her supplies and began to rinse and chop vegetables at the sink. Motioning to Jess, she tossed over a garlic press.

"Sauté, if you would."

Obliging, he approached the stove and peeled a large garlic clove. He mashed the sharp, pungent juices into a sauté pan, added diced onions and finally, deli sausage. The pan sizzled as he stirred, still humming the punky melody of the *Capriccio*.

Mikavlov uncorked the bottle of Chianti and poured them each a glass. He held his up high.

"To the best," the Russian declared proudly.

Coming into the kitchen in her faded cut-offs and purple shirt imprinted with a measure of Beethoven's Ninth, Zoë blushed furiously.

Mikavlov bowed deeply to her.

"To the best cellist, best young lady, best..." he paused and cleared his throat roughly, "best young *friend I* have pleasure to know."

He tipped his glass to the thirteen year old and winked gravely.

Zoë deepened the color of a tomato, but her eyes sparkled with pleasure. She leaned over and tasted Sarah's wine, puckering as she made a face. And Mikavlov chuckled as his protégé yanked open the refrigerator door and pulled out a root beer instead.

"Here's to us all," Zoë said.

Jess handed Sarah her wine. The small kitchen filled with tantalizing smells.

The mood became festive and lively, Sarah pouring readily from the bottle of Chianti. Half-listening to Mikavlov and Zoë rehash the audition, Jess pondered the events of the last few hours. He sneaked a glance at Zoë, sprawled in her chair, her bare feet propped up on the edge of the table. Hard to believe it was the same kid. For over an hour the girl had played her heart out before a panel of stone-faced men, who did no more than nod or murmur amongst themselves. And even though the results of her audition had not been announced, the teen seemed tranquil, unconcerned.

He understood. Still, he marveled at the self-possession of this youngster who cast the dice so firmly, who breathed and laughed as number sixes spun and spun on their corners. Oddly, it was Sarah who seemed the most anxious, her smile over-bright.

"Alexei?" Sarah asked as she scooped red and yellow peppers from the chopping board into Jess' sauté pan. "When will we hear from the school?"

The Russian leaned back in his chair. He glanced at Zoë, twiddling with the braid of a multicolored lanyard she was weaving. She raised her head and fixed passive green eyes on her teacher.

"Soon, I think," the maestro's gray head bobbed quickly, his eyebrows scooped to hopeful dashes. "We are fortunate to come at end of audition, I think. All have been heard. Most," he patted the air lightly with his hand, "will take many weeks to decide. Not so for us." He smiled benignly at his pupil with happy tiredness.

Sarah stirred the sauce, adding in diced tomatoes and mushrooms. Steam billowed from the nearby pasta kettle. She peeked into the pot, increasing the heat to a boil.

Jess moved out of Sarah's way, leaning comfortably against the cabinet drawers as he sipped his wine. Good enough in its way, but lacking the simple satisfaction of a cold, bitter beer. Jess rolled up the cuffs of his flax-colored shirt, opening the buttons at the neck.

"Anyone mind?" he asked, and pulled open the back door, grateful for the evening air. The scents of honeysuckle and star-jasmine mingled with Italian herbs.

"It was good wasn't it? The audition, I mean?" Sarah looked over her shoulder at Mikavlov and Zoë, braiding the lanyard. "I mean really *quite* good?"

Zoë shrugged, not taking her eyes off her intricate finger work. "I lost my fingering at the mezzo movement in the Foss for a second. Thank God Wendy heard me. She held her next measure."

Alexei Mikavlov placed his light, graceful hand over hers.

"No, Zoë," he shook his head, smiling. "Your best on the Bach I think, and the Foss...it was huge! A true sound, yes." Wine had loosened the Russian's 'r's and his expression crinkled with pleasure.

Zoë put down her braiding, crossing to the stove and sniffing appreciatively over the pan of simmering sauce.

"Set the table, Wonder Girl," Sarah prompted, lugging the boiling pasta toward the sink.

Jess hid a smile as Zoë carted plates to the table, marveling at the transition from mercurial teenager to self-assured young woman on the audition stage. She bent like light around life. And here she was now, padding about the kitchen in her bare feet, cradling dinner plates with the same grace with which she played the violoncello.

Jess impulsively set his glass down and excused himself, disappearing upstairs. A second later he slipped back into the kitchen, the Contax SLR clasped in his hands. He ignored Sarah's surprised look and addressed the two musicians.

"Could I bother you two for an image?" he asked directly. "I'd like one of the two of you, together. A practice pose like the other night."

"Jess! The eye patch!" Sarah barked with alarm.

"Won't nudge it, promise."

"But dinner...."

"Let it simmer," Jess countered impatiently.

Mikavlov glanced at Zoë, who grinned back.

Jess set up the shot in the living room, re-directing the overhead track lights to imitate a semblance of studio lighting. He sat Zoë down in her practice chair holding her cello, bow in hand, and then directed Mikavlov to stand a few feet behind her, his face turned in profile, hand clasped about his chin as if listening.

"Okay. This works," Jess muttered, checking his light meter and exposure, squinting with his right eye. "Now Zoë, just play! Alexei, you listen, or do whatever you do. Engage with Zoë as you would in practice."

Zoë looked at Jess, her eyes wide in consternation. "But Jess, what should I play?"

"Well, anything! How about that little Rachmaninoff from Arizona?"

Zoë shot a grin at the maestro. "The *Vocalise*? We recorded that on the chamber tape!"

Alexei Mikavlov nodded.

Sarah wandered in from the kitchen, her hands buried in a blue-striped kitchen towel. A sheen of perspiration shone on her face and she pushed her hair back irritably.

Jess held up a finger. "Just a sec, Sarah. I promise."

Zoë glanced at her mother and began to play a little self-consciously, while Mikavlov stood fixed in his pose like a post. Jess said nothing, letting the two grow gradually absorbed in the music, forgetting the camera. Zoë danced into the open, romantic melody of the piece, and Alexei fell to listening, his eyes half-closed, foot tapping imperceptibly. Jess pressed the shutter. Three, four times more. The little piece ended and Zoë looked up, exuberant and flushed. Jess pressed the shutter again.

"Are you done? Should I play something else? That was fun!"

Alexei Mikavlov patted his pupil on the shoulder. "You play, I pose. Not so hard for me, I think."

Jess laughed and replaced the lens cover.

"All done, and thanks."

He had gotten a great image. He knew it! Mikavlov half in the shadow, his great aquiline beak a dark silhouette behind Zoë, his face absorbed and distracted as he listened. And the girl, tucked in close about her cello with one small hand curled about the neck of her instrument, the bow in flight across the strings. The two faces of music Jess intuited, deeply excited. The listening self, lost in an inner song, contrasted with the body at play, the physical, musical dance.

"Well pasta everyone." Sarah interrupted firmly, shepherding the three back to the kitchen and their places at the table.

She bustled about, setting out a deep tureen of sauce, thrusting a wooden bowl of greens into Jess hands, instructing him to serve the table. He did so, still preoccupied with thoughts of the photograph.

They sat down to their meal, the four of them.

"This is quite something, Sarah," Jess commented appreciatively. Alexei grunted in agreement, his napkin already tucked in at his neck.

"As Zoë will tell you, I do two basics. Pasta, and an English Christmas feast with plum pudding." She poured more wine before taking her seat. "Red taught me the pasta."

Zoë forked in a mouthful of spaghetti, eyeing her mother in surprise.

"And, I have a toast to make," Sarah declared solemnly, lifting her goblet. Her voice, softened by wine, had rumpled down to a charming slur. "First, to my daughter, who made me so very proud today. May all your dreams come true!"

Sarah held her daughter's gaze before she faced Alexei, and then, Jess. Her voice toughened, "And for those of you who suppose I *never* believed in Zoë, well, you're wrong! I always believed. That's the terror of it...."

Zoë leaned forward in fascination, a streak of sauce smudged at the corner of her mouth, her fork poised over her dish.

"I never doubted you for a moment, baby. Never," Sarah confessed. "But this talent. It's so big. You are first of all *mine*, not the world's."

She shook her head. "How could I live without you, baby?" Her face twisted in a sad, soft smile. "It's always been just the two of us. But Jess made me see how selfish I've been."

Jess cleared his throat, but Sarah threw up a hand.

"No, I *was* wrong, Jess. Selfish and stupid." She shook her head in pained embarrassment. "I can't force it out of her, can't make her into something she's not. I won't delude myself any longer that doing so would benefit anyone but me."

The maestro had put his glass down to listen, and laced his fingers together over his plate.

Zoë's eyes flicked back to her mother nervously.

"Maestro Mikavlov," Sarah sighed, placing both hands solemnly on the table. "It is to you I owe the biggest apology of all. I...." Finally she glared at the table in annoyance, her cheeks flaming. "I guess that's all."

She picked up her wine and slugged the contents down, wiping her lips primly with one finger.

Mikavlov reached across the table and patted Sarah's hand.

"Zoë, she play with exuberant heart today. You hear this? There is much freedom, much joy in how she plays this day. This too, judges hear." He studied the rim of his glass. Then he looked up at Sarah, his eyes inscrutable. "Zoë plays for you, Mrs. Doctor."

Sarah's face glowed with the tribute.

Zoë slunk down in her chair, close to disappearing under the table with embarrassment. She stuck the tip of her tongue out, draping her napkin over her face dramatically.

Jess leaned sideways. "Learn to live with it, kiddo. You can't duck just praise."

Zoë dug into her pasta, firmly ignoring them all.

The meal finished around talk of the Institute, and the music history of Philadelphia. No one mentioned Jess eye, and except for the itch of the eye-patch, he had pretty much forgotten it himself. Tomorrow the patch would come off and he'd catalog his own initial assessment; thumbs up, or thumbs down.

"Coffee anyone?" Sarah asked, laying down her napkin.

"Count me out," her daughter yawned. "I'm wiped. 'Night everyone."

Kissing everyone quickly on the cheek, Zoë hopped the stairs to her room two at a time, a teen video tucked under her arm.

After clearing the table, the men washed the dishes.

Mikavlov turned to Jess, his hands deep in the soapy water. "This picture over desk in hall, this is yours, yes?"

"Yes, Alexei," Sarah answered for Jess. She lingered at the table, her feet up on a chair.

"I think is quite goot," Mikavlov nodded approvingly.

"But who is the woman, Jess?" Sarah mused, finishing her last glass of wine. "I've always wondered, you know. You can't tell anything about her from the back. Not her age, or anything, although she certainly appears rather exotic."

Jess methodically stacked the dry plates to one side.

"A good friend of mine. A painter," he finally muttered. "She sometimes modeled for me."

"Interesting pose," Alexei murmured, draining the water from the sink. "To be seated at open window, without clothes, and much snow! Cold, yes?" His hands cupped imaginary breasts, and he shivered. His eyes twinkled as he drained the last of the Chianti bottle into his glass.

He sat down next to Sarah.

She was staring fixedly at Jess. "She wouldn't be *Venezuela*, would she, Jess?"

He stiffened.

Sarah clucked her tongue against her teeth, shaking her head over her wine. "Ah, the mystery woman. Why Jess, you *do* have a personal life after all! Zoë and I were beginning to believe that dog of yours was the sole love of your life."

Half-drunk, Mikavlov grunted something prosaic under his breath. He tilted his head back and glanced at the ceiling, as if addressing the muses.

"Very romantic, yes? Only art or only woman, what matter?"

Sarah laughed, hiccupping with delight.

Jess threw down the towel, nodding brusquely.

"You two will have to excuse me. I'm beat."

Sarah grinned wolfishly and Jess unaccountably feared the bold, uncontained gleam in her eye.

"Turned her back on you, did she? Li-literally!" she giggled callously, still hiccupping. "Ah, romance *is* rather messy. Everything should be kept at the pr-pr-proper distance. Depth of f-field, I'd say." Her laugh rang out. "At least I gave things a proper fight with Red...s'truth."

She plucked away a strand of hair caught in the corner of her mouth, gazing at Jess pityingly. "You ought to read Venezuela's letters, Mister Photographer. You ought to, you know, try life *in front of* the lens."

"Butt out, Sarah!" Jess responded curtly.

Mikavlov shrugged, politely averting his gaze.

"Well, what are you running from?" Sarah countered. "What's *Venezuela* to you?"

"Nothing, damn it!" he snapped, regretting having given her the satisfaction of an answer.

Mikavlov ran his hand down the side of his cheek, sighing philosophically.

"Time to go, I think," he muttered tactfully to no one in particular. "I call soon as I hear from school."

He stood up. "Good night, friends. *Spasebo*. Thank you for dinner!"

Sarah followed Mikavlov to the front door, where they exchanged a few murmured words on the doorstep before Mikavlov drove away.

Jess had escaped halfway up the stairs to the guest room before Sarah called out after him.

"Jess! Do you know why I bought that particular photograph?"

He hesitated on the step before he swung around, his face set.

"No, Sarah. Why?"

"Because it was so sad," she whispered, her voice falling, barely reaching him where he stood. "Because it's all about love, and so much distance."

She approached the bottom of the stairs, her hand resting on the newel post as she gazed up at him.

"You're still trapped there, aren't you?"

"You can't grasp the moon."

"But you *can* catch the light," she rebuked solemnly as he turned away. "Yes. You can, Jess."

Gradient Light

Her and her shadow, Imogen Cunningham, 1936

The gravity of the body.

A nude lies on her back, reclining away from the viewer, the breasts and ribs and thigh rendered as landscape. The form, and the form's shadow, a vigorous bodyscape of the gravid beauty of earth. The familiar and simple subtracted from the nude, and recombined in the language of shadow and gradient light.

Jess recalled only one encounter with Imogen Cunningham in San Francisco, a decade before her death in 1976. It was chance, certainly, and unforgettable. *Her and Her Shadow*, the famous Cunningham's imprimatur, stamped forever on his young soul.

Jess had been moonlighting from a photography workshop, making a few bucks as a barman at a society fundraiser at the San Francisco Museum of Modern Art. Cunningham, the guest of honor, and without question the Grand Dame of West Coast photography, held court somewhere in the room, answering questions about her work. Jess circled about in his

247

borrowed suit, a tray of drinks in his hand, soaking up the rich and surprising works presented at the auction.

He stopped before a matted image displayed on a small easel, coincidentally paired up next to a tiny, turtle-like woman in whose wrinkled face were imbedded two pebbly eyes. The old woman hunched before the easel, peering over the rim of her large glasses, her face inches from the selenium image. The photograph was of a large shell, one of Weston's Jess suspected, although he couldn't determine for sure as the woman blocked most of the photograph from view.

"Damn good job of copying," the aged socialite spit from the corner of her mouth.

"Excuse me?" Jess stammered. He shifted his tray of drinks to one side to avoid clipping the lady as she straightened up.

"*I* did shells. Long before Edward," she grumbled in disgust. "Leave it to him to make even *that* natural object erotic."

Jess offered a wobbly smile, unconvinced this crabby dame had anything to do with photography.

"Who are you, Ma'am?" he inquired politely.

The old woman flashed him a disgruntled, sour look. "Never you mind. Suppose you photograph, too! Cameras hanging off people like zippers. Well just remember young man, everything in nature is connected by a common beauty. And that has nothing to do with lust!"

With a searing look that brooked no rebuttal, she marched across the room, disappearing into the crowd. Only much later, when three early works including *Her and Her Shadow* fetched the highest bids of any offered at the auction, did Jess realize he had been standing by none other than Imogen Cunningham herself.

The only other person to make the seashell famous!

He never forgot the irascible photographer's words. It became a thread between them that resonated years later, when critics routinely commented of Jess work, "*This emerging artist explores elements of interconnectivity...he reaches for a common language of symbol and content, seemingly independent of object".*

Jess had discovered his theme in the relationship of the nude and her shadow.

Note from the Daybook:
I have met a child of genuine gift. The rest of us lesser gods all.

The hour was early. Jess had slept poorly, and he awoke before the dawn, searching for something to read on Sarah's bookshelf before finally settling on a slim volume of poetry. Bravo poetry, the steadfast soldier in the empty hours. After browsing restlessly for a half hour, Jess replaced the book on the shelf and dressed silently. He focused on the digital clock, testing his vision. His good right eye registered five-thirty on the dial; his left, a Salvador Dali five, melted and folded over onto a sideways three.

He tucked in his shirt and put the eye patch in his pocket.

Coming down the stairs, he was rather surprised to find Sarah sitting in the kitchen in her blue robe, nursing her perennial cup of coffee. The doctor looked like a train wreck, her hair in a clumpy tangle.

She looked up as Jess entered and smiled wanly. "Early riser?"

Absently scratching the stubble on his chin, Jess poured himself a cup of coffee and headed out the back of the kitchen into the chill morning air of the garden. He wasn't ready to face Sarah. To be truthful, the way she had come after him the night before had hurt. He paused beneath the climbing roses, breathing deeply of their brazen, dime-store perfume, awash in sudden memories of Kentucky, and the red, red roses that climbed his mother's porch.

Sarah padded out behind him and shivered, inching her feet deeper into her wool mules as she sat down at the iron table. For a few moments she said nothing, then she grimaced slightly, delicately itching her brow with a nail.

"Mikavlov called after you went upstairs last night. The committee called."

Jess sipped his coffee.

"They accepted Zoë."

Jess half-turned his head. "Congratulations! I thought they would."

Sarah nodded, distracted. "Yes...but the offer is contingent on satisfactory living arrangements. The school administration requires minors to live with a parent or guardian. They want to know Zoë's planned arrangements."

"And those would be?"

"I don't know," Sarah confessed. "If I go with her, I must completely rethink my practice and my position here. Honestly, find a home and work in Philadelphia? I haven't even considered it! If I don't go with her, then Zoë must live with Red's sister and her husband, and we hardly know them."

Jess set his empty cup on the small table, gazing at Sarah thoughtfully. He waited. The gray morning light had brightened by degrees to a band of silver above the roofline of the cottage. Upstairs the lights in Zoë's room were dark.

Sarah curled forward in her chair, moaning. "What do I do?"

"How would I know, Sarah? Figure out how you feel."

"Oh, like you do?"

"Why is what I do so important to you?"

"Because," Sarah pulled her robe around her irritably, "it would be damn nice if *one* of us made the right choice."

"Stop feeling sorry for yourself and move on to Plan B, whatever that is, Doc. A surgeon of your reputation should be able to find a position or a practice in Philly. So go! Or don't, and be glad Zoë has family to pick up where you leave off."

Sarah gripped her coffee mug tightly. "You're awfully harsh," she stuttered under her breath.

"Those are the facts, Sarah."

"Jess, I'm forty-seven years old! Change comes at a cost."

"Try sixty-three. And it comes, like it or not."

Suddenly tired of the conversation, tired of everything, Jess stood up.

"Why don't you ask Zoë what she'd like? She's a smart girl. But what she doesn't know is what's more important to you, being her mother, or being Doctor Harte-Valentine."

Sarah clenched her fists and buried them in the pockets of her robe. Leaving the cups on the table, she marched up the back steps and disappeared inside the house.

Jess returned from his walk an hour later, and found Sarah waiting for him in the living room. She had already showered and changed into tan slacks and a striped green shirt, her hair held back from her forehead with a leather headband. Despite the carefully applied make-up, she appeared distraught and visibly middle-aged.

Jess sidestepped around her and headed up the stairs.

"Jess--"

"No wait, *I'm* sorry, Sarah."

He faced her.

"Odd, but you and I apologize more to each other than we say hello. But you've done what you could for me, and I thank you for it."

"But Jess, that's what I'm trying to tell you," Sarah interrupted impatiently. "We need to do an Amsler this morning. I need to map out the immediate effects of the therapy. Another angiography will be due in six weeks to establish the treatment's overall effectiveness, and if necessary," she added determinedly, "we zap them again."

"This is absolutely necessary?"

"Don't you want to know if it worked?"

"It hasn't," Jess declared pensively. "The blur's still there."

Sarah gripped his forearm and pulled him back down the step. "That's a false conclusion, Cappello!" she berated, pushing him toward the kitchen. "Improvements are subtle at first. It takes time for the body to reabsorb the destroyed blood vessels, and for the retina to lie smooth again. It's far too soon to judge!"

Jess yielded to her bullying, and slumped down at the kitchen table with a sigh. In front of him Sarah had arranged another Amsler grid. He reached into his shirt pocket and retrieved his eye patch.

"Where's Zoë? She up yet?" He asked offhandedly.

"No, still sleeping. She's exhausted. Mikavlov tells me she has a full summer schedule ahead of her with the youth symphony, and the Carmel Bach Festival is penciled in. I confess I had no idea." She concentrated, refitting the eye patch over Jess' untreated eye, blocking his vision.

She slid over the grid.

"Okay. I want you to mark any area of blur or distortion that you see on the grid. Here's the pencil. Be as precise as you can, Jess, it's important."

She took a seat opposite him and waited.

Jess squinted at the grid, located the point of the pencil near the center of the graph and began to outline a shape about the size of a hazel nut. He rested his eye, before slightly reshaping the marks on the graph paper.

"There," he grunted, and peeled off the eye patch.

Sarah took the grid. She compared it to the previous one, spread out on the table in front of her.

"Well?" Jess demanded.

Sarah looked up too quickly, her smile wavering.

"Better!" she enthused. "This area here," she pointed to a corner on the second grid, "seems to have shrunk, and the upper far left has pulled into just this clump near the center." She placed the two grids side by side. "See the difference?"

He studied them before he nodded, and leaned back in his chair.

Sarah leaned forward across the table, eyeing Jess intently.

"Remember, any improvement, however slight, is a step in the right direction. We've surely arrested the neovascularization, and possibly prevented further damage. It's likely you'll stabilize."

"Sarah," Jess inquired slowly, detached. "Do you believe in God?"

She sat back, obviously nonplussed. Then after a moment she shrugged. "Well, I suppose I do," she responded uncomfortably, her tone cautious.

Jess traced the shape on the Amsler grid with a gnarled forefinger. Over and over his finger ran the connected lines. He could almost feel on his skin the shape of his loss. He stopped abruptly and rested the flat of his hand over the mark on the grid, meeting the doctor's puzzled frown.

"God's thumbprint."

Sarah looked at the grid completely confused.

"God's own thumbprint," Jess muttered. "The mark of one man's destiny, Doctor. All the tragedies and failures that have encompassed a life, my life. There it is you see? God's calling card. Smack on a grid for all to see."

Sarah blinked. "It's a clump of blood vessels, Jess, not religious theory."

"Think so? God holds a full house. The big guy wins."

"You think random circumstance is some kind of religious sign of damnation? The great seal of judgment?"

Jess laughed soundlessly. "Maybe. I surely do know what it is to be damned."

"Don't be ridiculous!" Sarah sputtered incredulously.

She pushed away from the table and walked briskly into the living room, returning with the framed image of *Snowbank* gripped tightly in her hands. She thrust the picture under Jess nose.

" Look!" she ordered. "Look at it. *That* is God's thumbprint! Your *talent.*"

Jess averted his face, refusing to look at his own work.

"Promise me you'll commit to the follow-up angiography," Sarah persisted.

He shook his head. "No, Sarah. I won't be coming back."

"You have to, Jess!" She burst out, alarmed. She stepped closer, the photograph forgotten and unnoticed in her hands.

"Let me live with what I've got," Jess sighed heavily, glancing sternly at her. "Let it be."

"But, Jess--" Sarah objected, nearly speechless with frustration. "You have to be re-checked, at least once a year! At least commit to that," she pleaded.

Jess smiled gently. The Englishwoman quite honestly cared.

"I'll call if I notice any changes, Sarah."

He shoved back from the table, whacking his shin on the table leg. He winced, rubbing the injury absently.

"I'm going to collect my things. And if I didn't adequately say so before, thanks."

Aperture

Olive Grove at Hidden Villa, Jess Cappello, 1998

Time stands still.

The image is a small sepia print of washed copper tones, taken in an olive grove several hundred years old. The black tree trunks, smooth and skeletal, flow toward the sky as though a forest of kelp, floating toward the light. The ground is a carpet of silver leaves, and amongst the standing trees, a fallen trunk, split and ruined. The image is haunting, peaceful, and oddly sacred. Far back in the tunnel of trees, a fox watches.

Only Jess knows he is there.

Note from the Daybook:
There is no entry.

Sarah and Zoë stood entwined on the sidewalk, watching in mute regret as Jess threw in the last of his gear and locked down the box in the truck bed. He worked silently, quickly, not looking at the pair. Finished, he grabbed his thermos of coffee from Sarah with nod, and straightened his shoulders, and turned to say his goodbyes.

"Good luck in Philadelphia, Zoë," Jess said sincerely to the girl. "I suspect one of these days I'll be hearing your name at Carnegie Hall." He made an effort to smile, but Zoë would have none of it. She flung herself into his arms and hugged him tightly.

"Jess, don't go," she begged, her voice muffled in his shirt.

Jess lifted a hand and stroked her spiky red hair, his face pained. "Got to. We're going different places, Zoë. And besides, I'm far too old to audition on the ukulele."

He heard her giggle into his shirt. He pulled away and Sarah stepped up. She wrapped an arm around her daughter's shoulders gently.

Jess touched a fingertip to his forehead gravely. A slow salute.

"Job well done, Doc. Don't blame yourself for your patient's mule-headedness."

Sarah smiled tightly, her eyes troubled.

"I wish you'd reconsider, Jess."

He opened the truck door, slid onto the seat, and placed the thermos at his side. As he started the engine, Sarah let go of her daughter, and stepped forward. She gripped the door before Jess could shut it.

"Remember what I said, Jess. Don't confuse mere circumstance with gift."

He tugged the door from Sarah's fingers and shut it firmly, then rolled down the window and leaned out.

"Send a Christmas card, you two."

"Give Ansel a big treat, Jess," Zoë called.

He waved, and disappeared back inside the cab as the truck rumbled away from the curb.

Zoë and Sarah stood on the sidewalk, watching as the old pickup lumbered down Tennyson Lane, made a right at the corner, and vanished. Zoë lifted her face to her mother.

"What's he going to do, Mum?"

Sarah shook her head. "I don't know, baby. I just don't know."

Together they turned back toward the house and climbed the steps, Zoë tucked into the shoulder of her mother.

"Well, kiddo," Sarah changed tacks, as they looked back one more time down the empty street. "We need to call the Curtis people and get the names of some decent neighborhoods near the school. I was thinking of an old brownstone, like my Mum and Dad had. You know, an upstairs-downstairs arrangement, so you could practice without bothering the neighbors..."

Deep in the cool night, Jess crossed the empty wastes of Death Valley. He nursed a cup of coffee as he drove the empty highway, the truck's high beams illuminating the occasional jackrabbit and tumbleweed crisscrossing the road. His eyes ached with concentration: behind the wheel ten hours already, and at least fourteen to go. Leaning over the rim of the window, Jess let the warm desert air wick the sweat off his neck. Waves of blistering air feathered his skin as he attempted to stay awake.

He fiddled with the radio dial as the reception spit and sputtered out of range, and then unexpectedly caught a classical station out of Los Angeles, deciding to let the muted symphony occupy the long, empty drive. The pickup chugged alongside massive eighteen-wheelers, past the occasional exit signs to towns huddled in clusters of lights against the black sands. On and on he drove, the engine pegged at a steady fifty-five, his eyes dwelling in the incredible brilliance of the night sky. The stars were chips of quartz, he thought, embedded in an obsidian night.

The radio music was a melancholy piece, almost as painful in its beauty as his first impression of *Moonrise,* and oddly enough, a cello solo.

Faure, the radio announcer said as it ended, *Lamento.*

Even in the blackness, he could feel the earth cracked open like a baked potato.

He thought of his mother some, how she liked to sing in the kitchen, and make an apple tart on Sundays. How they always said her name "Han-*naw*", and she'd correct them, wearing on her face such a look of pained particularity they laughed, knowing how she hated their country accents. He remembered that they always wore the same shoes until the Thanksgiving Day department store sales, when she would flip their old, scuffed ones in the trash, and treat herself and the boys to a new pair.

He thought of Louis back when he was young, and how he could crack a bat lengthwise from the middle to the end hitting a baseball past the reservoir fence. And how Louis could twist his arm so hard he'd cry, his brother conversing in a pleasant tone of voice with their mother in the other room, twisting and twisting. He thought of Louis coming home in a box, sealed with tape. Aunt Shelby burying the box under the flowering crabapple in her back yard because they couldn't afford a proper burial, and she knew Hannah would not want her boy in a military cemetery, one pebble more in a wide beach of white, nameless stones.

Jess twisted open the thermos and refilled his coffee cup, listening to the hum of the tires as he steered with one finger and leaned back in the worn seat. He'd never really figured out why Gianni took the same lunch every day into the mines. The same damn sandwich of fried Spam and catsup, a twist of jerky and two pickles.

If that prison scuffle hadn't killed him, Jess was pretty sure the mines would have. Every night he'd hear the old man coughing upstairs in the bedroom. That dry, musty cough, drawn deep from the lungs, the miner's ailment. Doubled over until the old man coughed up enough to spit, and grow quiet.

All the other Cappello brothers he knew of had been miners: tough, illiterate, violent, and short-lived.

All dead, and nobody sorry.

How long he'd been on his own, he thought, emptying the thermos cup. More years now than he'd been part of his own family. But never enough years to forget the family, although he often wished he could.

He didn't dwell much on the thing with his eyes. There was no need for it. He understood, finally. He'd gotten at the truth, and in an odd, tranquil way, the facts tempered the loss, bore regret down the road even as the mountains of California fell away to the desert, and beyond, waited the pines of the Continental Rockies. Peace settled his brain, his thoughts shaped with tiredness, giving everything to the simple essence of the journey.

As the hours passed, he thought of Zoë occasionally, wondering if Sarah would ever understand the nature of the girl's genius. Zoë's life would never be customary, but bent to the demands of a talent so extraordinary there would be little room for anything minor. The vine of such a gift might be tenacious, but the flower was fragile. She couldn't survive on her own. Sarah was exactly what Zoë needed. He shook his head. He hoped she'd do the right thing. The English doctor could be tough as nails, a damn stalwart lattice her daughter could cleave to.

Jess caught a shooting star leap the horizon.

Why hand a small human being a destiny lit from one end like a roman candle? Burns *and* brilliance, why both?

He considered Sarah Harte-Valentine then, amusing himself with images of her frozen, aggrieved expressions, and her odd, bullying way. He wished he'd had a chance to photograph Sarah. What would have stepped from that image, the cool, professional surgeon, or the embattled, fearful mother? Red's jilted lover, perhaps? In the end, the thing he would associate with her the most, was the way she'd stitched up Ansel. There was genuine kindness there.

Halfway through the desert, his radio reception faltered for good and he lost Los Angeles. The station settled into a hissing buzz and Jess shut it off. The silence in the truck good company with the empty night. And after a time, he found himself humming something.

What was it? That little piece of Zoë's, he realized, the Rachmaninoff. He smiled in the dark. Astounding how the universe could rearrange itself in a few short weeks.

Ahead of him he could see the orange glow of Barstow in the distance, and beyond, the dark outline of distant peaks.

Jess reached into his shirt pocket and pulled out a creased envelope. He turned it over and glanced again at the spidery handwriting on the address, the colorful stamps from Venezuela. He had not opened the envelope nor read its contents, although he had thought he would. Now he just squinted at the paper in his fingers, absorbing the outmost shape of her hand, divining what thoughts she held of him as she traced the letters of his name. There wasn't much he could identify in the dim light of the instrument panel, but it was all, every bit of it, desperately familiar. Catalina's handwriting was a familiar conversation, somehow even carried the clean-earth scent of her skin, the careless way she would toss her hair and laugh. She was all there. Whispering to him, laughing.

Shifting his body to hold the wheel steady with his knees, Jess roughly tore the letter into tiny shreds. He scooped the scraps from his lap and drizzled the pieces out the open window. He flew down the highway, bits of paper whirling in the wake of the truck.

A desert snow, a beautiful confetti of abandoned love.

Provenance

U Buy U Sell bulletin board, Mike's Market, Santa Fe.

Post date August 7, 2000.
Lowel Tota-lights (2 avail. with filter frames) $75ea, Lowel VIP Pro lights with lamps, barn doors and scrims (2 avail) $175ea, Lowel Grips (set of 3 for $75) Lowel Light stands (set of 6 for $300) New FDN lamps (set of 5 $40) New GCA lamps (set of 3 $35) New DYS lamps (set of 3 $25) 40" round folding gold/white reflector with case $35, Lowel umbrella $50, Cardilini clamps (set of 6 for $150) Closing studio due to eye disease.

Abe Santos stood in the doorway of Jess studio, surveying the room in surprise, Ansel's leash dangling from his hand.

"Lord, what happened here?"

Jess looked up from an opened portfolio box spread across stacks of similar, dusty boxes he had hauled out of the attic. He grunted, shrugging at the mess.

"Abe. Didn't expect to see you here. Grab a beer from the frig."

Abe returned with two, handing one cold, tall-neck bottle over the stacks of matted prints to Jess.

"What gives? You spring cleaning?" Abe pulled out a stool from under the work table and propped himself against the wall. He swiped his forehead with his ball cap. It was a blistering August afternoon, and sweltering inside the small room, even with the windows pulled open to draw in the stir of breeze off the cottonwoods.

"Seems like it," Jess acknowledged, taking a long drink of beer. "Haven't organized this stuff in years—just threw it in the boxes. Damn if *View Camera* magazine didn't call, asking for a print of mine they ran back in '91. Can't find it."

"Well, I ain't helping," Abe grinned sourly. "I just finished the garage for Carly. One genuine horror," he shook his head. "Hadn't realized we'd painted the house so many different colors—must've unearthed thirteen cans of Benjamin Fuller."

"Your house is white."

"Yeah. Now it is."

Abe angled his neck to get a better look at the date on one of the stacked archival boxes. *1967.* "Shoot, Jess. These are ancient history. This stuff oughta go to the Art Center for storage, or one of those museums. Don't they hound you for this stuff? I'd call UPS, man."

Jess snorted, edging several cartons aside with the toe of his boot to make a space to sit on the bare floor. "Not labeled 'stuff' they don't."

"I can see it now—*Retrospective II, The Scrapbook.*"

"This isn't your Grandma's photo tin."

Jess returned to sorting through the matted prints, sliding some into protective sleeves, inexplicably tossing other prints into a wood crate. Abe reached over and retrieved the last toss-off, a portrait of a portly New York cop staring down at a vagrant huddled in the doorway of a brick building. Abe examined the print, nursing his beer.

He considered the events of the past few months. Jess had been home a week before they'd known of it–he and Carly startled to see the photographer knocking at the door one night, come by for Ansel. Since then, Jess had kept to himself, until finally, Abe had driven over on the pretext of returning the dog's leash.

"This print's good. Why toss it?" he asked. The image had the haunting tonal clarity that was Jess trademark. It puzzled Abe that Jess had not made more portraits, choosing instead the less personal landscape. This particular photograph had legs—between the suspicious cop and the surly vagrant lay a glimpse of stark, unsentimental empathy, a picture with a dialog all its own. Why discard good work?

"Old. Inferior. Trite." Jess spoke without looking up from his task, using his box cutter to slit open the seal on another box.

Abe studied Jess from under the brim of his cap. His friend had lost weight, what little he had to pad his skeletal frame, and had either stopped shaving entirely, or intended an eventual beard, for his cheeks and chin were bristled white.

"You all right?" he demanded abruptly.

"Hell, yes. Why ask?" Jess answered, distracted.

"Because you holed up here soon's you got back from California, and I haven't heard one word on the doc, the kid, or your eyeballs."

Jess shrugged, meeting Abe's intense gaze calmly. "Zoë's on her way to a bang-up music school, and as to the rest—the doc's done her best."

"And–?"

"Fact is, nothing's changed. It didn't take. Whole thing was useless."

"You don't say." Abe digested this, waiting for Jess to elaborate.

After a lengthy silence marked only by the sound of strapping tape and a dove, lonesome by the back door, Jess stood up and stretched. He looked across the small room at the Ansel Adams image on the wall over his working table, his face hardening imperceptibly. Stepping over the stacks of prints and bins of trash, Jess slipped his thumb behind the picture and unhooked *Moonrise Over Hernandez* from the wall. He held it in his hands. He turned to Abe.

"I want you to have this."

"Hell no, you say!" Abe's expression went slack in disbelief.

"Take it, Abe."

"Cappello, you've had that picture in this studio as long as I've known you. You love that picture. And, it's worth a frickin' fortune," he grumbled under his breath.

"I'm tired of looking at it," Jess said softly. "Take it, or I'll send it off with the rest to the Art Center."

"Sure, an Ansel Adams in the Men's Room. What's gotten into you? Doc rearrange your brains?" Abe shook his head firmly. "No way, Jess. That image is part of you. It belongs here, where you work."

Jess stared thoughtfully at Abe, rubbing his jaw, before he turned and laid *Moonrise* face to the wall, returning to his opened portfolios on the floor. A moment later he looked up, his expression smooth and untroubled in the late afternoon light.

"You're a good man, Abe."

The other man shifted on his stool, putting his beer down on the floor. "And you're a good photographer," he answered, standing up. He laid the discarded photograph back in the wooden crate reluctantly, shaking his head.

"Remember that old saw from class? About the importance of the trashcan? Well, don't over do it."

"I know what to keep, Abe. After all these years, that much I know."

Abe nodded and moved toward the doorway. He hesitated at the threshold.

"Say, Jess...."

Jess looked up and smiled faintly, two prints in his hands.

"Kids want to know if Ansel can come this weekend. Kind of a play date thing, what you'd call 'visitation rights'. Truth is, we've gotten kind of fond of the pup." He reddened, crumpling his cap in his hand. He was still holding onto the dog's leash.

"This all right with Carly?"

"Yep."

"Fine by me, then. See you Saturday."

Abe let himself out, and the rumble of his truck faded down the driveway. Jess stuck to his task, opening sealed decades of his work, his face set and grim.

Twilight crept deep into the folds of the sage green hills, until bone-tired, Jess left the studio for the cool of the front porch, settling with a fresh beer on the broken log by the juniper. Thinking better of it, he went back in for the fine old Mexican tequila Catalina had given him on his last birthday. Carrying the bottle under one arm, he propped himself on the soft ground, leaning back against the log. Light spilled in yellow pools out of the opened windows of the studio, a soft comfort in the growing dark.

Ansel nosed up and laid down close against Jess leg, whining slightly. Jess stroked the collie behind the ear.

"Not been much fun around here lately, eh pal? Want to see Carly's kids again?"

The collie's tail thumped the dust.

"Saturday, then." Jess nodded to himself, splashing a shot of tequila down his throat, growling at the harsh golden burn. "We'll take us a short break and then back to work."

A half moon tipped low over the hills, pale and hesitant against the deepening night. Jess watched as the light danced into shadow, into the universal textures Adams had first taught him to love: the darkest line of canyon against a grayer hill, the warm brown smudge of plain below empty, glassy sky. The last values of light lingered in the darkness, shadows to suggest, obscure, identify.

He lit a cigarette, comfortable against the rough log, pouring another tequila. It didn't matter that he really couldn't see the etched, velvet black canyon. That his left eye had grown dimmed, as though webbed in lint, and that his right eye seemed at a loss to compensate, throwing off his depth perception, distorting even the nearest images. No, it didn't matter that he could no longer see the exquisite range of contrasts. There existed a selenium print, his boyhood witness to the remarkable light on a snowy night in Korea. It didn't matter he couldn't see the light now. He remembered it all.

AP Wire-August 28, 2000. Albuquerque, New Mexico. The well-known American landscape photographer Jess Cappello died Thursday in a fire at his home and studio in Tesuque, New Mexico. Investigators in Santa Fe stated they suspect the cause of fire to be a lit cigarette in a trash receptacle located in the artist's studio.

Cappello, a native of Eastern Kentucky, and a veteran of the Korean War, was most widely known for his platinum and palladium landscape prints of the Southwest. Cappello began his photographic career as an Air Force aerial reconnaissance photographer, and later as a civilian, debuted his first major work in Manhattan during the 1960s.

Selections of Jess Cappello's work have been procured by major art institutions including the Smithsonian, New York's Museum of Modern Art, the Eastman Institute, and the

Center for Photography in Tucson. The Museum of Modern Art in San Francisco recently mounted a Retrospective of the artist, which he keynoted with his presence. His prints are widely available in galleries throughout the United States and Europe.

Cappello has been lauded by critics for his focus on the elements of interconnectivity in nature. It was his stated intention to demonstrate a common language of symbol and content independent of object.

The art world considers the loss of Mr. Cappello, as well as the artist's personal portfolio of work and extensive private collection of rare and remarkable prints, irreplaceable. Mr. Cappello never married and had no living relatives. He was sixty-three years old.

Sarah put down the San Francisco Chronicle with a dull gasp. Stunned, she blinked rapidly, taking a series of short breaths. She was certain Zoë had already seen the obituary, for the house had been filled for hours with music, the haunting elegy, Bruch's *Kol Nidrei*.

Faced with the reality of this shocking news, the aching sorrow of Zoë's playing hurt Sarah's ears so badly she wanted to scream at her daughter. *Stop, oh stop*! she thought, pressing her hands to her ears. Instead, she took a deep breath and walked into the living room.

She touched Zoë on the shoulder.

The girl lifted her pale, swollen face and waited, unable to speak.

"I have Jess' camera, Zoë."

"You have his camera?" she stuttered, not comprehending, wiping her eyes with the back of her hand.

"Yes. He left it here. The Contax, remember? The one he took the pictures of you and Alexei with."

Sarah shivered.

"I meant to send it to him, but I hadn't a chance yet. What do you think I should do? They say everything is lost!"

"Except that." Zoë pointed to the framed image above the desk.

"Yes, and others like it, in collections and private homes, I suppose. But who would I send the film to, even if I knew what to do with it?"

Zoë bowed her head. She was silent for several seconds. Then she looked up, her gaze fixed on her mother. "You should take that darkroom class and develop them, Mum."

Sarah glanced at her daughter, startled.

"Why, baby?"

"He'd want you to. He was great, Mum. Jess Cappello was *great*. Who else would he trust to do it."

"Abe, maybe?"

Sarah paced away from her daughter to gaze blankly out the living room window.

"Do you think he did it on purpose?" Zoë whispered, her eyes bright with tears.

Sarah whirled around. "Start a fire on purpose? No, Zoë! How could you think that? However badly Jess may have felt about losing his vision he was not a quitter. And he'd never have harmed Ansel."

Zoë shook her head angrily. "You don't understand. He was a *photographer.*"

Sarah averted her face, her arms folded stiffly.

Zoë laid her cello on its side and slipped out of the room. Sarah heard the creak of the front door and the racket of the bike banging against the side of the house, and knew *Zoë* was headed to Mikavlov's to tell him, if he hadn't already heard, the unbelievable news that Jess Cappello was dead.

Sarah crossed the room and stood beneath the image she loved so much. She studied the photograph, looking past the model, out toward the cold moon. Then she opened the drawer of her desk and lifted out Jess' camera. Carrying it in her hands, she sank into a chair in the living room, and stared at the black autofocus SLR resting heavily in her lap.

Well, Jess? Was the diminishing light more than your soul could bear?

Sarah's lips trembled. She refused to believe it. Jess Cappello was the stuff of rock. Never would such a man crack.

Abruptly, she thought of something Jess had said to the students in the Santa Fe workshop.

The best tool in an artist's kit is the trashcan. What you throw away matters more than what you keep...only then do you understand your own work, what is good and what is not.

Sarah bowed her head over the camera and wept.

The door on the truck swung shut behind him as Abe Santos walked toward the abandoned char of Jess adobe. He stood at the edge of the rubble, crushed and disbelieving. The studio wing was gone, burned to a tangle of collapsed blackened support beams, hulks of metal cabinetry melted in the extreme heat. Piles of ash and unidentifiable debris marked the old wood foundation.

Abe had gotten the call in the stark hours of morning. Jaspar Buckman, the burly ex-rodeo champ, bartender at the Wicked Coyote and volunteer for the Fire Department, had called him from the fire.

"It's Jess' place, man. Come when you can."

The Santa Fe Fire Department and the Emergency Response teams had left by first light. Ribbons of yellow tape were knotted between the still standing front porch and the half-burnt trees, snapping lightly in the fresh breeze. The archivist dispatched from the Art Center, Abe's first call, had gone as well, his station wagon loaded with scorched, water damaged boxes that might yield an intact file or protected portfolio, a spared print.

Head bowed beneath the bright sun, Abe crossed the blackened earth. He could barely breath, fighting a grief so strong his teeth ached in the suppression of it. Jess, the studio, everything gone.

He kicked aside stucco and wallboard. Hearing the crush of glass under foot, he bent down and swept aside the ash, uncovering a photograph frame, face down on the ground. Abe turned the frame carefully over. He recognized the seared, water-stained image instantly. *Moonrise.*

Closing his eyes, he turned the print back over and stood up. He reminded himself why he'd come back, to find Ansel. No one had seen the dog. No animal corpse had been found in the aftermath of the fire. Abe figured the collie was out there somewhere, scared but alive. Straightening his shoulders, he whistled clearly; turned toward the cottonwood creek and whistled again.

Abe circled the debris, moving toward the standing half of the house, skirting the half-collapsed walls of the bedroom wing and approaching the house through the front door. He pushed on the buckled door and it gave easily. He entered uncertainly. Odors of sulphur and chemical retardants mixed with the char of water on wood made him cough, and his eyes sting. The standing walls of the hall were filmy with smoke, a queer half-light penetrating from the damaged roof into the still rooms.

Abe searched carefully for the dog, but finding no evidence of the animal backed his way out, disheartened. He must have been wrong. He'd just been so sure, felt it in his bones he'd find the pup. Hesitating just inside the front door, he whistled again, ready to give up.

A black and white shadow caught his eye.

"Here, boy. Come, Ansel."

Wet and matted, the dog belly-crawled from the direction of Jess bedroom. The collie was shaking, dragging the leg the cougar ruined, approaching Abe with stark, frightened eyes.

Abe bent down and cradled the pup's head in his knees, rubbing his ear gently. The collie whimpered.

"No place for you here now, Ansel. Come home with me and the kids."

Abe stood, and the dog folded in beside him as he turned to leave. Through the smoky shadows, a glint of light sparkled in the dim interior, somewhere behind the half-opened door. Abe stopped and shifted the door slightly, revealing the photograph half-hidden behind it.

Despite the heat of the fire, despite the merciless efforts of the fire crew wielding water and axe to extinguish the flames, one picture had survived. The solitary, cloistered image Jess had loved so well–*Triangles*, intact on the wall.

Without a second thought, Abe lifted the photograph down.

"C'mon, Lady. You, too."

Abraham Santos left the ruined house.

Acknowledgements

I am indebted to a number of talented and hardworking individuals in the writing of this novel. First and foremost, to my talented children Katy and David I offer a deep bow of respect for inspiration, encouragement, and loyalty. Another bow to my late husband Kenneth Grunzweig, the frame for all that I love and respect about the darkroom image. To my NYC agent Barbara Braun, who offered valuable assistance readying the book for publication, my gratitude: there is no savvier agent in publishing. And to Kimberley Cameron, another extraordinary agent, every writer needs just such a champion. And dearest friends, salut!

Most importantly, to the fine art photographers, musicians and composers who form the spine and heart of this novel, thank you for what you do. History thanks you.

Acknowledgement and recognition is due the *Curtis Institute of Music* in Philadelphia for its world-renowned and remarkable music education. All creative liberties taken, including descriptions of faculty and audition practices, as presented here are strictly fiction.

Source Books

This list is offered by the author as a partial resource for the interested reader in photography. Photographs referenced in this novel may be viewed in these resources and other collections, with the exception of those fictional images attributed to the main character, Jess Cappello. *Olive Grove at Hidden Villa* is the work of the late Kenneth Grunzweig, a fine-art photographer.

A New History of Photography, Michael Frizot, Konemann Publishers, Koln, Germany, 1994.

Advanced Photography, Michael Langford, Focal Press, Oxford, London, 1989.

Ansel Adams: A Biography, Mary Street Allinder, Henry Holt, NY, 1996.

Ansel Adams, Examples: the Making of 40 Photographs, Bullfinch Press, Boston, 1963.

Beyond Basic Photography, Henry Haverstein, Little, Brown & Co., NY, 1973.

Brad Cole: The Last Dream, Center for Photography, Carmel, CA, 1998.

Camera Lucida, Roland Barthes, Hill and Wang, Boston, 1981.

Edward Weston: Photographer, Aperture Foundation, NY, 1978.

Georgia O'Keefe: A Portrait by Alfred Stieglitz, Metropolitan Museum of Art, NY, 1978.

Gordon Parks, A Poet and His Camera, Viking Press, NY, 1968.

Henri Cartier Bresson: Photographer, Little, Brown and Co., NY, 1979.

Imogen Cunningham, On the Body, Richard Lorenz, Bullfinch Press, Boston, 1998.

Imogen Cunningham, The Poetry of Form, Edition Stemmel, Germany, 1970.

Masters of Photography, Beaumont and Nancy Newhall, Castle Books, NY, 1958.

Minor White: Rites and Passages, Aperture Foundation, NY, 1978.

Nude Photography: Masterpieces from the Past 150 Years, Peter Cornell-Richter, Prestel-Verleg, Germany, 1998.

Occam's Razor, Billy Jay, Nazraeli Press, Germany, 1992.

On Being a Photographer, David Hurn, Lenswork Publishing, NY, 1997.

On Photography, Susan Sontag, Anchor Books, NY, 1989.

Paul Strand, National Gallery of Art/Aperture Foundation, NY, 1990.

Radiant Identities, Photographs by Jock Sturges, Aperture Foundation, NY, 1994.

Photography, Barbara London and John Upton, Harper Collins, NY, 1994.

Steichen: A Life in Photography, Museum of Modern Art, Doubleday and Co., New York, 1963.

The Art of Photographic Lighting, Michael Buselle, David and Charles, UK, 1993.

The Daybooks of Edward Weston: I Mexico and II California, ed. Nancy Newhall, Aperture Foundation, NY, and Center for Creative Photography, Board of Regents, University of Arizona, 1961.

The Enchanted Landscape: Wynn Bullock, Photographs 1940-1975, Aperture Foundation, NY, 1993.

The Eternal Body: Ruth Bernhard, Chronicle Books, San Francisco, 1986.

The Photograph Collectors Guide, Lee Witkin and Barbara London, New York Graphic Society, 1979.

View Camera, The Journal of Large-Format Photography, Sacramento, CA, May/June 2002.

Why People Photograph, Robert Adams, Aperture Foundation, NY, 1994.

About the Author

Glenda Burgess was born in New Mexico and lives in the mountain Northwest. She spent her early life traveling the world, falling in love with customs and cultures, and eventually, the photographer Kenneth Grunzweig. Her work encompasses the complexities and mysteries of human passion engaged in art. Also by the author, the novel Loose Threads (1998), and a forthcoming novel on sculpture and the vineyards of Argentina.

Printed in the United States
40187LVS00010B/37